VAL McDERMID

Val McDermid grew up in a Scottish mining community then read English at Oxford. She was a journalist for sixteen years, spending the last three years as Northern Bureau Chief of a national Sunday tabloid. Now a full-time writer, she lives in Cheshire.

Star Struck is the last of six novels featuring Kate Brannigan. It won the 1998 French Grand Prix des Romans d'Aventure.

Val is also the author of three tense psychological thrillers featuring criminal profiler Tony Hill. The first of these, *The Mermaids Singing*, was awarded the 1995 Gold Dagger Award for Best Crime Novel of the Year, while the second, *The Wire in the Blood*, lends its name to the acclaimed ITV series featuring Robson Green as Tony Hill. She has also written three standalone thrillers, *Killing the Shadows*, *A Place of Execution* and *A Distant Echo*, and six novels featuring journalist-sleuth Lindsay Gordon.

VAL McDERMID

Star Struck

HarperCollins*Publishers*

HarperCollins*Publishers*
77–85 Fulham Palace Road
London, W6 8JB

The HarperCollins website address is:
www.harpercollins.co.uk

First published in Great Britain by
HarperCollins*Publishers* 1998

This paperback reissue edition published 2003

1

Copyright © Val McDermid 1998

The author asserts the moral right to
be identified as the author of this work

ISBN: 978-0-00-787982-3

Typeset in Meridien by Palimpsest Book Production Limited,
Polmont, Stirlingshire

Printed and bound in Great Britain by
Clays Ltd, St Ives plc

ACKNOWLEDGEMENTS

I was a journalist for many years on a newspaper that became increasingly obsessed with the world of soaps. As a result, I have forgotten more than any respectable person would want to know about the private lives of many household names. Nevertheless, the fictional soap *Northerners* and its cast are entirely creatures of my imagination. Any resemblances to the real or fictional characters of any actual regular drama series are entirely coincidental and purely accidental. Besides, I'm not worth suing.

The legal advice came from Brigid Baillie, Jai Penna and Paula Tyler; any errors are either deliberate mistakes for dramatic effect, or just plain stupidity. Jennifer Paul also provided crucial information, in exchange for which I promise never to tell the story about the golden retriever.

Thanks too to my agents Jane Gregory and Lisanne Radice and my editors Julia Wisdom and Karen Godfrey who, because of the wonders of e-mail, were able to shower me with queries the length and breadth of three continents.

For Tessa and Peps, the Scylebert Twins
(aka Margaret & Nicky)
Thanks for all the laughter – we'll
never feel the same about Isa.

Prologue

Extract from the computer database of
Dorothea Dawson, Seer to the Stars

Written in the Stars for Kate Brannigan,
private investigator.

Born Oxford, UK, 4th September 1966.

* Sun in Virgo in the Fifth House
* Moon in Taurus in the Twelfth House
* Mercury in Virgo in the Fifth House
* Venus in Leo in the Fourth House
* Mars in Leo in the Fourth House
* Jupiter in Cancer in the Third House
* Saturn retrograde in Pisces in the Eleventh House
* Uranus in Virgo in the Fifth House
* Neptune in Scorpio in the Sixth House
* Pluto in Virgo in the Fifth House
* Chiron in Pisces in the Eleventh House
* Ascendant Sign: Gemini

1

SUN IN VIRGO IN THE 5TH HOUSE

On the positive side, can be ingenious, verbally skilled, diplomatic, tidy, methodical, discerning and dutiful. The negatives are fussiness, a critical manner, an obsessive attention to detail and a lack of self-confidence that can disguise itself as arrogance. In the 5th House, it indicates a player of games.

From *Written in the Stars*, by Dorothea Dawson

My client was about to get a resounding smack in the mouth. I watched helplessly from the other side of the street. My adrenaline was pumping, but there was no way I could have made it to her side in time. That's the trouble with bodyguarding jobs. Even if you surround the client with a phalanx of Rutger Hauer clones and Jean Van Damme wannabes in bulletproof vests, the moment always comes when they're vulnerable. And guess who always gets the blame? That's why, when people come looking for a minder, the house rule at

Brannigan & Co: Investigations & Security states, 'We don't do that.'

But Christmas was coming and the goose was anorexic. Business had been as slow as a Post Office queue and even staff as unorthodox as mine expect to be paid on time. Besides, I deserved a festive bonus myself. Eating, for example. So I'd sent my better judgement on an early Yuletide break and agreed to take on a client who'd turned out to be more accident prone than Coco the Clown.

For once, it wasn't my fault that the client was in the front line. I'd had no say in what was happening out there on the street. If I'd wanted to stop it, I couldn't have. So, absolved from action for once, I stood with my hands in my pockets and watched Carla Hardcastle's arm swing round in a fearsome arc to deliver a cracking wallop that wiped the complacent smirk off Brenda Barrowclough's self-satisfied face. I sucked my breath in sharply.

'And cut,' the director said. 'Very nice, girls, but I'd like it one more time. Gloria, loved that smug little smile, but can you lose it at the point where you realize she's actually going to thump you? And let us see some outrage?'

My client gave a forbearing smile that was about as sincere as a beggar asking for tea money. 'Whatever you say, Helen, chuck,' she rasped in the voice that thrilled the nation three times a week as we shovelled down our microwave dinners in front of Manchester's principal contribution to the world of soap. Then she turned to me with an exaggerated wink and called, 'You're all right, chuck, it's only make believe.'

Everyone turned to stare at me. I managed to grin while clenching my teeth. It's a talent that comes in very handy in the private-eye business. It's having to deal with unscrupulous idiots that does it. And that's just the clients.

'That's my bodyguard,' Gloria Kendal – alias Brenda Barrowclough – announced to the entire cast and crew of *Northerners*.

'We'd all worked out it wasn't your body double,' the actress playing Carla said, apparently as sour in life as the character she played in the human drama that had wowed British audiences for the best part of twenty years.

'Let's hope you only get attacked by midgets,' Teddy Edwards added. He'd once been a stand-up comedian on the working men's club circuit, but he'd clearly been playing Gloria's screen husband for so long that he'd lost any comic talent he'd ever possessed. I might only be five feet three in my socks, but I wouldn't have needed to use too many of my Thai-boxing skills to bring a lump of lard like him to his knees. I gave him the hard stare and I'm petty enough to admit I enjoyed it when he cleared his throat and looked away.

'All right, settle down,' the director called. 'Places, please, and let's take it again from the top of the scene.'

'Can we have a bit of hush back there?' someone else added. I wondered what his job title was and how long I'd have to hang around the TV studios before I worked out who did what in a hierarchy that included best boys, gaffers and too many gofers to count. I figured I'd probably have long enough, the way things were going. There was a lot of time for idle reflection in this job. When Gloria was filming, silence was the rule. I couldn't ask questions, eavesdrop or burgle in pursuit of the information I needed to close the case. All there was for me to do was lean against the wall and watch. There was nothing remotely glamorous about witnessing the seventh take of a scene that was a long way from Shakespeare to start with. As jobs went, minding the queen of the nation's soaps was about as exotic as watching rain slide down a window.

It hadn't started out that way. When Gloria had swanned into our office, I'd known straight off it wasn't going to be a routine case. At Brannigan & Co, the private investigation firm that I run, we cover a wide spectrum of work. Previously, when I'd been in partnership with Bill Mortensen, we'd mostly investigated white-collar fraud, computer security, industrial espionage and sabotage, with a bit of miscellaneous meddling that friends occasionally dropped in our laps. Now Bill had moved to Australia, I'd had to cast my net wider to survive. I'd clawed back some process-serving from a handful of law firms, added 'surveillance' to the letterheading and canvassed insurance companies for work exposing fraudulent claims. Even so,

Gloria Kendal's arrival in our front office signalled something well out of the ordinary.

Not that I'd recognized her straight away. Neither had Shelley, the office administrator, and she's got the X-ray vision of every mother of teenagers. My first thought when Gloria had swept through the door on a wave of Estée Lauder's White Linen was that she was a domestic violence victim. I couldn't think of another reason for the wide-brimmed hat and the wraparound sunglasses on a wet December afternoon in Manchester.

I'd been looking over Shelley's shoulder at some information she'd downloaded from Companies House when the woman had pushed open the door and paused, dramatically framed against the hallway. She waited long enough for us to look up and register the expensive swagger of her mac and the quality of the kelly-green silk suit underneath, then she took three measured steps into the room on low-heeled pumps that precisely matched the suit. I don't know about Shelley, but I suspect my astonishment showed.

There was an air of expectancy in the woman's pose. Shelley's, 'Can I help you?' did nothing to diminish it.

The woman smiled, parting perfectly painted lips the colour of tinned black cherries. 'I hope you can, chuck,' she said, and her secret was out.

'Gloria Kendal,' I said.

'Brenda Barrowclough,' Shelley said simultaneously.

Gloria chuckled. 'You're both right, girls. But we'll just let that be our little secret, eh?' I nodded blankly. The only way her identity was ever going to stay secret was if she kept her mouth shut. It was clear from three short sentences that the voice that had made Brenda Barrowclough the darling of impressionists the length and breadth of the comedy circuit wasn't something Gloria took on and cast off as readily as her character's trademark bottle-blonde beehive wig. Gloria really did talk in broad North Manchester with the gravelly growl of a bulldozer in low gear.

'How can I help you, Ms Kendal?' I asked, remembering my manners and stepping out from behind the reception desk. She might not be a CEO in a grey suit, but she clearly had enough in the bank to make sure we all had a very happy Christmas.

'Call me Gloria, chuck. In fact, call me anything except Brenda.' After twenty years of TV viewing, the raucous laugh was as familiar as my best friend's. 'I'm looking for Brannigan,' she said.

'You found her,' I said, holding out my hand.

Gloria dropped a limp bunch of fingers into mine and withdrew before I could squeeze them – the professional sign of someone who had to shake too many hands in a year. 'I thought you'd be a bloke,' she said. For once, it wasn't a complaint, merely an observation. 'Well, that makes things a lot easier. I were wondering what we'd do if Brannigan and

Co didn't have women detectives. Is there some place we can go and talk?'

'My office?' I gestured towards the open door.

'Grand,' Gloria said, sweeping past me and fluttering her fingers in farewell to Shelley.

We exchanged a look. 'Rather you than me,' Shelley muttered.

By the time I closed the door behind me, Gloria was settled into one corner of the sofa I use for informal client meetings. She'd taken off her hat and tossed it casually on the low table in front of her. Her own hair was a subtle ash-blonde cut in a gamine Audrey Hepburn style. Somehow it managed not to look ridiculous on a woman who had to be nudging sixty. She had the clear skin of a much younger woman, but none of the Barbie-doll tightness that goes with the overenthusiastic face-lift. As I sat down opposite her, she took off the sunglasses and familiar grey eyes crinkled in a smile. 'I know it's ridiculous, but even though people stare at the bins, they don't recognize Brenda behind them. They just think it's some daft rich bitch with delusions of grandeur.'

'Living a normal life must be tough,' I said.

'You're not kidding, chuck. They see you three times a week in their living room, and they think you're a member of the family. You let on who you are and next thing you know they're telling you all about their hernia operation and the state of their veins. It's a nightmare.' She shrugged out of her coat, opened her handbag and took out a packet of those long skinny brown cigarettes that look like cinnamon sticks, and a gold Dunhill lighter. She looked around, eyebrows raised.

Stifling a sigh, I got up and removed the saucer from under the Christmas cactus. I'd only bought it two days before but already the buds that had promised pretty cascades of flowers were predictably starting to litter the windowsill. Me and plants go together like North and South Korea. I tipped the water from the saucer into the bin and placed it on the table in front of Gloria. 'Sorry,' I said. 'It's the best I can do.'

She smiled. 'I used to work in a cat food factory. I've put my fags out in a lot worse, believe me.'

I preferred not to think about it. 'Well, Gloria, how can I help you?'

'I need a bodyguard.'

My eyebrows rose. 'We don't normally . . .'

'These aren't normal circumstances,' she said sharply. 'I don't want some thick as pigshit bodybuilder trailing round after me. I want somebody with a brain, somebody that can figure out what the heck's going on. Somebody that won't attract attention. Half my life I spend with the bloody press snapping round my ankles and the last thing I need is stories that I've splashed out on a hired gun. That's why I wanted a woman.'

'You said, "somebody that can figure out what the heck's going on",' I said, focusing on the need I

8

probably could do something useful about. 'What seems to be the problem?'

'I've been getting threatening letters,' she said. 'Now, that's nothing new. Brenda Barrowclough is not a woman who minces her words, and there are a lot of folk out there as can't tell the difference between *Northerners* and the real world. You'd be too young to remember, but when I was first widowed in the series, back about fifteen years ago, I was snowed under with letters of condolence. People actually sent wreaths for the funeral, addressed to fifteen, Sebastopol Grove. The Post Office is used to it now, they just deliver direct to the studios, but back then the poor florists didn't know what to do. We had letters from cancer charities saying donations had been made to their funds in memory of Harry – that was my screen husband's name. Whenever characters move out, we get letters from punters wondering what the asking price is for the house. So whenever Brenda does owt controversial, I get hate mail.'

I dredged my memory for recent tabloid headlines. 'Hasn't there been some storyline about abortion? Sorry, I don't get the chance to watch much TV.'

'You're all right, chuck. Me neither. You know Brenda's granddaughter, Debbie?'

'The one who's lived with Brenda since she was about ten? After her mum got shot in the Post Office raid?'

'You used to be a fan, then?'

'I still watch when I can. Which was a lot more back when Debbie was ten than it is now.'

'Well, what's happened is that Brenda's found out that Debbie's had an abortion. Now, Brenda had a real down on Debbie's boyfriend because he was black, so the audience would have expected her to support Debbie rather than have a mixed-race grandson. But Brenda's only gone mental about the right to life and thrown Debbie out on her ear, hasn't she? So me and Sarah Anne Kelly who plays Debbie were expecting a right slagging off.'

'And that's what's happened?'

Gloria shook her head, leaving a ribbon of smoke drifting level with her mouth. 'Sort of,' she said, confusing me. 'What happens is the studio goes through our post, weeding out the really nasty letters so we don't get upset. Only, of course, you ask, don't you? I mean, you want to know if there's any real nutters out there looking for you.'

'And the studio told you there was?'

'No, chuck. It weren't the studio. The letters I'm worried about are the ones coming to the house.'

Now I was really confused. 'You mean, your real house? Where you actually live?'

'Exactly. Now, I mean, it's not a state secret, where I live. But unless you're actually a neighbour or one of the reptiles of the press, you'd have to go to a bit of trouble to find out. The phone's ex-directory, of course. And all the official stuff like electricity bills and the voters' roll don't come under Gloria Kendal. They come under my real name.'

'Which is?'

'Doreen Satterthwaite.' She narrowed her eyes. I didn't think it was because the smoke was getting into them. I struggled to keep my face straight. Then Gloria grinned. 'Bloody awful, isn't it? Do you wonder I chose Gloria Kendal?'

'In your shoes, I'd have done exactly the same thing,' I told her. I wasn't lying. 'So these threatening letters are coming directly to the house?'

'Not just to my house. My daughter's had one too. And they're different to the usual.' She opened her handbag again. I wondered at a life where it mattered to have suit, shoes and handbag in identical shades. I couldn't help my mind slithering into speculation about her underwear. Did her coordination extend that far?

Gloria produced a sheet of paper. She started to pass it to me, then paused. I could have taken it from her, but it was an awkward reach, so I waited. 'Usually, letters like this, they're semi-literate. They're ignorant. I mean, I might have left school when I were fifteen, but I know the difference between a dot and a comma. Most of the nutters that write me letters wouldn't know a paragraph if they woke up next to one. They can't spell, and they've got a tendency to write in green ink or felt-tip pens. Some of them, I don't think they're allowed sharp objects where they live,' she added. I've noticed how actors and audiences often

11

hold each other in mutual contempt. It looked like Gloria didn't have a whole lot of respect for the people who paid for the roof over her head.

Now she passed the letter across. It was plain A4 bond, the text printed unidentifiably on a laser printer. *'Doreen Satterthwaite, it's time you paid for what you've done. You deserve to endure the same suffering you've been responsible for. I know where you live. I know where your daughter Sandra and her husband Keith live. I know your granddaughter Joanna goes to Gorse Mill School. I know they worship at St Andrew's Church and have a caravan on Anglesey. I know you drive a scarlet Saab convertible. I know you, you bitch. And soon you're going to be dead. But there'll be no quick getaway for you. First, you're going to suffer.'* She was right. The letter sounded disturbingly in control.

'Any idea what the letter writer is referring to?' I asked, not really expecting an honest answer.

Gloria shrugged. 'Who the heck knows? I'm no plaster saint, but I can't think of anybody I've done a really bad turn to. Apart from my ex, and I doubt he could manage a letter to me that didn't include the words, "you effing bitch". He certainly can't manage a conversation without it. And besides, he wouldn't threaten our Sandra or Joanna. No way.' I took her response for genuine perplexity, then reminded myself how she made her living.

'Have there been many of them?'

'This is the third. Plus the one that went to

Sandra. That were about the sins of the mother. To be honest, the first couple I just binned. I thought they were somebody at the wind-up.' Suddenly, Gloria looked away. She fumbled another cigarette from the packet and this time, the hand that lit it shook.

'Something happened to change your mind?'

'My car tyres were slashed. All four of them. Inside the NPTV compound. And there was a note stuck under the windscreen wipers. "Next time your wardrobe? Or you?" And before you ask, I haven't got the note. It'd been raining. It just fell to bits in my hand.'

'That's serious business,' I said. 'Are you sure you shouldn't be talking to the police?' I hated to lose a potential client, but it would have verged on criminal negligence not to point out that this might be one for Officer Dibble.

Gloria fiddled with her cigarette. 'I told the management about it. And John Turpin, he's the Administration and Production Coordinator, he persuaded me not to go to the cops.'

'Why not? I'd have thought the management would have been desperate to make sure nothing happened to their stars.'

Gloria's lip curled in a cynical sneer. 'It were nowt to do with my safety and everything to do with bad publicity. Plus, who'd want to come and work at NPTV if they found out the security was so crap that somebody could walk into the company compound and get away with that?

Anyway, Turpin promised me an internal inquiry, so I decided to go along with him.'

'But now you're here.' It's observational skills like this that got me where I am today.

She flashed a quick up-and-under glance at me, an appraisal that contained more than a hint of fear held under tight control. 'You're going to think I'm daft.'

I shook my head. 'I don't see you as the daft type, Gloria.' Well, it was only a white lie. Daft enough to spend the equivalent of a week's payroll for Brannigan & Co on a matching out-fit, but probably not daft when it came to a realistic assessment of personal danger. Mind you, neither was Ronald Reagan and look what happened to him.

'You know Dorothea Dawson?' Gloria asked, eyeing me out of the corner of her eye.

' "The Seer to the Stars"?' I asked incredulously. 'The one who does the horoscopes in *TV Viewer*? The one who's always on the telly? "A horse born under the sign of Aries will win the Derby"?' I intoned in a cheap impersonation of Dorothea Dawson's sepulchral groan.

'Don't mock,' she cautioned me, wagging a finger. 'She's a brilliant clairvoyant, you know. Dorothea comes into the studios once a week. She's the personal astrologer to half the cast. She really has a gift.'

I bet she had. Gifts from all the stars of *Northerners*. 'And Dorothea said something about these letters?'

14

'I took this letter in with me to my last consultation with her. I asked her what she could sense from it. She does that as well as the straight clairvoyance. She's done it for me before now, and she's never been wrong.' In spite of her acting skills, anxiety was surfacing in Gloria's voice.

'And what did she say?'

Gloria drew so hard on her cigarette that I could hear the burning tobacco crackle. As she exhaled she said, 'She held the envelope and shivered. She said the letter meant death. Dorothea said death was in the room with us.'

2

SUN TRINE MOON

Creative thinking resolves difficult circumstances; she will tackle difficulties with bold resolution. The subject feels at home wherever she is, but can be blind to the real extent of problems. She will not always notice if her marriage is falling apart; she doesn't always nip problems in the bud.

From *Written in the Stars*, by Dorothea Dawson

Anybody gullible enough to fall for the doom and gloom dished out by professional con merchants like astrologers certainly wasn't going to have a problem with my expense sheets. Money for old rope, I reckoned. By Gloria's own admission, hate mail was as much part of the routine in her line of work as travelling everywhere with stacks of postcard-sized photographs to autograph for the punters. OK, the tyre slashing was definitely more serious, but that might be unconnected to the letters, an isolated act of vindictiveness. It was only because the Seer to the Stars had thrown a wobbler that this poison pen outbreak had been blown up to life-threatening proportions. 'Does she often sense impending death when she does predictions for people?' I asked, trying not to snigger.

Gloria shook her head vigorously. 'I've never heard of anybody else getting a prediction like that.'

'And have you told other people in the cast about it?'

'Nobody,' she said. 'It's not the sort of thing you go on about.'

Not unless you liked being laughed at, I reckoned. On the other hand, it might mean that the death prediction was one of Dorothea Dawson's regular routines for putting the frighteners on her clients and making them more dependent on her. Especially the older ones. Let's face it, there can't be that many public figures Gloria's age who go through more than a couple of months without knowing somebody who's died or dying. Gloria might have been catapulted into panic by her astrologer, but I couldn't imagine it being anything more than a stunt by Dorothea Dawson. Minding Gloria sounded like a major earner with no risk attached. Just what the bank manager ordered. I said a small prayer of thanks to Dorothea Dawson and told Gloria that for her, I'd be happy to make an exception to company policy. In fact, I would take personal responsibility for her safety.

The news seemed to cheer her up. 'Right then,

we'd better be off,' she said, stubbing out her cigarette and gathering her mac around her shoulders.

'We'd better be off?' I echoed.

She glanced at her watch, a chunky gold item with chips of diamond that glittered like a broken windscreen in a streetlight. 'Depends where you live, I suppose. Only, if I'm opening a theme pub in Blackburn at eight and we've both got to get changed and grab a bite to eat, we'll be cutting it a bit fine if we don't get a move on.'

'A theme pub in Blackburn,' I said faintly.

'That's right, chuck. I'm under contract to the brewery. It's straightforward enough. I turn up, tell a few jokes, sing a couple of songs to backing tapes, sign a couple of hundred autographs and off.' As she spoke, she was setting her hat at a rakish angle and replacing her sunglasses. As she made for the door, I dived behind the desk and swept my palmtop computer and my moby into my shoulder bag. I only caught up with her because she'd stopped to sign a glossy colour photograph of herself disguised as Brenda Barrowclough for Shelley.

Something terrible had happened to the toughest office manager in Manchester. Imagine Cruella De Vil transformed into one of those cuddly Dalmatian puppies, only more so. It was like watching Ben Nevis grovel. 'And could you sign one, "for Ted"?' she begged. I wished I had closed-circuit TV cameras covering the office. A video of this would keep Shelley off my back for months.

'No problem, there you go,' Gloria said, signing the card with a flourish. 'You right, Kate?'

I grabbed my coat and shrugged into it as I followed Gloria into the hall. She glanced both ways and down the stairwell before she set off. 'The last thing I need is somebody clocking me coming out of your office,' she said, trotting down the stairs at a fair pace. At the front door I turned right automatically, heading for my car. Gloria followed me into the private car park.

'This sign says, "Employees of DVS Systems only. Unauthorized users will be clamped,"' she pointed out.

'It's all right,' I said in a tone that I hoped would end the conversation. I didn't want to explain to Gloria that I'd got so fed up with the desperate state of car parking in my part of town that I'd checked out which office car parks were seldom full. I'd used the macro lens on the camera to take a photograph of a DVS Systems parking pass through somebody else's windscreen and made myself a passable forgery. I'd been parking on their lot for six months with no trouble, but it wasn't something I was exactly proud of. Besides, it never does to let the clients know about the little sins. It only makes them nervous.

Gloria stopped expectantly next to a very large black saloon with tinted windows. I shook my head and she pulled a rueful smile. I pointed the remote at my dark-blue Rover and it cheeped its usual greeting at me. 'Sorry it's not a limo,' I said to Gloria as we piled in. 'I need to be invisible most of the time.' I didn't feel the need to mention that the engine under the bonnet was very different from the unit the manufacturer had installed. I had enough horsepower under my bonnet to stage my own rodeo. If anybody was stalking Gloria, I could blow them off inside the first five miles.

I drove home, which took less than five minutes even in early rush-hour traffic. I love living so close to the city centre, but the area's become more dodgy in the last year. I'd have moved if I hadn't had to commit every spare penny to the business. I'd been the junior partner in Mortensen & Brannigan, and when Bill Mortensen had decided to sell up and move to Australia, I'd thought my career prospects were in the toilet. I couldn't afford to buy him out but I was damned if some stranger was going to end up with the lion's share of a business I'd worked so hard to build. It had taken a lot of creative thinking and a shedload of debt to get Brannigan & Co off the ground. Now I had a sleeping partner in the Cayman Islands and a deal to buy out his share of the business piecemeal as and when I could afford it, so it would be a long time before I could consider heading for the southern suburbs where all my sensible friends had moved.

Besides, the domestic arrangements were perfect. My lover Richard, a freelance rock journalist, owned the bungalow next door to mine, linked by a long conservatory that ran along the back of both properties. We had all the advantages of living together and none of the disadvantages. I didn't have to put up with his mess or his music-business cronies; he didn't have to deal with my girls' nights in or my addiction to very long baths.

Richard's car, a hot-pink Volkswagen Beetle convertible, was in its slot, which, at this time of day, probably meant he was home. There might be other showbiz journos with him, so I played safe and asked Gloria to wait in the car. I was back inside ten minutes, wearing a bottle-green crushed-velvet cocktail dress under a dark-navy dupion-silk matador jacket. OTT for Blackburn, I know, but there hadn't been a lot of choice. If I didn't get to the dry cleaner soon, I'd be going to work in my dressing gown.

Gloria lived in Saddleworth, the expensively rural cluster of villages that hugs the edges of the Yorkshire moors on the eastern fringe of Greater Manchester. The hills are still green and rolling there, but on the skyline the dark humps of the moors lower unpleasantly, even on the sunniest of days. This is the wilderness that ate up the bodies of the child victims of Myra Hindley and Ian Brady. I can never drive through this brooding landscape without remembering the Moors Murders. Living on the doorstep would give me nightmares. It didn't seem to bother Gloria. But why would it? It didn't impinge either on her or on Brenda Barrowclough, and the half-hour drive out to Saddleworth was long enough for me to realize these were the only criteria that mattered to her. I'd heard it said that actors are like children in their unconscious self-absorption. Now I was seeing the proof.

In the December dark, Saddleworth looked like a Christmas card, early fairy lights twinkling against a light dusting of snow. I wished I'd listened to the weather forecast; the roads out here can be closed by drifts when there hasn't been so much as a flake on my roof. Yet another argument against country living. Gloria directed me down the valley in a gentle spiral to Greenfield. We turned off the main street into a narrow passage between two high walls. I hoped I wouldn't meet something coming the other way in a hurry. About a hundred yards in, the passage ended in two tall wrought-iron gates. Gloria fumbled with something in her handbag and the gates swung open.

I edged forward slowly, completely gobsmacked. I appeared to have driven into the set of a BBC period drama. I was in a large cobbled court-yard, surrounded on three sides by handsome two-storey buildings in weatherworn gritstone. Even my untrained eye can spot early Indus-trial Revolution, and this was a prime example. 'Wow,' I said.

'It were built as offices for the mill,' Gloria said, pointing me towards a pair of double doors in the long left-hand side of the square. 'Leave the car in front of my garage for now. Then the mill became a cat food factory. Sound familiar?'

'The factory where you used to work?'

'Got it in one.' She opened the car door and I followed her across the courtyard. The door she stopped at was solid oak, the lock a sensible mortise. As we went in, a burglar alarm klaxoned its warning. While Gloria turned it off, I walked across the wide room that ran the whole depth of the building. Through the tall window, I could see light glinting off water. The house backed on to the canal. Suddenly life looked better. This house was about as impregnable as they come. Unless Gloria's letter writer had the Venetian skill of climbing a ladder from a boat, I was going to be able to sleep in my own bed at night rather than across the threshold of Gloria's bedroom.

'It's beautiful,' I said.

'Especially when your living room used to be the cashier's office where you picked up your wages every week smelling of offal,' Gloria said ironically.

I turned back to look round the room. Wall uplighters gave a soft glow to burnished beams and the exposed stone of the three outer walls. The furnishings looked like a job lot from John Lewis, all pastel-figured damask and mahogany. The pictures on the wall were big watercolour landscapes of the Yorkshire moorland and the expanse of stripped floorboards was broken up by thick pile Chinese rugs. There was nothing to quarrel with, but nothing that spoke of individual taste, unlike Gloria's clothes. 'You live here alone?' I asked.

'Thank God,' she said with feeling, opening a walk-in cupboard and hanging up her coat.

'Anyone else have keys?'

'Only my daughter.' Gloria emerged and pointed to a door in the far wall. 'The kitchen's through there. There's a freezer full of ready meals. Do you want to grab a couple and stick them in the microwave while I'm getting changed?' Without waiting for an answer, she started up the open-plan staircase that climbed to the upper floor.

The kitchen was almost as big as the living room. One end was laid out as a dining area, with a long refectory table and a collection of unmatched antique farm kitchen chairs complete with patchwork cushions. The other end was an efficiently arranged working kitchen, dominated by an enormous freestanding fridge-freezer. The freezer was stacked from top to bottom with meals from Marks and Spencer. Maybe country living could be tolerable after all, I thought. All you needed to get through the winter was a big enough freezer and an endless supply of computer games. I chose a couple of pasta dishes and followed the instructions on the pack. By the time they were thawed and reheated, Gloria was back, dressed for action in a shocking-pink swirl of sequins. All it needed was the Brenda Barrowclough beehive to define camp kitsch better than any drag queen could have.

'Amazing,' I said faintly, scooping chicken and pasta into bowls.

'Bloody awful, you mean,' Gloria said, sitting down in a flounce of candyfloss. 'But the punters are paying for Brenda, not me.' She attacked her pasta like an extra from *Oliver Twist*. She finished while I was barely halfway through. 'Right,' she said, wiping her mouth with the back of her hand. 'I'll be five minutes putting on me slap and the wig. The dishwasher's under the sink.'

With anyone else, I'd have started to resent being ordered around. But I was beginning to get the hang of Gloria. She wasn't bossy as such. She was just supremely organized and blissfully convinced that her way was the best way. Life would inevitably be smoother for those around her who recognized this and went along with it unquestioningly. For now, I was prepared to settle for the quiet life. Later, it might be different, but I'd deal with that when later rolled round. Meanwhile, I loaded the dishwasher then went outside and started the car.

The drive to Blackburn was the last sane part of the evening. Gloria handed me a faxed set of directions then demanded that I didn't mither her with problems so she could get her head straight. I loaded an appropriate CD into the car stereo and drove to the ambient chill of Dreamfish while she reclined her seat and closed her eyes. I pulled up outside the pub three-quarters of an hour later, ten minutes before she was due to sparkle. She opened her eyes, groaned softly and said, 'It's a bit repetitive, that music. Have you got no Frank

Sinatra?' I tried to disguise my sense of impending doom. I failed. Gloria roared with raucous laughter and said, 'I were only winding you up. I can't bloody stand Sinatra. Typical man, I did it my own bloody-minded way. This modern stuff's much better.'

I left Gloria in the car while I did a brief reconnaissance of the venue. I had this vague notion of trying to spot any suspicious characters. I had more chance of hitting the Sahara on a wet Wednesday. Inside the pub, it was mayhem on a leash. Lads with bad haircuts and football shirts jostled giggling groups of girls dressed in what the high-street chain stores had persuaded them was fashion. Mostly they looked like they'd had a collision with their mothers' cast-offs from the seventies. I couldn't think of another reason for wearing Crimplene. The Lightning Seeds were revealing that football was coming home at a volume that made my fillings hurt. Provincial didn't begin to describe it. It was so different from the city-centre scene I began to wonder if we could have slipped through a black hole and ended up in the Andromeda galaxy. What a waste of a good frock.

The special opening night offer of two drinks for the price of one had already scored a clutch of casualties and the rest of the partygoers looked like they were hellbent on the same fate. I ducked back out and collected Gloria. 'I'll try to stay as close to you as I can,' I told her. 'It's a madhouse in there.'

She paused on the threshold, took a swift look round the room and said, 'You've obviously led a very sheltered life.' As she spoke, someone spotted her. The cry rippled across the room and within seconds the youth of Blackburn were cheering and bellowing a ragged chorus of the theme song from *Northerners*. And then we were plunged into the throbbing embrace of the crowd.

I gave up trying to keep Gloria from the assassin's knife after about twenty seconds when I realized that if I came between her and her public, I was the more likely candidate for a stiletto in the ribs. I wriggled backwards through the crowd and found a vantage point on the raised dais where the DJ was looking as cool as any man can who works for the local building society during the day. I was scanning the crowd automatically, looking for behaviour that didn't fit in. Easier said than done, given the level of drunken revelry around me. But from what I could see of the people crammed into the Frog and Scrannage, the natives were definitely friendly, at least as far as Gloria/Brenda was concerned.

I watched my client, impressed with her energy and her professionalism. She crossed the room slower than a stoned three-toed sloth, with a word and an autograph for everyone who managed to squeeze alongside. She didn't even seem to be sweating, the only cool person in the biggest sauna in the North West. When she finally made it to the dais, there was no shortage of hands to help her up. She turned momentarily and swiftly handed the DJ a cassette tape. 'Any time you like, chuck. Just let it run.'

The lad slotted it into his music deck and the opening bars of the *Northerners* theme crashed out over the PA, the audience swaying along. The music faded down and Gloria went straight into what was clearly a well-polished routine. Half a dozen jokes with a local spin, a clutch of anecdotes about her fellow cast members then, right on cue, the music swelled up under her and she belted out a segued medley of 'I Will Survive', 'No More Tears', 'Roll With It' and 'No Regrets'.

You had to be there.

The crowd was baying for more. They got it. 'The Power of Love' blasted our eardrums into the middle of next week. Then we were out of there. The car park was so cold and quiet I'd have been tempted to linger if I hadn't had the client to consider. Instead I ran to the car and brought it round to the doorway, where she was signing the last few autographs. 'Keep watching the show,' she urged them as she climbed into the car.

As soon as we were out of the car park, she pulled off the wig with a noisy sigh. 'What did you think?'

'Anybody who seriously wanted to damage you could easily get close enough. Getting away might be harder,' I said, half my attention on negotiating a brutal one-way system that could commit us to Chorley or Preston or some other fate worse than death if I didn't keep my wits about me.

'No, not that,' Gloria said impatiently. 'Never mind that. How was I? Did they love it?'

It was gone midnight by the time I'd deposited Gloria behind bolted doors and locked gates and driven back through the empty impoverished streets of the city's eastern fringes. Nothing much was moving except the litter in the wind. I felt a faint nagging throb in my sinuses, thanks to the assault of cigarette smoke, loud music and flashing lights I'd endured in the pub. I'd recently turned thirty; maybe some fundamental alteration had happened in my brain which meant my body could no longer tolerate all the things that spelled 'a good night out' to the denizens of Blackburn's latest fun pub. Perhaps there were hidden benefits in aging after all.

I yawned as I turned out of the council estate into the enclave of private housing where I occasionally manage a full night's sleep. Tonight wouldn't be one; Gloria had to be at the studios by nine thirty, so she wanted me at her place by eight thirty. I'd gritted my teeth, thought about the hourly rate and smiled.

I staggered up the path, slithering slightly on the frosted cobbles, already imagining the sensuous bliss of slipping under a winter-weight feather-and-down duvet. As soon as I opened the door, the dream shattered. Even from the hallway I could see the glow of light from the conservatory. I could hear moody saxophone music and the mutter of voices. That they were in the conservatory rather than Richard's living room meant that whoever he was talking to was there for me.

My bag slid to the floor as my shoulders drooped. I walked through to the living room and took in the scene through the patio doors. Beer bottles, a plume of smoke from a joint, two male bodies sprawled across the wicker.

Just what I'd always wanted at the end of a working day. A pair of criminals in the conservatory.

3

VENUS SQUARES NEPTUNE

This is a tense aspect that produces strain in affairs of the heart because she has a higher expectation of love and comradeship than her world provides. She has a strong determination to beat the odds stacked against her.

From *Written in the Stars*, by Dorothea Dawson

It's not every night you feel like you need a Visiting Order to enter your own conservatory. That night I definitely wanted reinforcements before I could face the music or the men. A quick trip to the kitchen and I was equipped with a sweating tumbler of ice-cold pepper-flavoured Absolut topped up with pink grapefruit juice. I took a deep draught and headed for whatever Dennis and Richard had to throw at me.

When I say the conservatory was full of criminals, I was only slightly exaggerating. Although

Richard's insistence on the need for marijuana before creativity can be achieved means he cheerfully breaks the law every day, he's got no criminal convictions. Being a journalist, he doesn't have any other kind either.

Dennis is a different animal. He's a career criminal but, paradoxically, I trust him more than almost anyone. I always know where I am with Dennis; his morality might not be constructed along traditional lines, but it's more rigid than the law of gravity, and a hell of a lot more forgiving. He used to be a professional burglar; not the sort who breaks into people's houses to steal the video and rummage through the lingerie, but the sort who relieves the very rich of some of their ill-gotten and well-insured gains. Some of his victims had so many expensive status symbols lying around that they didn't even realize they'd been burgled. These days, he's more or less given up robbing anyone except other villains who've got too much pride to complain to the law. That's because, after his last enforced spell of taking care of business from behind high walls with no office equipment except a phone card, his wife told him she'd divorce him if he ever did anything else that carried a custodial sentence.

I've known Dennis even longer than I've known Richard. He's my Thai-boxing coach, and he taught me the basic principle of self-defence for someone as little as I am – one crippling kick to the kneecap or the balls, then run like hell. It's saved my life more than once, which is another good reason why Dennis will always be welcome in my house. Well, almost always.

I leaned against the doorjamb and scowled. 'I thought you didn't do drugs,' I said mildly to Dennis.

'You know I don't,' he said. 'Who's been telling porkies about me?'

'Nobody. I was referring to the atmosphere in here,' I said, wafting my hand in front of my face as I crossed the room to give Dennis a kiss on a cheek so smooth he must have shaved before he came out for the evening. 'Breathe and you're stoned. Not to mention cutting your life expectancy by half.'

'Nice to see you too, Brannigan,' my beloved said as I pushed the evening paper to one side and dropped on to the sofa next to him.

'So what are you two boys plotting?'

Dennis grinned like Wile E. Coyote. My heart sank. I was well past a convincing impersonation of the Road Runner. 'Wanted to pick your brains,' he said.

'And it couldn't wait till morning?' I groaned.

'I was passing.'

Richard gave the sort of soft giggle that comes after the fifth bottle and the fourth joint. I know my man. 'He was passing and he heard a bottle of Pete's Wicked Bohemian Pilsner calling his name,' he spluttered.

'Looking at the number of bottles, it looks more

like a crate shouting its head off,' I muttered. The boys looked like they were set to make a night of it. There was only one way I was going to come out of this alive and that was to sort out Dennis's problem. Then they might not notice if I answered the siren call of my duvet. 'How can I help, Dennis?' I asked sweetly.

He gave me the wary look of a person who's drunk enough to notice their other half isn't giving them the hard time they deserve. 'I could come back tomorrow,' he said.

'I don't think that'll be necessary,' I said repressively. 'Like the song says, tonight will be fine.'

Dennis gave me a quick sideways look and reached for his cigarettes. 'You never finished your law degree, did you?'

I shook my head. It was a sore point with my mum and dad, who fancied being the parents of the first graduate in the family, but all it brought me was relief that business could never be so bad that I'd be tempted to set up shop as a lawyer. Two years of study had been enough to demonstrate there wasn't a single area of legal practice that wouldn't drive me barking within six months.

'So you couldn't charge me for legal advice,' Dennis concluded triumphantly.

I raised my eyes to the heavens, where a few determined stars penetrated the sodium glow of the city sky. 'No, Dennis, I couldn't.' Then I gave him the hard stare. 'But why would I want to?

34

We've never sent each other bills before, have we? What exactly are you up to?'

'You know I'd never ask you to help me out with anything criminal, don't you?'

''Course you wouldn't. You're far too tight to waste your breath,' I said. Richard giggled again. I revised my estimate. Sixth bottle, fifth joint.

Dennis leaned across to pick up his jacket from the nearby chair, revealing splendid muscles in his forearm and a Ralph Lauren label. It didn't quite go with the jogging pants and the Manchester United away shirt. He pulled some papers out of the inside pocket then gave me a slightly apprehensive glance. Then he shrugged and said, 'It's not illegal. Not as such.'

'Not even a little bit?' I asked. I didn't bother trying to hide my incredulity. Dennis only takes offence when it's intended.

'This bit isn't illegal,' he said firmly. 'It's a lease.'

'A lease?'

'For a shop.'

'You're taking out a lease on a shop?' It was a bit like hearing Dracula had gone veggie.

He had the grace to look embarrassed. 'Only technically.'

I knew better than to ask more. Sometimes ignorance is not only bliss but also healthy. 'And you want me to cast an eye over it to see that you're not being ripped off,' I said, holding a hand out for the papers.

Curiously reluctant now, Dennis clutched the

papers to his chest. 'You do know about leases? I mean, it's not one of the bits you missed out, is it?'

It was, as it happened, but I wasn't about to tell him that. Besides, since I'd quit law school, I'd learned much more practical stuff about contracts and leases than I could ever have done if I'd stuck it out. 'Gimme,' I said.

'You don't want to argue with that tone of voice,' Richard chipped in like the Dormouse at the Mad Hatter's tea party. Dennis screwed his face up like a man eating a piccalilli sandwich, but he handed over the papers.

It looked like a bog standard lease to me. It was for a shop in the Arndale Centre, the soulless shopping mall in the city centre that the IRA tried to remove from the map back in '96. As usual, they got it wrong. The Arndale, probably the ugliest building in central Manchester, remained more or less intact. Unfortunately, almost every other building within a quarter-mile radius took a hell of a hammering, especially the ones that were actually worth looking at. As a result, the whole city centre ended up spending a couple of years looking like it had been wrapped by Christo in some bizarre pre-millennium celebration. Now it looked as if part of the mall that had been closed for structural repairs and renovation was opening up again and Dennis had got himself a piece of the action.

There was nothing controversial in the document, as far as I could see. If anything, it was skewed in favour of the lessee, one John Thompson, since it gave him the first three months at half rent as a supposed inducement. I wasn't surprised that it wasn't Dennis's name on the lease. He's a man who can barely bring himself to fill in his real name on the voters' roll. Besides, no self-respecting landlord would ever grant a lease to a man who, according to the credit-rating agencies, didn't even exist.

What I couldn't understand was what he was up to. Somehow, I couldn't get my head round the idea of Dennis as the natural heir of Marks and Spencer. Karl Marx, maybe, except that they'd have had radically different views of what constituted an appropriate redistribution of wealth. I folded the lease along its creases and said, 'Looks fine to me.'

Dennis virtually snatched it out of my hand and shoved it back in his pocket, looking far too shifty for a villain as experienced as him. 'Thanks, love. I just wanted to be sure everything's there that should be. That it looks right.'

I recognized the key word right away. Us detectives, we never sleep. 'Looks right?' I demanded. 'Why? Who else is going to be giving it the once-over?'

Dennis tried to look innocent. I've seen hunter-killer submarines give it a better shot. 'Just the usual, you know? The leccy board, the water board. They need to see the lease before they'll connect you to the utilities.'

'What's going on, Dennis? What's really going on?'

Richard pushed himself more or less upright and draped an arm over my shoulders. 'You might as well tell her, Den. You know what they say – it's better having her inside the tent pissing out than outside pissing in.'

I let him get away with the anatomical impossibility and settled for a savage grin. 'He's not wrong,' I said.

Dennis sighed and lit a cigarette. 'All right. But I meant it when I said it's not criminal.'

I cast my eyes upwards and shook my head. 'Dennis O'Brien, you know and I know that "not criminal" doesn't necessarily mean "legal".'

'Too deep for me,' Richard complained, reaching for another bottle of beer.

'Let's hear it,' I said firmly.

'You know how I hate waste,' Dennis began. I nodded cautiously. 'There's nothing more offensive to a man like me than premises standing empty because the landlords' agents are crap at their job. So I had this idea about making use of a resource that was just standing idle.'

'Shop-squatting,' I said flatly.

'What?' Richard asked vaguely. 'You going to live in a shop, Den? What happened to the house? Debbie thrown you out, has she?'

'He's not going to be living in the shop, dope-head,' I said sarcastically.

'You keep smoking that draw, you're going to

have a mental age of three soon,' Dennis added sententiously. 'Of course I'm not going to be living in the shop. I'm going to be selling things in the shop.'

'Take me through it,' I said. Dennis's latest idea was only new to him; he was far from the first in Manchester to give it a try. I remembered reading something in the *Evening Chronicle* about shop-squatting, but as usual with newspaper articles, it had told me none of the things I really wanted to know.

'You want to know how it works?'

Silly question to ask a woman whose first watch lasted only as long as it took me to work out how to get the back off. 'Was Georgie Best?'

'First off, you identify your premises. Find some empty shops and give the agents a ring. What you're looking for is one where the agent says they're not taking any offers because it's already let as from a couple of months ahead.'

'What?' Richard mumbled.

Dennis and I shared the conspiratorial grin of those who are several drinks behind the mentally defective. 'That way, you know it's going to stay empty for long enough for you to get in and out and do the business in between,' he explained patiently.

'Next thing you do is you get somebody to draw you up a moody contract. One that looks like you've bought a short-term lease in good faith, cash on the nail. All you gotta do then is get into the shop and Bob's your uncle. Get the leccy and the water turned on, fill the place with crap, everything under a pound, which you can afford to do because you've got no overheads. And the Dibble can't touch you for it, on account of you've broken no laws.'

'What about criminal damage?' I asked. 'You have to bust the locks to get in.'

Dennis winked. 'If you pick the locks, you've not done any damage. And if you fit some new locks to give extra security, where's the damage in that?'

'Doesn't the landlord try to close you down?' Richard asked. It was an amazingly sensible question given his condition.

Dennis shrugged. 'Some of them can't be bothered. They know we'll be out of there before their new tenant needs the premises, so they've got nothing to lose. Some of them have a go. I keep somebody on the premises all the time, just in case they try to get clever and repo the place in the night. You can get a homeless kid to play night watchman for a tenner a time. Give them a mobile phone and a butty and lock them in. Then if the landlord tries anything, I get the call and I get down there sharpish. He lays a finger on me or my lad, he's the criminal.' Dennis smiled with all the warmth of a shark. 'I'm told you get a very reasonable response when you explain the precise legal position.'

'I can imagine,' I said drily. 'Do the explanations come complete with baseball bat?'

'Can people help it if they get the summons

when they're on their way home from sports training?' He raised his eyebrows, trying for innocent and failing dismally.

'Profitable, is it?' I asked.

'It's got to be a very nice little earner, what with Christmas coming up.'

'You know, Dennis, if you put half the effort into a straight business that you put into being bent, you'd be a multimillionaire by now,' I sighed.

He shook his head, rueful. 'Maybe so, but where would the fun be in that?'

He had a point. And who was I to talk? I'd turned my back on the straight version of my life a long time ago. If Dennis broke the law for profit, so did I. I'd committed burglary, fraud, assault, theft, deception and breaches of the Wireless and Telegraph Act too numerous to mention, and that was just in the past six months. I dressed it up with the excuse of doing it for the clients and my own version of justice. It had led me into some strange places, forced me into decisions that I didn't like to examine too closely in the harsh light of day. Once upon a time, I'd have had no doubt whether it was me or Dennis who could lay claim to the better view from the moral high ground.

These days, I wasn't quite so sure.

4

MOON SQUARES MARS

An accident-prone aspect, suggesting she can harm herself through lack of forethought. She is far too eager to make her presence felt and doesn't always practice self-control. Her feelings of insecurity can manifest themselves in an unfeminine belligerence. She has authoritarian tendencies.

From *Written in the Stars*, by Dorothea Dawson

Anyone can be a soap star. All you need is a script-writer who knows you well enough to write your character into their series, and you're laughing all the way to the BAFTA. I'd always thought you had to be an actor. But two hours on the set of *Northerners* made me realize that soap is different. About ten per cent of the cast could play Shakespeare or Stoppard. The rest just roll up to the studios every week and play themselves. The lovable rogues are just as roguish, the dizzy blondes are just as empty-headed, the salts of the earth make you thirst just as much for a long cold alcoholic drink and the ones the nation loves to hate are every bit as repulsive in the flesh. Actually, they're more repulsive, since anyone hanging round the green room is exposed to rather more of their flesh than a reasonable person could desire. There was more chance of me being struck by lightning than being star struck by that lot of has-beens and wannabes.

They didn't even have to learn their words. TV takes are so short that a gnat with Alzheimer's could retain the average speech with no trouble at all. Especially by the sixth or seventh take most of the *Northerners* cast seemed to need to capture the simplest sentiment on screen.

The main problem I had was how to do my job. Gloria had told everyone I was her bodyguard. Not because I couldn't come up with a decent cover story, but because I'd weighed up both sides of the argument and decided that if there was somebody in cast or crew who was out to get her it was time for them to understand they should back off and forget about it. Gloria had been all for the cloak and dagger approach, hoping I could catch the author of her threatening letters in the act of extracting vengeance, but I pointed out that if I was going to stay close enough to protect her, I'd be an obvious obstacle to nefarious doings anyway.

Besides, members of the public weren't allowed on the closed set of *Northerners*. The storylines were supposed to be top secret. NPTV, the company who made the soap, were so paranoid they made New Labour look relaxed. Everyone who worked on the programme had to sign an agreement that disclosure of any information relating to the cast characters or storylines was gross misconduct, a sacking offence and a strict liability tort. Even I had had to sign up to the tort clause before I was allowed into the compound that housed the interior and exterior sets, as well as the production suite and admin offices. Apart from location shooting to give the show that authentic Manchester ambience, the entire process from script conference to edited master tapes took place behind the high walls that surrounded NPTV's flagship complex.

A fat lot of good it did them. *Northerners* generated more column inches than any other TV programme in the country. The fuel for the flames had to come from somewhere, and tabloid papers have always had deep pockets. There's not a tabloid journalist I've ever met who couldn't explain in words of one syllable to a nervously dithering source that the NPTV legal threat of suing for civil damages was about as solid as the plyboard walls of Brenda Barrowclough's living room.

But NPTV insisted on their power trip, and I'd persuaded Gloria it would be simpler all round if we were upfront. The downside of being out in the open was that everyone was on their guard. Nobody was going to let anything slip accidentally. If my target was a member of the *Northerners* team, they'd be very careful around me.

In order to be effective protection for my client, I had to be visible, which meant that I couldn't even find a quiet corner and catch up with my e-mail and my invoices. If Gloria was in make-up, I was in make-up. If Gloria was on set, I was hovering round the edges of the set, getting in everybody's way. If Gloria was having a pee, I was leaning against the tampon dispenser. I could have made one of those video diary programmes that would have had any prospective private eye applying for a job as a hospital auxiliary.

I was trying to balance that month's books in my head when a hand on my shoulder lifted my feet off the floor. Spot the alert bodyguard. I spun round and found my nose level with the top button of a suit jacket. I took a step back and looked up. The man must have been six-three, wide shouldered and heavy featured. The suit, whose tailoring owed more to Savile Row than to Armani, was cut to disguise the effects of too many business lunches and dinners, but this guy was still a long way off fat. On the other hand, he looked as if he was still only in his early forties and in the kind of trim that betrays a commitment to regular exercise. In a few years, when his joints started complaining and his stamina wasn't what it had been, he'd swiftly slip into florid flabbiness. I'd seen the type. Greed was always a killer.

The smile on his broad face softened the stern good looks that come with a square jaw, a broad brow and deep-set eyes under overhanging brows.

'You must be Kate Brannigan,' he said, extending a hand. 'I didn't mean to startle you. I'm John Turpin.'

For a man who'd gone out of his way to try to persuade Gloria to keep her problems in the family, he seemed amazingly cordial. 'Pleased to meet you,' I said.

'How are your investigations proceeding?' he asked, smiling down on me benevolently.

'I could ask you the same question.' If the guy was trying to win me over with his affable helpfulness, the least I could do was take advantage and trawl for some information.

His smile curved up at one corner, suddenly turning his expression from magnanimous to predatory. 'I'm afraid I'm more of a guardian of company confidentiality than Ms Kendal,' he said, with a note of acid in his voice.

'But you expect me to share with you?' I asked innocently.

He chuckled. 'Not really, but it never hurts to try. As you yourself so ably demonstrated. I had hoped we could keep Ms Kendal's little problem in-house, but if she insists on wasting her money on services we can provide more effectively and for free, I can't stop her.'

'Can I tell her when to expect the results of your internal inquiry?' I wasn't playing the sweetness and light game any more. It hadn't got me anywhere so I figured I might as well turn into Ms Businesslike.

Turpin thrust one hand into his jacket pocket, thumb sticking out like Prince Charles always has. 'Impossible to say. I have so many calls on my time, most of them rather more serious than the antics of some poison-pen writer.'

'She had her car tyres slashed. All four of them. On NPTV premises,' I reminded him.

'It's a bitchy business, soap,' he said calmly. 'I'm far from convinced there's any connection between the letters and the car tyres. I can't believe you find it hard to credit that Ms Kendal could annoy a colleague enough for them to lose their temper and behave so childishly.'

'You're really not taking this seriously, are you?' I said, struggling to keep the incredulity out of my voice.

'That's what you're being paid for, Ms Brannigan. Me, I've got a television production company to run.' He inclined his head and gave me the full charm offensive again. 'It's been a pleasure.'

I said nothing, just watched his retreating back with its double-vent tailoring that perfectly camouflaged the effects of too many hours sitting behind a desk. If our conversation was par for the course around here, the only surprise was that it had taken Gloria so long to get round to hiring me.

In spite of Turpin's intervention, by lunchtime I was more bored than I'd been in the weeks before I finally managed to jettison A level Latin. If anyone had asked, I'd have admitted to being up for any distraction. I'd have been lying, as I discovered when my moby rang, right in the middle of the fifth run-through of a tense scene between my client and the putative father of her granddaughter's aborted foetus.

Mortified, I twisted my face into an apologetic grimace as the actor playing opposite Gloria glared at me and muttered, 'For fuck's sake. What is this? Fucking amateur city?' The six months he'd once spent on remand awaiting trial for rape (according to the front page of the *Sun* a couple of months back) hadn't improved his word power, then.

I ducked behind a props skip and tucked my head down into my chest as I grunted, 'Hello?'

'Kate? I've been arrested.' The voice was familiar, the scenario definitely wasn't. Donovan Carmichael was a second-year engineering student at UMIST. He'd just started eking out his pathetic student grant by working part time for me as a process-server, doing the bread and butter work that pays his mother's wages. Did I mention Shelley the office tyrant was his mother? And that she hated the thought that her highly educated baby boy might be tempted to throw it all away to become a maverick of the mean streets like her boss? That probably explained why said boy was using his one phone call on me rather than on his doting mother.

'What for?'

'Being black, I think,' he said angrily.

'What happened?'

'I was in Hale Barns.' That explained a lot. They don't have a lot of six-feet-three-inch black lads in Hale Barns, especially not ones with shoulders wider than the flashy sports cars in their four-car garages. It would lower the property values too much.

'Doing what?'

'Working,' he said. 'You know? Trying to make that delivery that came in yesterday afternoon?' His way of telling me there were other ears on our conversation. I knew he was referring to a domestic violence injunction we'd been hired to serve. The husband had broken his wife's cheek-bone the last time he'd had a bad day. If Donovan succeeded in serving the paper, there might not be a next time. But there were very good reasons why Donovan was reluctant to reveal his target or our client's name to the cops. Once you get outside the high-profile city-centre divisions that are constantly under scrutiny, you find that most policemen don't have a lot of sympathy for the victims of domestic violence. Especially when the guy who's been doing the battering is one of the city's biggest football stars. He'd given a whole new meaning to the word 'striker', but that wouldn't stop him being a hero in the eyes of the boys in blue.

'Are they charging you with anything?'

'They've not interviewed me yet.'

'Which nick are you in?'

'Altrincham.'

I looked at my watch. I stuck my head round the side of the skip. They were about to go for a take. 'I'll get someone there as soon as I can. Till then, say nothing. OK?' I said in a low voice.

I didn't wait for a reply, just ended the call and tiptoed back to the set. Gloria and the idiot boy she was acting opposite went through their interaction for the eighth time and the director announced she was satisfied. Gloria heaved a seismic sigh and walked off the set, dragging Brenda's beehive from her head as she approached me. 'That's me for today, chuck,' she said. 'Drop me at home and you can have the rest of the day off.'

'Are you staying in?' I asked, falling into step beside her as we walked to the dressing room she shared with Rita Hardwick, the actress who played Thelma Torrance, the good-time girl who'd never grown up.

'I am that. I've got to pick up next month's scripts from the office on the way out. I'll be lying in the Jacuzzi learning my lines till bedtime. It's not a pretty sight, and I don't need a spectator. Especially one that charges me for the privilege,' she added with an earthy chuckle.

I tried not to look as pleased as I felt. I could have sent a lawyer out to rescue Donovan, but it didn't sound as if things had reached the point where I couldn't sort it out myself, and lawyers cost either money I couldn't afford or favours I didn't want to owe.

*   *   *

Two hours later, I was walking Donovan back to my car. The police don't like private eyes, but faced with me threatening a lawsuit for false imprisonment and racial harassment, they were only too happy to release Donovan from the interview room where he'd been pacing the floor for every one of the minutes it had taken me to get there.

'I didn't do anything, you know,' Donovan complained. His anger seethed just below the surface. I couldn't blame him, but for all our sakes, I hoped the cycle ride back into town would get it out of his system.

'According to the copper I spoke to, one of the neighbours saw you sneaking round the back of the house and figured you for a burglar,' I said drily.

'Yeah, right. All I was doing was checking if he was in the snooker room round the back, like his wife said he usually is if he's not training in the morning. I reckoned if he was there, and I walked right up to the French windows, he'd be bound to come over and open up, at least to give me a bollocking. When I saw the place was empty, I came back down the drive and went and sat on a wall down the road, where I could see him come home. It's not like I was hiding,' he continued. 'They only arrested me because I'm black. Anybody black on the street in Hale Barns has got to be a burglar, right?'

'Or a drug dealer. The rich have got to get their coke and heroin from somewhere,' I pointed out reasonably. 'Where's your bike?'

'Hale Barns. Chained to a lamppost, I hope.'

'Let's go back out there and do it,' I sighed.

The leafy lanes of Hale Barns were dripping a soft rain down our necks as we walked along the grass verge that led to our target's house. Wrought-iron gates stood open, revealing a long drive done in herringbone brick. There was enough of it there to build a semi. At the top of the drive, a matching pair of Mercedes sports cars were parallel parked. My heart sank. 'I don't believe it,' I muttered.

We walked up the drive towards a vast white hacienda-style ranch that would have been grandiose in California. In Cheshire, it just looked silly. I leaned on the doorbell. There was a long pause, then the door swung silently open without warning. I recognized his face from the back pages of the *Chronicle*. For once, I didn't have to check ID before I served the papers. 'Yeah?' he said, frowning. 'Who are you?'

I leaned forward and stuffed the papers down the front of the towelling robe that was all he was wearing. 'I'm Kate Brannigan, and you are well and truly served,' I said.

As I spoke, over his shoulder, I saw a woman in a matching robe emerge from an archway. Like him, she looked as if she'd been in bed, and not for an afternoon nap. I recognized her from the *Chronicle* too. From the diary pages. Former model

Bo Robinson. Better known these days as the wife of the man I'd just served with the injunction her solicitor had sweated blood to get out of a district judge.

Now I remembered what I'd hated most about my own days as a process-server.

The last thing Donovan had said before he'd pedalled off to the university library was, 'Don't tell my mum I got arrested, OK? Not even as a joke. Not unless you want her to put the blocks on me working for you again.'

I'd agreed. Jokes are supposed to be funny, after all. Unfortunately, the cops at Altrincham weren't in on the deal. What I didn't know was that while I'd been savouring the ambience of their lovely foyer (decor by the visually challenged, furnishings by a masochist, posters from a template unchanged since 1959) the desk sergeant had been calling the offices of Brannigan & Co to check that the auburn-haired midget and the giant in the sweat suit really were operatives of the agency and not a pair of smart-mouthed burglars on the make.

I'd barely put a foot inside the door when Shelley's voice hit me like a blast furnace. 'Nineteen years old and never been inside a police station,' came the opening salvo. 'Five minutes working with you, and he might as well be some smackhead from Moss Side. That's it now, his name's on their computer. Another black bastard who's got away with it, that's how they'll have him down.'

I raised my palms towards her, trying to fend off her fury. 'It's all right, Shelley. He wasn't formally arrested. They won't be putting anything into the computer.'

Shelley snorted. 'You're so street smart when it comes to your business. How come you can be so naive about our lives? You don't have the faintest idea what it means for a boy like Donovan to get picked up by the police! They don't see a hard-working boy who's been brought up to respect his elders and stay away from drugs. They just see another black face where it doesn't belong. And you put him there.'

I edged across reception, trying to make the safe haven of my own office without being permanently disabled by the crossfire. 'Shelley, he's a grown man. He has to make his own decisions. I told him when I took him on that serving process wasn't as easy as it sounded. But he was adamant that he could handle it.'

'Of course he can handle it,' she yelled. 'He's not the problem. It's the other assholes out there, that's the problem. I don't want him doing this any more.'

I'd almost reached the safety of my door. 'You'll have to take that up with Don,' I told her, sounding more firm than I felt.

'I will, don't you worry about that,' she vowed.

'OK. But don't forget the reason he's doing this.'

Her eyes narrowed. 'What are you getting at?'

'It's about independence. He's trying to earn his own money so he's not dipping his hand in your pocket all the time. He's trying to tell you he's a man now.' I took a deep breath, trying not to feel intimidated by the scowl that was drawing Shelley's perfectly shaped eyebrows into a gnarled scribble. My hand on the doorknob, I delivered what was supposed to be the knockout punch. 'You've got to let him make his own mistakes. You've got to let him go.'

I opened the door and dived for safety. No such luck. Instead of silent sanctuary, I fell into nerd heaven. A pair of pink-rimmed eyes looked up accusingly at me. Under the pressure of Shelley's rage, I'd forgotten that my office wasn't mine any more. Now I was the sole active partner in Brannigan & Co, I occupied the larger of the two rooms that opened off reception. When I'd been junior partner in Mortensen & Brannigan it had doubled as Bill Mortensen's office and the main client interview room. Now, it was my sanctum.

These days, my former bolthole was the computer room, occupied as and when the occasion demanded by Gizmo, our information technology consultant. In our business, that's the polite word for hacker. And when it comes to prowling other people's systems with cat-like tread, Gizmo is king of the dark hill. The trade off for his computer acumen is that on a scale of one to ten, his social skills come in somewhere around absolute zero. I'm convinced that was the principal reason he was made redundant from his job as systems wizard with Telecom. Now they've become a multinational leading-edge company, everybody who works there has to pass for human. Silicon-based life forms like Gizmo just had to be downsized out the door.

Their loss was my gain. There had had to be changes, of course. Plain brown envelopes stuffed with banknotes had been replaced with a system more appealing to the taxman, if not to the company accountant. Then there was the personal grooming. Gizmo had always favoured an appearance that would have served as perfect camouflage if he'd been living on a refuse tip.

The clothes weren't so hard. I managed to make him stop twitching long enough to get the key measurements, then hit a couple of designer factory outlets during the sales. I was planning to dock the cost from his first consultancy fees, but I didn't want it to terrify him too much. Now he had two decent suits, four shirts that didn't look disastrous unironed, a couple of inoffensive ties and a mac that any flasher would have been proud of. I could wheel him out as our computer security expert without frightening the clients, and he had a couple of outfits that wouldn't entirely destroy his street cred if another of the undead happened to be on the street in daylight hours to see him.

The haircut had been harder. I don't think he'd

spent money on a haircut since 1987. I'd always thought he simply took a pair of scissors to any stray locks whose reflection in the monitor distracted him from what he was working on. Gizmo tried to make me believe he liked it that way. It cost me five beers to get him to the point where I could drag him across the threshold of the city centre salon where I'd already had to cancel three times. The stylist had winced in pain, but had overcome his aesthetic suffering for long enough to do the business. Giz ended up with a seriously sharp haircut and I ended up gobsmacked that lurking underneath the shambolic dress sense and terrible haircut was a rather attractive man. Scary.

Three months down the line, he was still looking the business, his hollow cheeks and bloodshot eyes fitting the current image of heroin addict as male glamour. I'd even overheard one of Shelley's adolescent daughter's mates saying she thought Gizmo was 'shaggable'. That *Trainspotting* has a lot to answer for. 'All right,' he mumbled, already looking back at his screen. 'You two want to keep the noise down?'

'Sorry, Giz. I didn't actually mean to come in here.'

'Know what you mean,' he said.

Before I could leave, the door burst open. 'And another thing,' Shelley said. 'You've not done a new client file for Gloria Kendal.'

Gizmo's head came up like it was on a string.

'Gloria Kendal? *The* Gloria Kendal? Brenda Barrow-clough off *Northerners*?'

I nodded.

'She's a client?'

'I can't believe you watch *Northerners*,' I said.

'She was in here yesterday,' Shelley said smugly. 'She signed a photograph for me personally.'

'Wow! Gloria Kendal. Cool! Anything I can do to help?' The last time I'd seen him this excited was over an advance release of Netscape Navigator 3.0.

'I'll let you know,' I promised. 'Now, if you'll both excuse me, I have some work to do.' I smiled sweetly and sidled past Shelley. As I crossed the threshold, the outside door opened and a massive basket of flowers walked in. Lilies, roses, carnations, and a dozen other things I didn't know the names of. For a wild moment, I thought Richard might be apologizing for the night before. He had cause, given what had gone on after Dennis had left. The thought shrivelled and died as hope was overtaken by experience.

'They'll be from Gloria Kendal,' Shelley predicted.

I contradicted her. 'It'll be Donovan mortgaging his first month's wages to apologize to you.'

'Wrong address,' Gizmo said gloomily. Given the way the day had been running, he was probably right.

'Is this Brannigan and Co?' the flowers asked. For such an exotic arrangement, they had a remarkably prosaic Manchester accent.

'That's right,' I said. 'I'm Brannigan.' I stepped forward expectantly.

'They're not for you, love,' the voice said, half a face appearing round the edge of the blooms. 'You got someone here called Gizmo?'

5

JUPITER IN CANCER IN THE 3RD HOUSE

Jupiter is exalted in Cancer. She has a philosophical outlook, enjoying speculative thinking. She is good humoured and generous, with strong protective instincts. Her intuition and imagination are powerful tools that she could develop profitably. She has a good business sense and communicates well in that sphere. She probably writes very thorough reports.

From *Written in the Stars*, by Dorothea Dawson

It was hard to keep my mind on Gloria's monologue on the way in to the studios the next morning. The conundrum of Gizmo's mysterious bouquet was much more interesting than her analysis of the next month's storylines for *Northerners*. When the delivery man had announced who the flowers were for, Shelley and I had rounded on Gizmo. Scarlet and stammering, he'd refused to reveal anything. Shelley, who's always been quick on her feet, helped herself to the card attached to the bouquet and ripped open the envelope.

All it said was, 'www gets real'. I know. I was looking over her shoulder. The delivery man had placed the flowers on Shelley's desk and legged it. He'd clearly seen enough blood shed over bouquets to hang around. 'So who have you been chatting up on the Internet?' I demanded. 'Who's the cyberbabe?'

'Cyberbabe?' Shelley echoed.

I pointed to the card. 'www. The worldwide web. The Internet. It's from someone he's met websurfing. Well, not actually met, as such. Exchanged e-mail with.'

'Safer than body fluids,' Shelley commented drily. 'So who's the cyberbabe, Gizmo?'

Gizmo shook his head. 'It's a joke,' he said with the tentative air of a man who doesn't expect to be believed. 'Just the guys trying to embarrass me at work.'

I shook my head. 'I don't think so. I've never met a techie yet who'd spend money on flowers while there was still software on the planet.'

'Honest, Kate, it's a wind-up,' he said desperately.

'Some expensive wind-up,' Shelley commented. 'Did one of your mates win the lottery, then?'

'There is no babe, OK? Leave it, eh?' he said, this time sounding genuinely upset.

So we'd left it, sensitive girls that we are. Gizmo retreated back to his hi-tech hermitage and Shelley shrugged. 'No use looking at me, Kate. He's not going to fall for the, "You can talk to me, I'm a woman, I understand these things," routine. It's down to you.'

'Men never cry on my shoulder,' I protested.

'No, but you're the only one around here who knows enough about computers to find who he's been talking to.'

I shook my head. 'No chance. If Gizmo's got a cybersecret, it'll be locked away somewhere I won't be able to find it. We'll just have to do this the hard way. First thing tomorrow, you better get on to the florist.'

Call me a sad bastard, but as I was driving Gloria to the studios, I was busy working out how we could discover Gizmo's secret admirer if she'd been clever enough to cover her tracks on the flower delivery. So I almost missed it when Gloria asked me a question that needed more than a grunt in response. 'So you don't mind coming along tonight?'

'No, that's fine,' I said, not quite certain what I'd agreed to.

'I'm really buggering up your social life, chuck,' she continued. 'If you've got a fella you want to bring along, you're welcome, you know.'

I must have shown how unlikely a prospect that was, since Gloria chuckled. 'He's a rock journalist,' I said.

She roared with laughter. 'Better not bring him anywhere I'm singing, then,' she spluttered. 'I'm too old to be insulted.'

By the time we reached the studios, the sky had clouded over and large raindrops were plopping on the windscreen. 'Oh bugger,' Gloria said.

'Problems?'

'We're supposed to be filming outside this morning. When it's raining like this, they'll hang on to see if it clears up and fill the time with the indoor scenes scheduled for this afternoon. I'm not in any of them, so not only do I lose an afternoon off but I get a morning hanging around waiting for the weather to change.' She rummaged in the bulging satchel that contained her scripts and pulled out a crumpled schedule. 'Let's see . . . Could be worse. Teddy and Clive are in the same boat. D'you play bridge, Kate?'

'Badly. I haven't played against humans since I was a student, and these days the computer usually gives me a coating.'

'You can't be worse than Rita Hardwick,' she said firmly. 'That's settled then.'

'Two spades,' I said tentatively. My partner, Clive Doran (Billy Knowles, the crooked bookmaker with an eye for his female employees) nodded approval.

'Pass,' said Gloria.

'Three hearts.'

'Doubled,' announced Teddy Edwards, Gloria's screen husband, the feckless Arthur Barrowclough, cowboy builder and failed gambler. I hoped he had as much luck with cards in real life as he did on screen. What Gloria had omitted to mention in the car was that we were playing for 10p a point. I suppose she figured she was paying me so much she needed to win some of it back.

I looked at my hand. 'Redoubled,' I said boldly. Clive raised one eyebrow. My bid passed round the table, and we started playing. I soon realized that the other three were so used to each other's game that they only needed a small proportion of their brains to choose the next card. The bridge game was just an excuse to gossip in the relative privacy of Gloria's dressing room.

'Seen the *Sun* this morning?' Clive asked, casually tossing a card down.

'It'd be hard to miss it,' Gloria pointed out. 'I don't know about where you live, but every newsagent we passed on the way in had a board outside. Gay soap star exposed: Exclusive. I sometimes wonder if this is the end of the nineteenth century, not the twentieth. I mean, who gives a stuff if Gary Bond's a poof? None of us does, and we're the ones as have to work with the lad.'

'They're bloody idle, them hacks,' Teddy grumbled, sweeping a trick from the table that I'd thought my ace of diamonds was bound to win.

Clive sucked his breath in over his teeth. 'How d'you mean?'

'It couldn't have taken much digging out. It's not like it's a state secret, Gary being a homo. He's always going on about lads he's pulled on a night out in the gay village.' Teddy sighed. 'I remember when it were just the red light district round Canal Street. Back in them days, if you fancied a bit, at least you could be sure it was a woman under the frock.'

'And it's not as if he's messing about with kids,' Gloria continued, taking the next trick. 'Nice lead, Teddy. I mean, Gary always goes for fellas his own age.'

'There's been a lot of heavy stories about *Northerners* lately,' I said. I might be playing dummy in this hand, but that didn't mean I had to take the job literally.

'You're not kidding,' Clive said with feeling, sweeping his thin hair back from his narrow forehead in a familiar gesture. 'You get used to living in a goldfish bowl, but lately it's been ridiculous. We're all behaving like Sunday-school teachers.'

'Aye, but you can be as good as gold for all the benefit you'll get if the skeletons are already in the cupboard,' said Gloria. 'Seventeen years since Tony Peverell got nicked for waving his willy at a couple of lasses. He must have thought that were dead and buried long since. Then up it pops on the front of the *News of the World*. And his wife a churchwarden.' She shook her head. I remembered the story.

'He quit the programme, didn't he?' I asked, making a note of our winning score and gathering the cards to me so I could shuffle while Gloria dealt the next hand with the other pack.

'Did he fall or was he pushed?' Clive intoned. It would have sounded sinister from someone who didn't have a snub nose and a dimple in his chin and a manner only marginally less camp than Kenneth Williams. It was hard to believe he was happily married with three kids, but according to Gloria, the limp-wristed routine was nothing more than a backstage affectation. 'And I should know,' she'd winked. I didn't ask.

'What do you mean?' I asked now.

'John Turpin's what he means,' Gloria said. 'I told you about Turpin, didn't I? The management's hatchet man. Administration and Production Coordinator, they call him. Scumbag, we call him. Just a typical bloody TV executive who's never made a programme all his born days but thinks he knows better than everybody else what makes good telly.'

'Turpin's in charge of cast contracts,' Clive explained, sorting his cards. 'So he's the one who's technically responsible when there's a leak to the press. He's been running around like all Four Horsemen of the Apocalypse rolled into one for the last six months. He threatens, he rants, he rages, but still the stories keep leaking out. One diamond.'

'Pass. It drives him demented,' Teddy said with a smug little smile that revealed rodent teeth.

'One heart?' I tried, wondering what message that was sending to my partner. When he'd asked what system of bidding I preferred, I'd had to smile weakly and say, 'Psychic?' He hadn't looked impressed.

'It's not the scandals that really push his blood pressure through the ceiling. It's the storyline leaks.' Gloria lit a cigarette, eyeing Teddy speculatively. 'Two clubs. Remember when the *Sunday Mirror* got hold of that tale about Colette's charity?'

'Colette Darvall?' I asked.

'That's right.'

'I must have missed that one,' I said.

'Two diamonds,' Clive said firmly. 'Off the planet that month, were you? When her daughter was diagnosed with MS, Colette met up with all these other people who had kids in the same boat. So she let them use her as a sort of figurehead for a charity. She worked her socks off for them. She was always doing PAs for free, giving them stuff to raffle, donating interview fees and all sorts. Then it turns out one of the organizers has been ripping the charity off. He legged it to the West Indies with all the cash. Which would have been nothing more than a rather embarrassing tragedy for everyone concerned if it hadn't been for the unfortunate detail that he'd been shagging Colette's brains out for the previous three months.'

'Oops,' I said.

'By heck, you private eyes know how to swear, don't you?' Teddy said acidly. 'I don't think "oops" was quite what Colette was saying. But Turpin was all right about that. He stuck one of the press officers on her doorstep night and day for a week and told her not to worry about her job.'

'That's because having a fling with somebody else's husband is sexy in PR terms, whereas flashing at schoolgirls is just sleazy,' Clive said. 'Have you taken a vow of silence, Teddy? Or are you going to bid?'

'Oh God,' Teddy groaned. 'Who dealt this dross? I'm going to have to pass. Sorry, Glo.'

'Pass,' I echoed.

'And I make it three in a row. It's all yours, Clive.' Gloria leaned back in her chair and blew a plume of smoke towards the ceiling. 'God, I love it when Rita's not here to whinge about me smoking.'

'Better not let Turpin catch you,' Clive said.

'He sounds a real prize, this Turpin,' I said. 'I met him yesterday and he was nice as ninepence to me. Told me nothing, mind you, but did it charmingly.'

'Smooth-talking bastard. He did the square root of bugger-all about sorting out my security. Bloody chocolate teapot,' Gloria said dismissively. 'At least this latest furore about the future of the show has stopped him going on about finding out who's leaking the storylines to the press.'

'The future of the show? They're surely not going to axe *Northerners*?' It was a more radical suggestion than abolishing the monarchy, and one that would have had a lot more people rioting in the streets. For some reason, the public forgave the sins of the cast of their favourite soap far more readily than those of the House of Windsor, even though they paid both lots of wages, one via their taxes, the other via the hidden tax of advertising.

'Don't be daft,' Gloria said. 'Of course they're not going to axe *Northerners*. That'd be like chocolate voting for Easter. No, what they're on about is moving us to a satellite or cable channel.'

I stared blankly at her, the cards forgotten. 'But that would mean losing all your viewers. There's only two people and a dog watch cable.'

'And the dog's a guide dog,' Teddy chipped in gloomily.

'The theory is that if *Northerners* defects to one of the pay-to-view channels, the viewers will follow,' Clive said. 'The men in suits think our following is so addicted that they'd rather shell out for a satellite dish than lose their three times weekly fix of an everyday story of northern folk.'

'Hardly everyday,' I muttered. 'You show me anywhere in Manchester where nobody stays out of work for more than a fortnight and where the corner shop, the fast-food outlet and the local newsagent are still run by white Anglo-Saxons.'

'We're not a bloody documentary,' Teddy said. He'd clearly heard similar complaints before. His irritation didn't upset me unduly, since it resulted in him throwing away the rest of the hand with one hasty lead.

'No, we're a fantasy,' Clive said cheerfully, sweeping up the next trick and laying down his cards. 'I think the rest are ours. What we're providing, Kate, is contemporary nostalgia. We're harking back to a past that never existed, but we're translating it into contemporary terms. People feel alienated and lonely in the city and we create the illusion that they're part of a community. A community where all the girls are pretty, all the lads have lovely shoulders and any woman over thirty-five is veneered with a kind of folk wisdom.'

I was beginning to understand why Clive hid behind the camp manner. Underneath it all there lay a sharper mind than most of his fellow cast members ever exhibited. He was just as self-absorbed as they were, but at least he'd given some thought to how he earned his considerable living. I bet that made him really popular in a green room populated by egos who were each convinced they were the sole reason for the show's success. 'So you reckon the tug of fantasy is so strong that the millions who tune in three times a week will take out their satellite subscriptions like a bunch of little lambs?' I said, my scepticism obvious.

'*We* don't, chuck,' Gloria said, lighting a fresh cigarette while Clive dealt the cards. 'But the management do.'

'That's hardly surprising,' Teddy said. 'They're the ones who are going to make a bomb whatever happens.'

'How come?' I asked.

'The contract NPTV has with the ITV network is due for renegotiation. The network knows NPTV have been talking to satellite and cable companies with a view to them buying first rights in *Northerners* for the next three years. So the network knows that the price is going to have to go up. There's going to be a bidding war. And the only winners are going to be the management at NPTV, with their pocketfuls of share options. If they're wrong and the viewers don't follow the programme in droves, it doesn't matter to them, because they'll already have their hot sticky hands on the cash,' Clive explained.

'So Turpin needs to plug the storyline leak,' Gloria said, examining her cards.

'I'm not sure I follow you. Surely any publicity is good publicity?'

'Not when it involves letting the public know in advance what's going to happen,' Teddy said, raising his eyes to the heavens as if I was stupid. I didn't react. After all, I wasn't the one who was currently fourteen quid out of pocket.

Clive took pity on my puzzlement. 'If people know the big storylines in advance, a lot of them think it won't be the end of the world if they miss a few eps, because they know what they'll be missing. Once they get out of the habit of watching every ep religiously, their viewing habits drift.'

'They find other programmes on at the same time that they get to like. They don't bother setting the video to watch us because they think they already know what's going to happen. Or they just go down the pub. Before you know it, they've lost touch with the programme,' Gloria continued. 'One heart.'

'Especially now we're three times a week. You dip out for two, three weeks and when you come back, you don't know some of the faces. I'm going to pass this time.'

Teddy tugged at his shirt collar, a mannerism either he'd borrowed from Arthur Barrowclough or the character had borrowed from him. 'Two hearts. And every time the viewing figures drop, John Turpin sees his share of the profits going down.'

'And we get to watch his blood pressure going up,' Gloria said. 'Three hearts,' she added, noting my shake of the head.

'I'd have thought he'd be on to a loser, trying to find out who's behind it. It's too good an earner for the mole to give it up, and no journalist on the receiving end of a series of exclusives like that is going to expose a source,' I said.

'It won't be for want of trying,' Gloria said. 'He's even got every script coded so that any photocopied pages can be traced back. I hope whoever it is really is making a killing, because they're not going to earn another shilling off NPTV if they're caught.'

'You'll never work in this town again,' Teddy drawled in a surprisingly convincing American accent. I was so accustomed to him behaving in character I'd almost forgotten he was an actor.

'And speaking of making a killing, Gloria, any more news from your stalker?'

Gloria scowled. 'By heck, Clive, you know how to put a girl off her game. No, I've heard nowt since I took Kate on. I'm hoping we've frightened him off.'

'How do you know it's a he?' Clive said.

'Believe me, Clive, I know.'

We played out the hand in silence for a moment. In bridge as in life, I've always been better at defence than attack. Clive also seemed to relish the taste of blood and we left Gloria and Teddy three tricks short of their contract. My client raised her eyebrows and lit another cigarette. 'She lied so beautifully, Teddy. I really believed her when she said she was crap at this.'

'Don't tell Turpin,' Teddy said sharply. 'He'll hire her out from under you.'

'My dears, for all we know, he's done that already,' Clive said archly.

I should be so lucky, I thought as they all stared at me. I'm not proud about whose money I take. Maybe I should engineer another encounter with Turpin the hatchet man and kill two birds with one stone. Gloria's eyes narrowed, either from the smoke or because she could see the wheels going round in my head. 'Don't even think about it,' she warned me. 'Chances are it's one of our brain-dead mates who's ratting to the vampires, and I don't want that on my conscience.'

I nodded. 'Fair enough. Whose deal is it?'

6

VENUS IN LEO IN THE 4TH HOUSE

She can show great extravagance, both practical and emotional, to those she cares for. She is loyal but likes to dominate situations of the heart. She has creative ability, which can sometimes lead to self-dramatization. Her domestic surroundings must be easy on the eye.

From *Written in the Stars*, by Dorothea Dawson

My second evening bodyguarding Gloria Kendal taught me that I really should pay more attention to the client. The evening engagement I'd so blithely agreed to turned out to be another of the nights from hell that seemed to be how Gloria spent her free time. That night, she was guest of honour at the annual dinner dance of the ladies' division of the North West branch of the Association of Beverage and Victuals Providers. I've never been in the same room as that much hairspray. If taste were IQ, there would only have been a handful of them escaping Special Needs education. I'd thought the Blackburn outfit would have blended in nicely at a women-only dinner, but I was as flash as a peahen at a peacock convention. I should have realized Gloria wasn't wearing those sequins and diamanté for a bet.

About ten minutes after we arrived in Ormskirk, I sussed this wasn't one of those dinners you go to for the food. I know '70s food is coming back into fashion, but the Boar and Truffle's menu of prawn cocktail, boeuf bourguignon and, to crown it all, Black Forest gateau, owed nothing to the Style Police or the foodies. You could tell that every cooking fashion in the intervening twenty years had passed them by. This was a dinner my Granny Brannigan would have recognized and approved of. It wasn't entirely surprising; nobody who had any choice in the matter would spend a minute longer than they had to in a town characterized by a one-way system that's twice the size of the town centre itself. It's the only place I know where they're so proud of their back streets they have to show them to every unwary motorist who gets trapped there on the way to Southport.

The landladies, most of whom almost certainly served better pub grub back home, didn't care. The only function of the food they were interested in was its capacity to line the stomach and absorb alcohol. It wasn't a night to be the designated driver, never mind bodyguard.

Gloria was on fine form, though. She'd heeded

what I'd said about keeping her back to the wall and trying to make sure there was a table between her and her admirers. It wasn't easy, given how many of the female publicans of the North West desperately needed to have their photographs taken in a clinch with my client. But she smiled and smiled, and drank her gin and made a blisteringly funny and scathing speech that would have had a rugby club audience blushing.

'I'm sorry you've been landed with all this ferrying me around,' she said as I drove across the flat fields of the Fylde towards the motorway and civilization.

'Who normally does it?' I asked.

'A pal of mine. He got the sack last year for being over fifty. He's not going to get another job at his age. He enjoys the driving and it gives him a few quid in his back pocket.' She yawned and reached for her cigarettes. It was her car, so I didn't feel I could complain. Instead, I opened the window. Gloria shivered at the blast of cold air and snorted with laughter. 'Point taken,' she said, shoving the cigarettes back in her bag. 'How much longer do you think we're going to have to be joined at the hip?'

'Depends on you,' I said. 'I don't think you've got a stalker. I've seen no signs of anybody following us, and I've had a good look around where you live. There's no obvious vantage point for anybody to stake out your home –'

'One of the reasons I bought it,' Gloria interrupted.

'Those bloody snappers with their long lenses make our lives a misery, you know. All those editors, they all made their holier-than-thou promises after they hounded Princess Di to her death, but nothing's changed, you know. They're still chasing us every chance they get. But they can't catch me there. Not that I'm likely to be doing anything more exciting than planting out my window boxes, but I'm buggered if the *Sun's* readers have any right to know whether I'm having Busy Lizzies or lobelia this year.'

'So that probably confirms that whoever has been sending the letters is connected to the show; they can keep tabs on you because they see you at work every day. And they can pick up background details quite easily, it seems to me. The cast members talk quite freely among themselves and you don't have to set out to eavesdrop to pick up all sorts of personal information. I've only been on the set for a couple of days and already I know Paul Naylor's seeing an acupuncturist in Chinatown for his eczema, Rita Hardwick's husband breeds pugs and Tiffany Joseph's bulimic. Another week and I'd have enough background information to write threatening letters to half the cast.' What I didn't say was that another week among the terminally self-obsessed, and threatening letters would be the least of what I'd be up for.

'It's not a pretty thought, that. Somebody that knows me hates me enough to want me to be frightened. I don't like that idea one little bit.'

'If the letters and the tyre slashing are connected, then it almost certainly has to be somebody at NPTV, you know. Of course, it is possible that the tyre slasher isn't the letter writer, just some sicko who took advantage of your concern over the letters to wind you up. I've asked you this before, but you've had time to think about it now: are you sure there isn't anybody you've pissed off that might just be one scene short of a script?'

Gloria shook her head. 'Come on, chuck. You've spent time with me now. You've seen the way I am with the folk I work with. I'm a long way off perfect, but I don't wind them up like certain other people I could mention.'

'I'd noticed,' I said drily. 'The thing is, now everybody at NPTV knows you're taking what Dorothea said seriously. The person who wrote you those letters is basking in a sense of power, which means that he or she probably won't feel the need to carry the threats through any further. Besides, they won't know whether I'm off the case altogether or I've taken the surveillance undercover. Much as I'd love to be on this hourly rate indefinitely, I'd be inclined to give it another couple of days and then I'll pull out.'

'You're sure I'll be safe? I'm not a silly woman, in spite of how I come across, but what Dorothea said really scared me, coming on top of the business with the tyres. She's not given to coming the spooky witch, you know.'

'When is she in next?'

'Day after tomorrow. Do you want to see her?'

'I want to interview her, not have a consultation,' I said hastily.

'Oh, go on,' Gloria urged. 'Have it on me. You don't have to take it seriously.' She opened her bag and took out a pen and one of the postcard-sized portraits of herself she carried everywhere for the fans who otherwise would have had her signing everything from their library books to any available part of their anatomies. 'Give us your time, date and place of birth.' She snapped on the interior light, making me blink hard against the darkness. 'Come on, sooner you tell me, the sooner you get the light off again.'

'Oxford,' I said. 'Fourth of September, 1966.'

'Now why am I not surprised you're a Virgo?' Gloria said sarcastically as she turned off the light. 'Caligula, Jimmy Young, Agatha Christie, Cecil Parkinson, Raine Spencer and you.'

'Which proves it's a load of old socks,' I said decisively. A couple of miles down the road, it hit me. 'How come you can rattle off a list of famous Virgoans?'

'I married one. Well, not a famous one. And divorced him. I wish I'd known Dorothea then. Virgo and Leo? She'd never have let it happen. A recipe for disaster.'

'Aren't you taking a bit of a chance, working with me?'

Gloria laughed, that great swooping chuckle that

80

gets the nation grinning when things are going right for Brenda Barrowclough. 'Working's fine. Nobody grafts harder than a Virgo. You see the detail while I only get the big picture. And you never give up. No, you'll do fine for me.'

It's funny how often clients forget they've said that when a case doesn't work out the way they wanted it to. I only hoped Gloria wouldn't live to regret her words. I grunted noncommittally and concentrated on the road.

It was almost one when I walked through my own front door. Both my house and Richard's were illuminated only by the dirty orange of the sodium streetlights. I'd hoped he'd be home; I was suffering from what my best friend Alexis calls NSA – Non-Specific Anxiety – and my experience of self-medicating has told me the best cure is a cuddle. But it looked like he was doing whatever it is that rock journos do in live music venues in the middle of the night. It probably involved drugs, but Richard never touches anything stronger than joints and these days all the cops do with cannabis is confiscate it for their own use, so I wasn't worried on that score.

I turned on the kitchen light, figuring a mug of hot chocolate might prevent the vague feeling of unease from keeping me awake. I couldn't miss the sheet of paper stuck under a fridge magnet. 'Babysitting for Alexis + Chris. Staying over. See you tomorrow. Big kisses.' I didn't need to be a handwriting expert to know it was from my besotted lover. The only problem was, it wasn't me he was besotted with.

I'd know how to fight back if it was a beautiful blonde waving her perfectly rounded calves at him. But how exactly can a woman keep her dignity and compete with a nine-month-old baby girl?

The following day, we were let out to play. Because *Northerners* traded so heavily on its connection to Manchester, the city of cool, they had to reinforce the link with regular exterior and interior shots of identifiable landmarks. It had led to a profitable spin-off for NPTV, who now ran *Northerners* tours at weekends. The punters would stay in the very hotel where Pauline Pratt and Gordon Johnstone had consummated their adulterous affair, then they'd be whisked off on a walking tour that took in sites from key episodes. They'd see the tram line where Diane Grimshaw committed suicide, the alley where Brenda Barrowclough was mugged, the jewellery shop that was robbed while Maureen and Phil Pomeroy were choosing an engagement ring. They'd have lunch in the restaurant where Kamal Sayeed had worked as a waiter before his tragic death from streptococcal meningitis. In the afternoon, they visited the sets where the show was filmed, and a couple of cast members joined them for dinner, persuaded by veiled threats and large fees.

To keep that particular gravy train running, the show had to film on the streets of the city at least once a month. That day, they were filming a series of exterior shots at various points along the refurbished Rochdale Canal. According to Gloria, a new producer was determined to stamp his authority on the soap with a series of themed episodes. The linking theme of this particular week was the idea of the waterway providing a range of backdrops, from the sinister to the seriously hip. Gloria had drawn the short straw of an argument with Teddy outside Barca, Mick Hucknall's chic Catalan bistro. On a summer afternoon, it might have been a pleasant diversion. On a bleak December morning, it was about as much fun as sunbathing in Siberia. It took forever to film because trains and trams would keep rattling across the high brick viaducts above our heads when the cameras were rolling.

I couldn't even take refuge in the cast or crew buses, since I needed to keep a close eye on Gloria. In spite of what I'd said the night before, I hadn't entirely ruled out the possibility of an obsessive fan who was stalking her. The fact that she spent so much of her time inaccessible might actually fuel his derangement. He could be planning to take action against her only when she was in a public place and in character.

I huddled under the awning of the catering truck where a red-haired giant with a soft Highland accent supervised the pair of young women who were responsible for making sure there was a constant flow of bacon, sausage and/or egg butties for anyone who wanted them. They served me with a steaming carton of scalding coffee, which I held under my chin. Not for long, though. If my nose thawed out too quickly, there was always the possibility of it shearing off from the rest of my face.

I half listened to the conversation in the van behind me. It was a lot more interesting than the script Teddy and Gloria were working their way through. The caterers were discussing that day's lunch menu and the cast members in roughly equal proportions. I can't think why, but they seemed not to have a lot of respect for their customers. I was stifling a giggle at one particularly scurrilous comment about the randiness of one of the show's young studs being in inverse proportion to the size of his equipment when I was aware that I had company under the awning. The Rob Roy lookalike had abandoned his assistants and slipped out for a fag. The environmental health department would have been impressed.

He grinned. Close up, he was even more attractive than he was with a steaming array of food between us. His thick red-gold hair was swept back from a high, broad forehead. Eyes the blue of the Windows 95 intro screen sparkled above high cheekbones. He had one of those mouths romantic novelists always describe as cruel, which lets you know the heroine's probably going to end up in the guy's arms if not his bed. 'Hiya,' he said. 'I'm Ross Grant. I own the location catering company.'

The coffee had defrosted my lips enough for me to return his smile. 'Kate Brannigan. I'm –'

'I know who you are,' he interrupted, sounding amused. 'You're Gloria's bodyguard. Dorothea Dawson, the Seer to the Stars, told her she was going to be murdered, and she hired you to protect her.'

'You've been watching too much television,' I said lightly. 'People don't lash out the kind of money I cost without having good reason.'

'I'm sorry,' he said. 'I didn't mean to insult your professionalism. Or to take the piss out of Dorothea. She's been really good to us.'

'Predicting a sudden rush on bacon butties, you mean?'

He gave a sheepish grin. 'Very funny. No, I mean it. You know how she's always on the telly? Well, she's recommended us to quite a few of the programmes she's been on. We've got a lot of work off the back of it. She's great, Dorothea. She really understands what it's like trying to make a living out of a business where you're constantly dependent on goodwill. So she goes out of her way for folk like us, know what I mean? Not like most of them round here, it's self, self, self. Working with people that are so full of themselves, we find it hard to take anything about them seriously.'

This time it was my turn to smile. 'They do lack a certain sense of proportion.'

'But you're more than just a bodyguard, aren't

you? Somebody said you're a proper private investigator.'

'That's right. In fact, I almost never do this kind
of work. But Gloria can be very persuasive.'

'Don't I know it. This is the woman that had
me up all night making petits fours for her granddaughter's birthday party. Is she really in danger,
then?'

I shrugged. 'Better safe than sorry.'

'I'm sorry to hear that. She's the best of the
bunch. I don't like to think of her in fear of her life.
I wasn't asking out of nosiness,' he added quickly.
'I just wondered how long you were going to be
tied up working for Gloria.'

'Why? Are you missing me already?'

He went that strange damson-purple that red-
heads go when they blush. 'Actually, I wanted to
hire you.'

'Hire me?' Suddenly this was a lot more interesting than a mild flirtation to keep the cold out.
'What for?'

'I don't know if you know, but *Northerners* has
got a mole. Somebody's been leaking stuff to the
press. Not just the usual sordid stuff about people's
love lives and creepy things they did twenty years
ago, but storylines as well.' All the humour had
left him now.

'I'd heard. John Turpin's supposed to be finding
out where the leak is.'

'Yeah, well, Turpin's trying to pin it on me or
my staff,' Ross said bluntly.

86

'Why would he do that?'

He inhaled sharply. 'Because we're convenient scapegoats. Our contract's up for renewal at the end of January, and Turpin seems to be determined to ditch me. Knowing that slimy bastard, he's probably in bed with one of the other firms tendering for the contract and he figures if he can blame me for the leaks he can feather his own nest easier.'

'But why would anybody believe him?' I asked.

Ross flicked his cigarette end on to a frozen puddle where it bounced once then sank through the hole it made. 'We're the outsiders, aren't we? We're not part of the team like the ones who work inside the compound are.'

'So how are you supposed to come by the advance storylines?' I objected.

'We're involved in location filming for the show nearly every week. With them filming four weeks ahead of transmission, it's not hard to pick up the direction the stories are heading. The cast are always standing round the food wagon shooting their mouths off about storylines they don't like, or taking the piss out of each other about what their characters are up to. If me or my lassies had a mind to, we could be moles. It would be dead simple. But we're not.'

'How can you be sure?'

'Well, I know it's not me. And I know it's not my wife.' He gestured towards the open side of the van with his thumb. 'She's the one with the red sweatshirt on. And I'd put money on it not being Mary, the other lassie, because she owns twenty per cent of the business and she's never been a woman who went for the short-term benefit.'

I sighed. 'I sympathize. But it's always impossible to prove a negative.'

'I know that,' he said. 'That's not what I want to hire you for. I want you to find out who the real mole is and get me off the hook.'

I shook my head. It nearly killed me, turning business down. 'I'm already fully occupied taking care of Gloria. You'd be better off going to another firm.' I gritted my teeth. 'I could probably recommend somebody.'

He shook his handsome head. 'There would be no point. Turpin would never let them on to the location shoots, never mind inside the compound. I'm amazed Gloria's got away with having you on set. That's why you're the only one who can help me. I'll pay the going rate, I don't expect anything less.'

I finished my coffee and tossed the cup in the nearby bin. 'No can do,' I said. 'I can't take money under false pretences. I'd be lying if I said I could investigate the leaks at the same time as taking care of Gloria.'

He looked as if he was going to burst into tears. His big shoulders slumped and his mouth turned down at the corners. I glanced back to the serving hatch in the side of the van and caught a murderous look from his wife. 'Look,' I sighed. 'I tell you what I'll do. I'll keep my eyes and ears open, maybe make a couple of phone calls. If I come up with anything, you can pay me on results. How does that grab you?'

Laughing boy was back. He grinned and clapped a beefy arm round my shoulders. I thought my lungs had collapsed. 'That's terrific. Fabulous. Thanks, I really appreciate it.' He leaned over and smacked a sloppy kiss on my cheek.

'Ross?' his wife called sharply. 'I need a hand in here.'

'No problem,' the big man said. 'I'll be hearing from you then, Kate.'

Somehow I doubted it. Before I could say anything more, I noticed Gloria rushing off the set and into the make-up caravan. Grateful for the chance to get out of the northerly wind that was exfoliating the few square centimetres of skin I had allowed to be exposed, I ran across and climbed aboard.

Gloria was sitting in front of a mirror, blowing on her hands as a make-up artist hovered around her. 'Here she is,' Gloria announced. 'Me and my shadow,' she sang in her throaty contralto. 'Are you as cold as I am?'

'How many fingers have you got left?'

Gloria made a show of counting. 'Looks like they're all still here.'

'In that case, I'm colder,' I said, waving a hand with one finger bent over.

'Freddie, meet Kate Brannigan, my bodyguard.

Kate, this is Freddie Littlewood. It's his job to stop me looking like the raddled old bag I really am.'

'Hi, Freddie.'

He ducked his head in acknowledgement and gave me a quick once-over in the mirror. He had a narrow head and small, tight features framed by spiky black hair. With his black polo neck and black jeans like a second skin, he looked as if he'd escaped from one of those existential French films where you don't understand a bloody word even with subtitles. 'Honestly, Gloria,' he said. 'I don't know why you listen to that Dorothea Dawson.' His voice was surprising. There wasn't a trace of the high camp of his physical appearance. He could have read the radio news without a complaint.

'It's surprising how often she gets things right,' Gloria said mildly as he expertly applied powder to her cheeks.

'And how often she causes trouble,' he added drily. 'All those sly little hints that people take a certain way and before you know it, old friends are at each other's throats. You watch, now she's got you all wound up and scared witless, I bet this week she'll tell you something that starts you looking out the corner of your eye at one of your best friends.'

'I don't know why you've got it in for Dorothea,' Gloria said. 'She's harmless and we're all grown-ups.'

'I just don't like to see you upset, Gloria,' he said solicitously.

'Well, between me and you and the wall, Freddie, it wasn't what Dorothea said that upset me. I was already in a state. I'd been getting threatening letters. I'd had my tyres slashed to ribbons. All Dorothea did was make me realize I should be taking them seriously.'

I could have clobbered her. I'd told her to carry on keeping quiet about the threatening letters and the vandalism, to let everyone think it was Dorothea's eerie warning that was behind my presence. And here she was, telling all to the man perfectly placed to be the distribution centre of the rumour factory. 'Nice one, Gloria,' I muttered.

It's not the people you go up against that make this job a bitch; it's the clients, every time.

7

SUN CONJUNCTION WITH MERCURY

She has a lively mind. Her opinions are important to her and she enjoys expressing them. Objectivity sometimes suffers from the strength of her views. Exchanging and acquiring information which she can subsequently analyse matters a lot.

From *Written in the Stars*, by Dorothea Dawson

When she finally finished filming her outdoor scene with Teddy, Gloria announced we were going shopping. I must have looked as dubious as I felt. 'Don't worry, chuck,' she laughed as I drove her into the NPTV compound. 'We won't get mobbed. How do you think I manage when I've not got you running around after me?'

I was gobsmacked by the result. I'd seen her in plain clothes already, not least when she'd first come to the office. But this was something else again. I thought I was the mistress of disguise until

I met Gloria. When she emerged from her dressing room after a mere ten minutes to slough off Brenda Barrowclough, I nearly let her walk past me. She'd cheated; this wasn't the outfit she'd worn when I'd driven her to work that morning. Wearing jeans and cowboy boots under a soft nubuck jacket that fell to mid-thigh, the image was entirely different. On her head perched a designer version of a cowboy hat, tilted to a jaunty angle. Instead of sunglasses, she'd gone for a pair of slightly tinted granny glasses that subtly changed the shape of her face. She looked twenty years younger. I wasn't going to be the only person who wouldn't instantly recognize Gloria now she'd ditched the wig and adopted a wardrobe that didn't include polyester.

Thankfully, she didn't have a major expedition in mind. Her granddaughter had been invited to a fancy dress party and she wanted to go as Esmeralda from *The Hunchback of Notre Dame*. 'They've got outfits at the Disney store, but they cost a fortune and I could make better myself,' Gloria explained as I squeezed the car into a slot in the Arndale Centre car park. She never ceased to amaze me. This was a woman who could afford a hundred Esmeralda outfits without noticing the dent in her bank balance. But her pretence of meanness didn't fool me. Making the costume wasn't about saving money; it was about giving her granddaughter something of herself. It was also a way, I suspected, of reminding herself of the life she had come from.

We descended a claustrophobic concrete stair-well that reeked so strongly of piss it was a relief to step out into the traffic fumes of High Street. Gloria led me unerringly through the warren of Victorian warehouses that house the city's rag trade till we fetched up at a wholesaler who specialized in saris. Judging by the warmth of the welcome, she was no stranger. Merely because I was with her, I was offered tea too. While Gloria sipped from a thick pottery mug and browsed the dazzling fabrics, I hung around near the door, peering into the street with the avidity of the truly paranoid. The only people in sight were hurrying through the dank cold of the dying December day, coat collars turned up against the knife edge of the wind that howled through the narrow streets of the Northern Quarter. It wasn't a day for appreciating the renaissance of yet another part of the inner city. Nobody was going to be browsing the shop windows today. The craft workers must have been blessing their good fortune at having an enclosed market.

We emerged on the street just as darkness was falling, me staggering two steps behind Gloria toting a bale of fabric that felt heavy enough to clothe half of Lancashire. As we approached the Arndale from a slightly different angle, I realized we must be close to Dennis's latest venture. I couldn't help smiling at the thought of the double act Dennis and Gloria would be. It had been a long week, and I felt like some light relief, so I said, 'A mate of mine has just opened a shop this end of the Arndale. Do you mind if we just drop in to say hello?'

'What kind of shop?'

'You remember what they used to say about how cheap it was to shop at the Co-op? On account of you could never find anything you wanted to buy?'

Gloria chuckled. 'That good, eh? Oh well, why not? We've got nowt else on till tomorrow morning.'

'I don't think it'll take that long.'

It wasn't hard to spot Dennis's establishment. Sandwiched between a cut-price butcher and a heel bar in the subterranean section of the mall, it was notable for the dump bins of bargains virtually blocking the underpass and the muscle-bound minder keeping an eye on potential shoplifters. All he was wearing was a pair of jogging pants and a vest designed to show off his awesome upper body development. 'High-class joint, then,' Gloria remarked as we followed the chicane created by the dump bins, artfully placed to funnel us past whitewashed windows proclaiming, 'Everything Under a Pound!' and into the shop.

By the door were three tills, all staffed by slack-jawed teenagers. The girls were the ones with the mascara. I think. Dennis was up near the back of the shop, stacking shelves with giant bottles of lurid green bath foam. We squeezed up a narrow aisle packed with weary shoppers who had the look and smell of poverty. My awkward parcel of material earned me a few hard words and a lot of harder looks.

Of course, I didn't get anywhere near Dennis before he noticed us. I swear that man has eyes in the back of his head. 'Kate,' he said, his face creasing up in a delighted grin. 'Fabulous!' He cleared a way through for us, telling his customers to kindly move their arses or take the consequences. 'So, what do you think?' he asked almost before I was within bear-hug reach.

I gave the shelves the quick once-over. Exactly what I'd expected. Cheap and nasty, from the toys to the toiletries. 'I think you're going to make a mint,' I said sadly, depressed at the reminder of how many skint punters there are out there who needed to fill Christmas stockings on a weekly budget of the same amount that most MPs spend on lunch.

'Are you not going to introduce us, chuck?' Gloria said. I half turned to find her giving Dennis the appraising look of a farmer at a fatstock show. That was all I needed. Dennis has a habit of forgetting he's married, which is fine by me as long as I'm not personally involved with aiding and abetting it. I'm very fond of his wife Debbie, even if she doesn't have the brains God gave a lemming.

'I don't think so,' I said. 'This is just a flying visit.'

I was too late. Dennis was already sliding round me and extending a hand to Gloria. 'Dennis O'Brien at your service, darling,' he said. Gloria slid her hand into his and he raised it to his lips, all the time fixing her with the irresistible sparkle of his intense blue eyes. I groaned.

'I'm Gloria Kendal.'

His smile reminded me of crocodiles at feeding time. 'I know,' he said.

'It's the voice,' I muttered. 'Total giveaway.'

'It's got nothing to do with the voice,' he said. 'It's because this lovely lady's with you. I can read, you know, Kate.'

'What do you mean, it's because she's with me?'

Dennis cast his eyes heavenwards. 'Tonight's *Chronicle*. You mean you've not seen it?'

'No. What about it?'

He jerked his head towards a door at the rear of the shop. 'Through the back. It's in my ski-jacket pocket.'

I looked at him. I looked at the door. I looked at Gloria. 'On you go, chuck,' she said. 'I think I'm in safe hands here.'

'That's all you know,' I mumbled. But I dumped the fabric parcel on Dennis and left them to it while I went to chase whatever he'd seen in the evening paper. I didn't have to look hard. There wasn't much room in the bare concrete back shop to hide anything as big as Dennis's ski jacket, which was draped over one of two folding chairs by a cardboard computer carton doing a bad impersonation of a table. The paper was sticking out of a pocket and the story I was clearly supposed to be looking for was splashed across the front page. **'*NORTHERNERS'* STAR IN DEATH THREAT DRAMA,'** I read.

> *'Gloria Kendal, busybody Brenda Barrowclough in top soap* Northerners, *is at the heart of a real-life drama tonight. The award-winning actress has been warned that threatening letters sent to her home could mean death.*
>
> *'The desperate warning was spelled out by her personal astrologer Dorothea Dawson, the TV Seer to the Stars. But following a savage act of vandalism on her Saab sports car, Ms Kendal has taken the danger to heart and has hired top local private investigator Kate Brannigan to act as bodyguard.*
>
> *'The star of the Manchester-based soap has vowed not to be driven underground by the vicious poison-pen writer . . .'*

I skimmed to the end of the article, but there didn't seem to be any more meat on the bones. There were a couple of paragraphs mentioning previous cases where my name had unfortunately made it into the press, but nothing too damaging. What I couldn't figure out, apart from where the story had come from, was why nobody had called me all afternoon about it. Shelley should have been straight on to me the minute the paper landed, I thought. I was almost glad of the rare opportunity to put her in the wrong.

Then I took my moby out of my bag and realized

I'd forgotten to switch it back on after I'd had it muted for the filming.

There were fourteen messages. I wasn't strong enough to deal with them yet. Besides, if the situation was out in the open, I needed to get my client away from the public eye as fast as possible. The last thing I needed was for some care-in-the-community case to hit on the idea of making a name for himself by metamorphosing into the secret stalker.

I hurried back to the shop, clutching the paper. I was too late. When I opened the door, it looked as if a small riot had enveloped the shop. At the eye of the storm was Dennis, standing on a counter with Gloria perched next to him. The massive bouncer had moved inside the store and was brandishing one of the red plastic under-a-pound fun cameras like King Kong with a fire engine. 'Did you get that, Keith? Did you get that?' Dennis kept asking.

The shoppers had lost all interest in Dennis's wares, but for once he didn't care. 'Melody, get on the blower to the *Sun* and tell them we've got exclusive pictures to sell of Gloria Kendal defying death threats and shopping in Manchester's best value-for-money store.'

'Ah, shit,' I muttered, lowering my head and thrusting through the crowd. Getting through to Gloria was a lot harder than Moses parting the Red Sea. Eventually I managed it, but only by elbowing a couple of elderly ladies in the ribs and stepping hard on the instep of a teenage girl who was still yelping in complaint minutes later. 'Come on, Gloria, time to go home,' I said grimly.

'I was just starting to enjoy myself,' she complained good-naturedly, pushing herself to her feet.

'You're not whisking this wonderful woman off before we've had the chance to get to know each other?' Dennis demanded, sounding aggrieved.

'That's as good a reason as any,' I grunted, trying to force a way through the clamouring crowd to the door.

Gloria turned to wiggle her fingers at him. 'See you around, Dennis. I hope.'

'Keith,' I shouted. 'Stop poncing around pretending to be David Bailey and give us a hand here. I need to get Gloria home.'

The big bouncer looked to Dennis for guidance. He gave a rueful smile and nodded. 'Sort it,' he said.

Keith picked up the parcel of fabric and carved a path to the door in seconds flat. One look at biceps the size of cannonballs, and the obstructive punters just melted into the shelves. Gloria signed postcards as she walked, automatically passing them into the grasping hands of the fans. Out in the underpass, Keith thrust the bundle into my arms and I hustled Gloria towards a nearby bank of lifts that would take us back to the car park. 'I like your friend,' she said as we crammed in beside a pushchair and a harassed-looking woman who was too busy pacifying her toddler to care who was in the lift with her.

'He obviously likes you too. But then, his wife's a big fan of *Northerners*,' I said drily.

'That's a pity,' she said.

'I thought you needed all the viewers you could get just now.'

Gloria raised her eyebrows, not entirely amused by my deliberate misunderstanding. 'I meant, the existence of a wife. I was going to ask you for his number, but if he's a married man, I'm not interested.'

'Worried about the press?'

She shook her head. 'It's not fear of the *Sun* that stops me having affairs with married men. There are enough people out there ready to make women's lives a misery without me joining in.'

The lift doors opened and Gloria stepped out, turning to give the young mother a hand with her pushchair. 'You never cease to amaze me, Gloria,' I said as we crossed the car park. 'You must have *some* bad habits.'

In response, she took out her cigarette packet and waved it at me. 'One for the road,' she said, climbing into the passenger seat of her Saab. 'And I like a drink,' she added as I started the engine. 'And I have been known to play the odd game of bingo.'

'You're too good for this world,' I said wryly.

She plucked the *Chronicle* from the pocket where

I'd stowed it and stared grim-faced at the front page. 'I flaming hope not,' she said.

After I dropped Gloria at home where she planned a quiet night in with her sewing machine and a stack of Fred Astaire and Ginger Rogers movies, there was only one logical place to go. Even if it did involve one of those cross-country routes that looks sensible on the map but suddenly develops a mind of its own as soon as all human habitation falls out of sight.

My best friend Alexis and her partner Chris live in the wilds of the Derbyshire Peak District. Alexis claims she can be in her office in central Manchester twenty-three minutes after leaving home, but that's only because she's the crime correspondent of the *Chronicle* and so she starts work around half past six in the morning. I always feel like I need a Sherpa and a St Bernard with a barrel of brandy to make it to the dream home they built themselves. Chris is an architect, and she designed the small development in exchange for the skills of her neighbours who did a lot of the heavy work as well as the plumbing and electrics. They ended up spending about eighty grand on a property that would sell for three times that on the open market.

Then they found the perfect way to spend all the money they'd saved. They had a baby. Chris actually did the bit that makes most people wince and cross their legs, but Alexis has just as much of a stake in Jay Appleton Lee. I'm about as fond of woodlice as I am of children, but even I have to admit – if only to myself – that I can see why Richard finds this particular baby as delightful as her parents do.

But that night I wasn't interested in admiring Jay's shock of black spiky hair or her latest tooth. It was Alexis I needed to see. I'd timed my arrival perfectly. Jay was en route from bath to bed, so all I had to do was make a few admiring noises before Chris whisked her away. Five minutes later, the three of us were installed in the comfortable living room, Chris and Alexis with dark smudges under their eyes that just about matched the glasses of Murphy's stout they were drinking.

'You having a night off, then, girl?' Alexis asked, her Scouse accent as rich as the creamy head on her glass. 'Rather you than me, minding a soap star for a living.'

'Just let me lie down for five minutes then I'll throw some pizza at the oven,' Chris said, stifling a yawn and stretching out on the sofa, dumping her feet in Alexis's lap. 'So what's she like, Gloria Kendal?'

'Brenda Barrowclough with a bit more insight, humour and style,' I said. 'At first, all I saw was that total self-absorption you get with actors. But the more I've got to know her, the more I've come to realize there's more to her than that. She's forthright, funny, generous. I'm amazed, but I actually like her.' I told them about our adventures with Dennis. They both knew him well enough to fill in the gaps for themselves.

'I wish I'd been there. It sounds like one to cut out and keep,' Alexis said, reaching for her cigarette packet. She took out a fag and began to go through the motions of smoking without actually lighting up. Another consequence of motherhood. She'd gone from fifty Silk Cut a day to smoking about a dozen and using a few others as the adult equivalent of a dummy. The only person who didn't see this as an improvement was Alexis herself.

'Thanks to the *Chronicle*.' I scowled.

'The newsdesk were on to me about it,' Alexis said. 'I told them there wasn't any point in me ringing you for a quote. Or in them ringing you for a quote. I gave them this whole spiel about how you've got this Philip Marlowe code of conduct and you'd never grass up a client.'

'Very noble of you,' Chris said drily. 'Respecting Kate's professional code. You really love pissing off the newsdesk, don't you?'

'Well,' Alexis drawled. 'They ask for it, don't they? So, is she really getting death threats?'

'I'll swap you,' I said. 'I'll give you some nonattributable background if you tell me where the story came from in the first place.'

Alexis pulled a face and flicked the nonexistent ash from her cigarette. 'You got me there, KB. You know I have as little to do with the brain-dead dickheads on the newsdesk as possible. And this didn't actually come as a tip directly to news. The story came through features, from Mack Morrissey who does the showbiz beat. It'll have come from a contact.'

'Any chance you could find out who?'

Alexis shrugged. 'I don't know. Mack's a bit precious, you know. He wouldn't let any of us hairy-arsed hacks anywhere near his valuable artistic contacts.'

'You could ask him,' Chris chipped in.

'I could,' Alexis admitted. 'But there's a better way of finding out. I can't believe he got a tale like this for free. He'll have had to put a payment through the credits book.'

'He won't have stumped up readies?' I asked.

Alexis shook her head. 'Not this amount. It'll have been a few hundred. I'm surprised his contact gave the story to us, to be honest. It would have been worth a lot more to the nationals.'

Another interesting piece of information to tuck away in the file marked, 'Makes no sense'. When the oddments of data reached critical mass, seemingly unrelated facts collided and rearranged themselves into logical sequences. It's a process normally called 'woman's intuition'.

'I'll check out the credits book in the morning,' Alexis promised. 'So what's the score with Gloria? Has she really had death threats? And does she really think you're going to throw yourself between her and the assassin's bullet?'

'How else will I catch it with my teeth?' I asked

innocently. 'People in Gloria's position are always getting hate mail. Recently, she's had a few letters that have seemed a bit more sinister than the usual run-of-the-mill stuff, and Dorothea Dawson threw some petrol on the flames. Bloody irresponsible, but what can you expect from a con merchant? None of these psychics and clairvoyants would earn a shilling if they had to stop preying on people's irrational fears. Take it from me, Alexis, nothing is going to happen to Gloria Kendal. All I'm there for is to put the frighteners on anybody who might be thinking about taking advantage of the situation.'

Alexis's eyebrows rose and she ran a hand through thick dark hair recently shorn from a wiry thicket to a shrubby bush less accessible to tiny grasping fists. Another consequence of motherhood. 'You've not met Dorothea yet, then?'

I frowned. 'No, but what difference does that make?'

'I didn't think you'd be calling her a con artist if you'd met her.'

I stared open-mouthed at Alexis. 'You're not telling me you believe in that crap, are you?'

'Of course not, soft girl. But Dorothea Dawson's not a charlatan. She's sincere about what she does. I interviewed her a few years back, when I was still working for features. Before I actually met her, I was saying exactly the same as you're saying now. And I had to eat my words. It wasn't that she told me anything world shattering, like I was going to meet a tall dark handsome stranger and do a lot of foreign travel. She didn't make a big production number out of it, just said very calmly that I had already met the love of my life, that my career was going to make a sideways move that would make me a lot more satisfied and it probably wouldn't be the fags that killed me but they wouldn't help.'

I shook my head. 'And this revelation turned you into a believer?' I said sarcastically.

'Yeah. Because she didn't grandstand. She was dead matter-of-fact, even apologized for not having anything more exciting to tell me. She came across as a really nice woman, you know? And she's not just in it for the money. Sure, she charges rich bastards like the *Northerners* cast an arm and a leg, but she does a lot of freebies for charity.'

'That's right,' Chris added. 'She donated a full personal horoscope to the Women's Aid charity auction last month. And you remember that mental health job I designed a couple of years ago?'

I nodded. It had been a major renovation project for Chris, turning an old mill in Rochdale into housing units for single homeless people with mental health problems. 'I remember,' I said.

'Well, I happen to know that Dorothea Dawson was the biggest single donor for that scheme. She gave them fifty grand.'

'You never told me that,' Alexis complained. 'That would have made a good diary piece.'

'That's precisely why I didn't tell you,' Chris

said drily. 'It was supposed to be confidential. She didn't want a big song and dance about it.'

'It's a lot of money,' I said diplomatically.

'So she can't be a con artist, can she?' Alexis demanded. 'They rip people off. They don't donate that sort of cash to charity. It's not like she'd need a tax loss, is it? I mean, a load of her earnings must be cash, so she could stash a bundle undeclared anyway.'

I held my hands up in submission. 'OK, I give in. Dorothea Dawson is a sweet little old lady, grossly misunderstood by cynical unbelievers like me. It must be written in my stars.'

'Anyway, KB, you sure taking care of Gloria isn't just a front?' Alexis demanded, changing tack in an obvious bid to wrong-foot me.

'For what?' I asked, baffled.

'Working for the management at NPTV. They've got a major mole in there, which is the last thing you need when you're trying to finesse a major deal with the networks. I heard they've got a mole hunt going on. You sure they've not hired you to find out who's stirring the shit for them?'

I shook my head. 'Sorry. You'll have to get your follow-up somewhere else.'

'I thought they'd be happy about all the press stories about the show,' Chris said. 'I'd have thought it would increase the ratings. I had to go to London the other day on the train, and the two women opposite me talked about *Northerners* nonstop.'

'I think the scandalous stories about the stars

108

whet people's appetites,' I said. 'According to my sources, what the management don't like are the storyline leaks. They reckon that makes people turn off.'

Before anyone could say more, my moby began to bleat insistently. 'Goodbye, pizza,' I said mournfully, grabbing my bag and reaching for the phone. 'Brannigan,' I grunted.

'It's me.'

My heart sank. 'Donovan, you've not been arrested again?'

8

MOON IN TAURUS IN THE 12TH HOUSE
The emotional swings of the moon are minimized in this placing, leading to balance between impulsiveness and determination. She is sociable, but needs to recharge her batteries in solitude which she seeks actively. Imaginative and intuitive, she has an instinctive rapport with creative artists though not herself artistic.

From *Written in the Stars*, by Dorothea Dawson

This time it was Alderley Edge, the village that buys more champagne per head of population than anywhere else in the UK. Donovan had been there to serve a subpoena on a company director who seemed to think the shareholders should fund the entire cost of his affair with a member of the chorus of Northern Opera. The detached house was in a quietly expensive street, behind tall hedges like most of its neighbours. Donovan had borrowed his mother's car and sat patiently parked a few doors down from the house for about an hour waiting for his target to return.

When the man came home, Donovan had caught him getting out of his car. He'd accepted service with ill grace and stormed into the house. Donovan had driven home via his girlfriend's student residence bedsit to pick up some tutorial handouts for the essay he was writing. He'd arrived home to find the police waiting. They hadn't been interested in an explanation. They'd just hauled him off in a police car to the local nick where they'd informed him he was being arrested on suspicion of burglary.

By the time I arrived, tempers were fraying round the edges. It turned out that at some point during the day, a neighbour of the company director had been burgled. And another nosy neighbour had happened to jot down Shelley's car number because, well, you just don't get black people sitting around in parked cars in the leafy streets of Alderley Edge. The neighbour had arrived home a few minutes after Donovan had driven off, discovered the burglary and called the police. When the nosy neighbour saw the police arrive (within five minutes, because Alderley Edge is middle-class territory, not a council estate where you wait half an hour for a response to a treble-niner reporting a murder in progress) he nipped across to tell them about the suspicious black man.

The police computer spat out Shelley's address in response to the car registration number, and the bizzies were round there in no time flat. Things were complicated by the fact that the bloke Donovan had served the subpoena on decided to get his own back and denied all knowledge of a young black process-server with a legitimate reason for being in the street.

It took me the best part of an hour to persuade the police that Donovan was telling the truth and that I wasn't some gangster's moll trying to spring my toy boy. Thighs like his, I should be so lucky.

The one good thing about the whole pathetic business was that Shelley had been out when the police had turned up. With luck, she'd still be out. As I drove him home, I said, 'Maybe this isn't such a good idea, you doing the process-serving.'

'I'm serving the papers properly, what's the problem?' he said defensively.

'It's not good for your image or your mother's blood pressure if you keep getting arrested.'

'I'm not letting those racists drive me out of a job,' he protested. 'You're saying I should just lie down and let them do it to me? The only places I have a problem are the ones where rich white people think that money can buy them a ghetto. People don't call the cops when *you* go to serve paper in Alderley Edge, or when I turn up on a doorstep in Hulme.'

'You're right. I'm sorry. I wasn't thinking it through,' I said, ashamed of myself for only seeing the easy way out. 'The job's yours for as long as you want it. And first thing tomorrow, I'll get your mother to have some proper business cards and ID printed up for you.'

'Fine by me. Besides, Kate, I need the money. I can't be scrounging off my mother so I can have a beer with my mates, or go to see a film with Miranda. The process-serving's something I can fit around studying and having fun. You can't do that with most part-time jobs.'

I grinned. 'You could always get an anorak and work with Gizmo on the computer security side of things.'

Donovan snorted. 'I don't think Gizmo'd let me. Have you noticed he's got well weird lately?'

'How can you tell?' I signalled the right turn that would bring me into the narrow street of terraced brick houses where the Carmichael family lived.

'Yeah, right. He's always been well weird. But this last few weeks, he's been totally paranoid android about his files.'

'He's always been secretive about his work,' I reminded him. 'And not unreasonably. A lot of what we do for clients on computer security is commercially sensitive.'

'There's secretive and there's mentally ill. Did you know you even need a password to get out of his screen savers?'

'Now you are exaggerating,' I said.

'You think so? You try it the next time he goes to the loo. Touch a key when one of the screen savers is running and you'll be asked for a password. You didn't know?' Donovan's eyebrows rose in surprise. He opened the car door and unfolded his long body into the street. Then he bent down and said anxiously, 'Check it out. I'm not making it up. Whatever he's up to, he doesn't want anybody else to know. And it is your hardware he's doing it on.'

'It'll be OK,' I said, trying to reassure myself as much as Donovan. 'Gizmo wouldn't take risks with my business.' Which was true enough, I thought as I drove home. Except that what Gizmo thought was fair game didn't necessarily coincide with the law's view. And if he didn't think it was wrong, why would he imagine it might be risky?

The response to the *Chronicle*'s story sharply polarized the *Northerners* cast in a way I hadn't seen before. Up to that point, I'd been beginning to wonder whether I could possibly be right about this being an inside job. Ten minutes in the NPTV compound that morning showed me the truth. People who had been all smiles and friendship the day before now had pursed lips and suddenly found they had somewhere else to look when Gloria passed. I actually heard one minor cast member say to another, supposedly apropos of something else, 'Too grand for the likes of us, of course.'

'What happened to that lot?' I asked as soon as Gloria closed the dressing room door behind us.

Rita Hardwick, who shared the room and played

114

rough and ready tart with a heart Thelma Torrance, paused in stitching the tapestry she passed the slack time with. 'Got the cold shoulder, did she?' she said with grim good humour.

'Yeah,' I said, not caring about showing my puzzlement. 'Yesterday, everybody's everybody's pal and today, it's like we've got a communicable disease.'

'It happens when you get a big show in the papers,' Gloria said, putting her coat on a hanger and subsiding into a chair. 'It's basically jealousy. The people below you in the pecking order resent the fact that you're important enough to make the front page of the *Chronicle* and have the story followed up by all the tabloids the next day.'

I'd already seen the evidence of Gloria's importance to the tabloids. When I'd arrived to collect her that morning, we'd had to run the gauntlet of reporters and photographers clustered round the high gates that kept Gloria safe from their invasive tendencies.

'Aye,' said Rita. 'And the ones above you in the pecking order reckon you need cutting down to size before you start snapping too close at their heels. Not that there's many above you these days, Glo.'

'Stuff like this shows you who your real friends are,' Gloria added.

'Aye, and we've all got precious few round here,' Rita said, thrusting her needle ferociously into the material. 'There's plenty would stab you in the

115

back soon as look at you if they thought they could get away with it.'

If a bit of newspaper coverage was all it took to create a poisonous atmosphere like the one we'd just walked through, I hated to think how Gloria's colleagues would react if someone actually did them serious damage. 'Have you had much personal publicity lately?' I asked, wondering if an excess of press attention had provoked one of her fellow cast members into sending her the original threatening letters.

Gloria shook her head. Rita disagreed. 'There's been a lot of stories about the abortion issue, Glo. Brenda and Debbie have been all over the tabloids.'

'But that's Brenda, not me. The punters don't know the difference, but the people who work here do.'

'It doesn't make any odds to some of that lot,' Rita said. 'Eaten up with jealousy, they are.' She glanced at her watch. 'Bloody hell, is that the time? I've got an appointment with Dorothea in five minutes.' She shoved her sewing into a tapestry bag.

'You're all right. I didn't see the van when we parked up.' Gloria gave me a considering look. 'You wanted a word with Dorothea, didn't you, chuck?'

Rita stared. 'By heck, Kate, I'd not have put you down as a lass who wanted her horoscope reading.'

I bristled. 'The only stars I want to ask Dorothea

Dawson about are the ones that work for *North-erners*.'

Rita giggled. 'If that crystal ball could talk . . .'

'Aye, but going to Dorothea's like going to the doctor. You can say owt you like and know it'll go no further,' Gloria said. 'Rita, chuck, do you mind if I just pop in ahead of you for a quick word with Dorothea, to see when she can fit Kate in?'

'Be my guest. I'll walk across with you.'

The three of us left the studio building and crossed the car park. Over at the far end, near the administration block, I noticed a camper van that hadn't been there when we'd arrived shortly before. It was painted midnight-blue, but as we drew closer, I could see there was a Milky Way of golden stars arcing across the cab door and the van's side. The door into the living section of the van had a zodiac painted on it in silver, the glyphs of the signs picked out in gold. Even I could recognize the maiden that symbolized my Virgo star sign. I also identified the familiar three-legged symbol of Mercedes Benz. I didn't need my background information from Chris to realize there was obviously serious money in Dorothea Dawson's profession.

Rita knocked and a familiar husky voice told us to come in. I expected a full blast of the histrionic mystic, complete with joss sticks and Indian cotton, but when it came to her personal environment, Dorothea clearly preferred the opulent to the occult. Leather, velvet, shag-pile carpet and wood panelling lined the luxurious interior. In the galley, I could see a microwave and a fridge. On a pull-out shelf sat a laptop and a portable colour printer, an ensemble that must have cost the thick end of three grand. Instead of a bloody awful tape of rainforest noises backed by Pan pipes and whales singing, the background music sounded like one of those 'not available in the shops' collections of Romantic Classics. The only concession to the mystic world of the zodiac was the dining table, surrounded on three sides by a bench seat. It was covered in a dark-blue chenille cloth and on it sat a massive crystal ball. If it had had a set of finger holes, we could have gone ten-pin bowling.

'Nice to see you all, ladies,' Dorothea Dawson said as we piled through the door. She was smaller than I expected from TV. But then, they all were. Her hair was pure silver, cut in a chin-length bob that hid the fact that her jaw was too heavy for her small features. Her skin was criss-crossed with the fine wrinkles of an apple that's been left lying around too long. Either she was older than she sounded or she'd loved the sun too much when she was younger. 'And you must be Kate Brannigan,' she said, acknowledging me with a nod, assessing me with eyes like amethyst chips.

'Saw me in your crystal ball, did you?' I asked more pleasantly than I wanted to. I've never liked charlatans.

'No, I saw you in the *Manchester Evening Chronicle*,' she said with wry amusement. I found myself liking her in spite of all my prejudices against people who prey on the gullible. 'You want to talk to me about my last session with Gloria?'

'Good guess,' I said.

'And I want you to cast her horoscope,' Gloria butted in, as usual incapable of holding her tongue.

Dorothea cocked her head, a knowing smile on her lips. 'Virgo, with . . . an air sign rising, at a guess. Probably Gemini, with such a smart mouth.'

I tried not to look as surprised as I felt. A one-in-twelve chance of getting my sun sign right multiplied up to a one-in-a-gross chance of hitting the sun sign and the ascendant. Not that I believed any of that rubbish; I only knew my rising sign because I'd spent half an hour the night before on the computer with some astrological chart-casting shareware I'd pulled down from the internet. But however she'd reached her conclusion, Dorothea was right. 'I couldn't say,' I lied, determined to show her my scepticism. 'Gloria can give you my details.'

'I have a very full diary today,' Dorothea said, sounding far more like a businesswoman than she had any right to. She looked businesslike too, in a high-necked Edwardian-style white blouse under a soft black wool crepe jacket. A silver and amethyst brooch the size of a credit card was pinned to the jacket, like an abstract representation of her hair and eyes. She flicked open a desk diary on the seat beside her while Gloria produced a piece of paper with a flourish. 'That's Kate's time, date and place of birth.'

Dorothea put it on the seat beside her without a glance. 'I couldn't possibly take you through your chart *and* answer your questions, Kate.'

'It's the answers to my questions I'm interested in.'

Dorothea raised one eyebrow. I used to do that, but I grew out of it. 'Pity. You should always seize opportunity when it presents itself. Who knows when you'll get a second chance to find out what really makes you tick?' She sounded amused.

'I'll manage somehow,' I said.

'I'm sure you will, and that's without reading your chart. Gloria, you're my final appointment today. How would it be if I saw Kate then? Or are you in a hurry to get home?'

'That's fine, Dor,' Gloria said. 'We'll get out your road now and let Rita get her money's worth. See you at half past five.'

She shooed me out ahead of her into the car park. 'We'd better get a move on,' she said. 'I'm due in make-up and I'm not frocked up yet.'

'Gloria, is Dorothea normally fully booked?' I asked, trailing in her wake.

'Oh aye. If you're not one of her regulars, you can wait a month or more for her to fit you in unless you're prepared to go to her consulting room.'

'All half-hour appointments?'

120

'That's right. From nine till half past five,' Gloria confirmed.

'Just as a matter of interest, how much does Dorothea charge?'

'For half an hour, she charges twice what you do for an hour, chuck.'

It was one of those bits of information that stops you dead in your tracks. I'm not cheap. Well, only where Richard's concerned, but even he hasn't worked that out yet. Four times my hourly rate was serious money. Sometimes I wonder if I'm in the right business.

The day passed. Wardrobe, make-up, rehearsal, film. No diverting phone calls, no murderous attacks on the client. No chance either of finding out who had written the poison-pen letters or the identity of the mole that Ross Grant wanted me to drag kicking and screaming into the daylight; thanks to the *Chronicle*, nobody was talking to me. I supposed the cast members had fallen out of love with me because for today I was more famous than them. The crew were just too busy and besides, the novelty of having a real live private eye about the place had worn off.

By the time five rolled around, I was beginning to think that I should start charging boredom money the way that some people charge danger money. I was convinced by now that whoever was writing threatening letters to Gloria was getting satisfaction from knowing they'd frightened her enough to hire me. Given the number of opportunities to cause her serious harm, even with me in tow, it was significant that we'd not even had so much as a near miss in the car. I'd accompany her on her weekend personal appearances, then I intended to call it a day.

Her face restored to street levels of make-up and Brenda's outfit back in wardrobe where it belonged, Gloria was ready for her session with Dorothea. 'Walk me across to the van, chuck,' she said. 'I'll see Dorothea on my own, but if you come over about five to six, you can walk me back to my dressing room then pop back to ask her whatever it is you want to know.'

An unrelenting sleet was falling as we joined the dozens of people scurrying across the car park, desperately seeking shelter. I'd helped myself to one of the umbrellas in an equipment skip by the entrance to the outdoor set, and I wrestled with the gusty wind to keep it over Gloria's head. At the caravan, I knocked. I heard Dorothea tell Gloria to come in. She disappeared inside and I closed the umbrella and sprinted for Gloria's car, parked only a few spaces away. Waiting for her there, I could at least listen to the radio.

I closed my eyes and leaned back in the seat, the day's news washing over me. The traffic reporter warned about drifting snow on trans-Pennine routes. 'Great,' I muttered, wondering how bad the road to Saddleworth would be. If the weather was going to close in, it might be worth suggesting to Gloria that she spend the night in my spare room to save myself the double journey over snowy moorland roads.

Almost before I knew it, the twenty-five minutes were up. I abandoned the condensation-fogged car and legged it for Dorothea's camper. I knocked on the door of the van and Gloria called, 'Just coming, chuck.' The door opened, the warm light from inside spilling on to the Tarmac and revealing the waterlogging that was creeping up the sides of my brown ankle boots. 'I'll send her right back,' Gloria said over her shoulder as she emerged, closing the door behind her.

I did my trick with the umbrella and escorted Gloria back to her dressing room. The production area already felt deserted. Nobody on *Northerners* loved their job so much they wanted to hang around after the end of filming on a Friday. I was slightly concerned about leaving Gloria vulnerable in her dressing room. Both Rita and Dorothea knew about my appointment with the astrologer, and either could have mentioned it unthinkingly to a third party. Given the speed rumour moved at in NPTV, the cleaners and secretaries all probably knew Gloria would be alone in a virtually empty building from six o'clock.

'I want you to lock the door behind me, OK?' I told her. 'And don't let anybody in except me. It doesn't matter how much you think you can trust them. If anyone turns up, tell them they'll have to wait until I get back. Promise?'

Gloria grinned. 'All right, boss. Whatever you say.'

I waited outside the door until I heard the Yale lock snap into place behind me. Then I hurried out of the building and ran back across the car park to Dorothea's van. There was no answer to my knock, but I knew she was expecting me to return. Besides, it wasn't the kind of night where you hang around in freezing sleet waiting for someone else to stop playing power games. I opened the door and stepped into the dimly lit interior.

Dorothea Dawson lay sprawled across her chenille tablecloth, one side of her head strangely misshapen and dark with spilled blood. A few feet away, her crystal ball glowed in the lamplight at the end of a flecked trail of scarlet clotting the deep pile of the champagne-coloured carpet.

I backed away momentarily, dragging my eyes from the compelling horror before me. I stared wildly around, checking there was no one else in the confined space. Then the thought hit me with the force of a kick to the stomach that Dorothea might still be alive. For a long moment I didn't know if I could bring myself to touch her.

But I knew that if she died because I'd been squeamish that the guilt would far outweigh the revulsion I felt now. I tried to swallow whatever it was that was preventing me from breathing and inched forward, carefully avoiding the track the crystal ball had left. I stretched my hand towards Dorothea's outflung arm and grasped her wrist.

Her skin was the same temperature as mine, which made it all the more horrible that I couldn't find a pulse.

I backed away, appalled. I'd been right to warn Gloria to take care. There was a killer out there.

I'd been catastrophically wrong about the target, though.

9

MARS OPPOSES THE MIDHEAVEN

She has a high opinion of herself and is not always diplomatic enough to hide it. She can be too bold and belligerent in pursuit of what she knows to be right. But this opposition provides great energy, allowing her to be enterprising and independent. Her speed and competitiveness often take the wind out of the sails of authority figures.

From *Written in the Stars*, by Dorothea Dawson

I didn't know what to do. I didn't think I could bear to stay in that confined space with Dorothea's corpse, but I couldn't just walk away leaving the camper van unsecured. Besides, I couldn't stand guard outside because I'd be soaked to the skin in minutes. It seemed important to me that I shouldn't face the police looking like a drowned rat.

The compromise I found was to move down to the cab. The passenger seat was designed so that it could either face out through the windscreen or swing round to act as an extra chair in the living section of the van. Luckily for my peace of mind, it was currently configured to face forwards.

I scrambled through the gap between the seats, surprised to find myself gasping for air as if I'd been running. I gripped the armrests and forced myself to breathe evenly. I wanted to make sure I didn't sound like an emergency operator's idea of a murderer. I concentrated on the tracks of the melting sleet slithering down the windscreen that blurred the floodlights around the car park and tried to forget the image branded on my mind's eye. Only when my breathing had returned to normal did I take out my phone and dial 999. Once I was connected to the police control room, I said, 'My name is Kate Brannigan and I am a private investigator. I want to report what appears to be a murder.'

The woman on the end of the phone had obviously assimilated her training well. With no apparent indication that this was any more extra-ordinary an occurrence than a burglary in progress, she calmly said, 'Where are you calling from?'

'My mobile. I'm in the car park of the *Northerners* compound. It's just off Alan Turing Way, near the velodrome.'

'And can you tell me what appears to have happened?'

'I'm in a camper van. It belongs to Dorothea Dawson. The astrologer? I'd arranged a meeting with her. I walked in and found her lying dead. It looks like someone's caved her head in with her crystal ball. I tried to find a pulse, but there's nothing.' I could hear my voice cracking and swallowed hard.

'Are you still there?'

'Yes. I'm in the camper van. You can't miss it. It's a big dark-blue Mercedes. Down the far end, away from the entrance. Most of the cars have gone now; there's just a few down this end of the car park.' I was gabbling, I knew, but I couldn't stop myself.

'We'll have some officers with you very soon. Please don't touch anything. Can you give me your number, please?'

I rattled off the number automatically. 'We will be with you very shortly,' she concluded reassuringly. I wasn't comforted. This was an opportunist killing. Normally, there would be people in the car park, chatting and gossiping on their way to their cars, pausing and taking notice. But tonight, the weather meant everyone had their heads down, rushing for shelter and paying no attention to anything except the quickest route to their wheels.

Then there was the time element. There had only been a gap of ten minutes at the very outside between Gloria and me leaving the van and me returning. But someone had been bold or desperate enough to seize that tiny window of opportunity to invade Dorothea's camper van. They'd caught her unawares, obviously, and smashed the heavy crystal ball into her skull so swiftly she'd had no time to react.

Then they'd slipped back into the night. No time to search or steal. Time only to kill and to disappear again. Suddenly, I realized the killer might only have been feet away from me as I pounded across the car park through the sleet. Minutes – no, seconds – earlier and I could have come face to face with someone ruthless enough to have killed me too.

The thought hit me like a blow to the heart. My mouth went dry and a violent shiver ran through me from head to foot. My stomach started to heave and I barely got the door open in time. Second-hand lunch splattered on to the puddled car park. I retched and retched long past the point where my stomach was empty, hanging on grimly to the door with one hand.

That's how the police found me. I hadn't even been aware of the approaching sirens. I figured they must have turned them off when they reached the security gates at NPTV. Now, it was only the flashing blue lights that announced their arrival. I looked up blearily, my hair stuck to my head with sleet and sweat, and took in two liveried police cars and an ambulance. The occupants were out and running almost before the cars came to a standstill.

They headed towards me. I straightened up and pointed weakly to the door that led directly into the living section. 'She's in there,' I croaked. Three of them shifted their angle of approach. The fourth moved towards me, blocking any getaway I might have planned. He wasn't to know we were on the same side. Not surprising; it was a role I found pretty unfamiliar myself. After a quick scan of his colleagues' faces to check there was no opposition, the first policeman opened the door and cautiously stuck his head inside the van. I heard the hiss of indrawn breath and a muffled curse.

Now the paramedics were also at the door, trying to get past the knot of police officers. 'Let us in,' I heard one of them say impatiently.

'No way,' the cop who'd seen the body said. 'That's a crime scene.'

'She could be alive,' the paramedic protested, attempting to shove through the barrier of blue uniforms.

'No way,' the policeman repeated. He looked about as good as I felt. 'Take it from me, there's nothing you can do for her.'

'She didn't have a pulse when I found the body,' I said.

'When was that?' the officer keeping an eye on me asked.

'About two minutes before I made the treble-niner.'

My unthinking use of a professional term won me a quizzical look. One of his colleagues was speaking into his radio, collar turned up against the wind-driven sleet. Grumbling, the paramedics headed back to the shelter of their ambulance. I inched back so that I was out of the worst of the weather, making sure I kept my hands in sight. I knew that right now I had to be their prime suspect. One being a prime number.

Another car splashed through the puddles, illuminating a couple of executives making for their cars, too worried about getting wet to care about the presence of police cars and ambulances. The new arrival skidded to a halt only feet away from the front of Dorothea's Mercedes. The doors swung open, switching on the interior light and the impossible happened.

Things got worse.

Twenty minutes later, I was sitting in the *Northerners* green room, instantly commandeered by the police as a temporary incident room until their own purpose-built caravan could be brought over. Opposite me sat Detective Sergeant Linda Shaw, her hands wrapped around a cardboard cup of instant coffee. I didn't mind Linda; she probably had more in common with me than she'd ever have with the hard-nosed bastard she worked for.

I suspected Detective Chief Inspector Cliff Jackson had an auburn-haired doll in his desk drawer. I was convinced he stuck pins into it at regular intervals. It was the only explanation I could think of for that stabbing pain I sometimes got in my left ankle. Jackson had been one of the senior murder detectives in the city for the last seven years or so. You'd think he'd be pleased that I've made a significant contribution to his clear-up rate. You'd be wrong. Now, whenever the planets really want to gang up on me, they send me an encounter with Jackson.

Linda Shaw stood between Jackson and me like a buffer zone between warring Balkan armies. As soon as he'd seen me pale-faced and shivering in the cab of Dorothea's van, the wheels had started going round in his head as he imagined the many ways he could use my presence at the murder scene to make my life hell. He'd sped across the intervening Tarmac without even pausing to put on his raincoat. 'What the fuck are you doing here?' he greeted me.

'Working,' I said. 'How about you?'

He turned scarlet. 'Don't push your luck, Brannigan,' he stormed. 'I'm here less than a minute and already you're looking at spending the night in the cells. You just don't know when to keep your smart mouth shut, do you?'

'If you want me to keep my mouth shut, that's fine by me. I'll make my one call to my solicitor and then you'll get "no comment" from here to eternity,' I snarled back. 'And as soon as I get home, I'll be on the phone to Alexis Lee. The world should hear how a material witness in the murder of the nation's favourite astrologer gets treated by Manchester's finest.'

'Sir.' Linda's voice was quiet but urgent. 'Sir, you're needed inside the van. The scene-of-crime lads are right behind us, and the rest of the team has just got here. Why don't I find a quiet corner and take a statement from Ms Brannigan? Then we'll have an idea where we're up to?'

'I don't want you sticking your nose in this, Brannigan,' Jackson snapped, straightening an electric-blue tie that clashed disturbingly with his lilac shirt. 'You give your statement to DS Shaw and then you bugger off out of it. That's not an invitation, it's an instruction. I'd love to arrest you for obstruction. But then, I shouldn't have to tell you that, should I? She's all yours, Detective Sergeant.'

I had led Linda from the van to the production building, suggesting it would be a good idea to get someone to contact John Turpin to tell NPTV what was going on and find out where we could talk. She'd got it sorted, right down to discovering where the nearest coffee machine was. Finally we had a moment to give each other the once-over. I saw a woman hovering around the crucial cusp of thirty, the skin around her eyes starting to show the attrition of long hours and late nights, the slight downturn to her mouth revealing the emotional price of dealing with people who have been violently bereaved, and the ones responsible for smashing those lives to smithereens.

I didn't want to think about what she saw. I opened the batting. 'Detective Sergeant, eh? Con-gratulations.'

'Thanks. I hear you've come up in the world too.

Brannigan and Co, not Mortensen and Brannigan any more.'

'Cliff keeps tabs on me, does he? At least I get to be my own boss. But you're still stuck being Jackson's bag carrier.'

'There are worse jobs in the police service,' she said drily.

'Especially if you're a woman.'

She inclined her head in agreement. 'So, help me to keep my job and tell me what happened here tonight?'

'You know I don't have any problem with you, Linda. Ask what you want. As long as you don't expect me to breach my client's confidentiality, I'll tell you all I can.'

She took me through the reason for my presence, then on to the precise circumstances of my discovery. We'd just got to the part where I described trying to find Dorothea's pulse when the door crashed open. Gloria staggered in dramatically, hair plastered to her head, eye make-up spreading like a bad Dusty Springfield impersonation. 'Kate,' she wailed. 'Thank God you're all right! Oh Kate, I can't believe it. Not Dorothea,' she continued, stumbling towards me. Think Vanessa Redgrave playing King Lear. I had no choice but to jump to my feet and support her. She'd have had no problem collapsing in a heap for effect. I had no doubt that she was sincerely upset, but being a thespian she couldn't help going over the top so much she made the Battle of the Somme look like a little skirmish.

I put an arm round her and steered her to the nearest sofa. Linda was staring at her with avid eyes. I didn't think it was Gloria's bedraggled appearance that had gobsmacked her. She was star struck. I've seen it happen. Normal, intelligent people faced with their heroes become open-mouthed, wittering wrecks. Back before she became crime correspondent, Alexis once got to interview Martina Navratilova for the features department. She claims the most intelligent question she managed to come out with was, 'What did you have for breakfast, Martina?'

So now I had a star struck detective, an hysterical soap star and a cop who wanted to arrest me for daring to find a murder victim. This was turning into the worst night for a very long time.

'I can't believe it,' Gloria was saying for the dozenth time. This time, however, she moved the narrative forward. 'I keep thinking, I must have been the last person to see her alive.'

The words brought Linda back to something approximating normality. 'What do you mean, Ms Kendal?' she asked gently, crossing to the sofa and sitting next to Gloria.

'Gloria, this is Detective Sergeant Shaw. She's involved in the inquiry into Dorothea's death.'

Gloria fixed Linda with eyes brimming with sooty tears. When this was all over, I'd have to speak to her about waterproof mascara. 'What happened, chuck? All they'd say out in the car park was that there had been an accident, that

Dorothea were dead. I'd gone out looking for you. You were gone so long, I was beginning to worry. I had this feeling . . .' Her voice tailed off into another whooping sob. 'Oh God, I can't believe it,' she wailed. I got up and silently fetched her a glass of water. She emptied it in a few swift gulps then clutched it histrionically to her bosom.

Linda patted her free hand. 'It's hard to grasp, losing a friend,' she said. 'But the best thing you can do for Dorothea now is to help us find the person responsible for this.'

'It wasn't an accident, then?' Gloria demanded. I saw an alertness spring into her eyes that hadn't been there a moment before.

Linda obviously hadn't. 'You'll have to brace yourself for a shock, I'm afraid, Gloria. It looks like Dorothea has been murdered.'

Gloria's face froze. The tears stopped as suddenly as they would when the director yelled, 'Cut'. 'Murdered?' she said, her voice an octave lower. 'I don't understand. Dorothea were fine when I left her. And Kate went right back to her. How could anybody have murdered her?'

'That's what we're here to find out,' Linda said reassuringly. Much more of this and I was going to throw up. A couple of generations ago, it was the professional classes who got this kind of veneration from the police. Before that, you had to have a title. But in Britain in the 1990s, the prerequisite for deference from Officer Dibble was celebrity.

I cleared my throat. 'Apart from the killer, it

seems likely that Gloria was the last person to see Dorothea alive.'

'Do you have any idea what time that might have been?' Linda asked Gloria.

'Just before six,' I said. 'I'd been sitting in Gloria's car in the car park, waiting for her to finish her half past five session with Dorothea. And before you ask, I didn't notice anyone hanging around suspiciously, just a lot of people rushing to their cars and a few others crossing from the production building to the admin block. At five to six, I left the car and went to the camper van. I knocked, and Gloria came out.'

'Did you see Dorothea?' Linda asked me. I couldn't believe she was getting into this with Gloria present. It broke all the unwritten rules about interviewing witnesses separately.

'No, I didn't enter the van.'

'Did you hear her voice?'

I shook my head. 'The wind was blowing, there were cars driving past, she wouldn't have been shouting anyway.'

I could see the implications registering with Linda. I could also see her dismissing the possibility that Gloria could have killed Dorothea for no more substantial reason than that Brenda Barrowclough could never have done such a thing. 'She said cheerio to me and said she'd expect Kate along in a few minutes. But Kate's right. She wasn't shouting. There was no reason why she should, and she wasn't one for raising her voice at the best of times,' Gloria said kindly, as if she was explaining something obvious to a child.

'Was the door on the latch, or did it automatically lock behind you?' Linda asked.

'Just on the latch. We'd all knock and walk in when it were time for our appointments,' Gloria said. 'She were strict about not overrunning, was Dorothea.'

'And how long was it before you got back to the van?' Linda asked me.

I'd already given the timing a lot of thought. 'Ten minutes, tops. Maybe three minutes to walk Gloria back to her dressing room, a few minutes to make sure she was going to lock the door behind me, then a couple of minutes back.'

'It's not long,' Linda observed.

Suddenly, Gloria burst into tears again. 'It's terrible,' she wailed. 'It's a warning. It's a warning to me. All those letters, and Dorothea's premonition. There's a killer out there and he's after me!'

I couldn't quite see the logic, but Gloria's fear seemed real enough. She sobbed and hiccuped and wailed. Linda and I exchanged desperate looks, neither sure how to deal with this. Then as abruptly as her hysterics had begun, they ended and she took control of herself. 'This is aimed at me,' Gloria said, her voice shaky. 'Everybody knew I relied on Dorothea. Everybody knew Dorothea had predicted there was death in the room that last time I saw her. She's been killed to put the fear of death into me.'

'I don't think that's likely,' Linda said soothingly. 'It's a very extreme thing to do if all this letter writer wants to do is frighten you. It's more likely that it's all just a horrible coincidence.'

'Oh aye?' Gloria sat upright, her shoulders straightening. It was a classic Brenda Barrowclough move that signalled to *Northerners* viewers that it was flak-jacket time. 'And is it just a horrible coincidence that I was the last person to see Dorothea alive? If somebody had it in for Dorothea, there must have been plenty of other times they could have killed her without taking the risk that somebody would see them going in or out of the van. Or even walk in on them. The only reason anybody would have for killing her when they did was to make it look like I was the killer. You mark my words, whoever killed my friend has got it in for me an' all.'

There was a moment's stunned silence. 'She has a point,' I said.

'So what are your lot going to do to protect me?' Gloria demanded.

Linda just stared.

'The short answer is, nothing,' I told her. 'Even if they had the bodies, you wouldn't be a priority, on account of your poison-pen letters don't actually threaten to kill you. That's right, isn't it, Linda?'

Linda made a strangled sort of noise. I figured she was agreeing with me.

'Right then,' said Gloria. 'I'll have to keep relying on Kate.' She gathered herself together. I suddenly understood the expression 'girding your loins'. Gloria stood up and said, 'Come on, chuck. I've had enough of this. I'm distraught and I need to go home and have a lie-down.'

She was halfway to the door when she looked behind to check I was following. I gave Linda a hapless shrug. 'We'll need formal statements,' Linda tried plaintively.

'Call my lawyer in the morning,' Gloria said imperiously. 'Kate, who's my lawyer?'

I grinned. Jackson was going to love this. 'Same as mine, of course. Ruth Hunter.'

The last thing I heard as the door swung shut behind us was Linda groaning, 'Ah, shit.' In grim silence we marched out of the building. The sleet had stopped, which was the one good thing that had happened since lunchtime. Gloria swept straight through the mêlée of activity around Dorothea's van, looking neither to right nor left. I scuttled in her wake, trying to look invisible to anyone who might be tempted to alert Jackson. We made it to the car without a challenge.

Once we'd got past the two bobbies working with the NPTV security men on the main gate, all the fight went out of Gloria. Her shoulders slumped and she reached for her cigarettes. 'This is an emergency,' she said. 'Don't you dare open that bloody window.' She inhaled deeply. 'You know I didn't kill Dorothea, don't you?'

I pulled a wry smile. 'You're an actress, Gloria. Would I know if you had?'

She snorted. 'I'm no Susan Sarandon. I play myself with knobs on. Come on, Kate, did I kill Dorothea?'

'I can't believe you did,' I said slowly.

'That'll do me. So you'll try and find out who's done this? Before he decides it's my turn? Or my granddaughter's?'

'Cliff Jackson, the cop that's in charge of this? He's not a bad investigator. But he's been wrong before. I'll give it my best shot.'

'I'll sleep easier knowing that,' she said, toking on her cigarette as if it gave life instead of stealing it.

'Speaking of sleep . . . Do you want to stay over at my place tonight? I'm thinking partly of the weather and partly from the security point of view.'

Gloria frowned. 'It's nice of you to offer, but I could do with being in my own space. I need to feel grounded. And I don't want to be under your feet. You're going to have to get stuck into your inquiries tomorrow, and I don't want to get in the road.'

'I don't want to leave you on your own. Even behind those high walls.' I thought for a moment, then pulled over to the roadside and took out my phone. A couple of phone calls and I had it sorted. It meant an awkward detour via the students' union, but as soon as Gloria saw Donovan in all his hulking glory, she was perfectly happy for me to hoof it the mile across town to my house while she disappeared over the hills and far away with the best-looking bodyguard either side of the Pennines. The only question was whether she'd still respect him in the morning.

I stepped out briskly. The temperature was plummeting now the sleet had stopped, the pavements rapidly icing over. Twice the only thing that saved me from crashing to the pavement was a handy lamppost. All I wanted was to curl up in my dressing gown with a very large amount of Absolut Citron and a smudge of grapefruit juice. With luck, Richard might be home early, preferably armed with a substantial Chinese. He always says Friday night is amateurs' night out as far as live music is concerned. I could almost taste the salt and pepper king prawns.

I should have known better. Nights like that just don't get better. The man I suppose I love was home all right. But not home alone. I found him fast asleep in his bed, his arms around someone else. When I walked into the room, her eyes snapped open. She took one look at me and screamed.

Sensible girl.

10

MERCURY IN VIRGO IN THE 5TH HOUSE

She can turn her hand to anything. She has a discriminating intellect but tends to be overcritical of herself and others in times of stress. She analyses problems with tenacity and is capable of painstaking research. She is logical, sceptical and can be obsessive.

From *Written in the Stars*, by Dorothea Dawson

Divorce may have deprived Richard of most of the last five years of his son Davy's life, but because a lot of his work is done at night, he did most of the daytime childcare for the first three. Thankfully the old skills hadn't deserted him. That meant I didn't have to take any responsibility for the most remarkable child on the planet (if you believed Alexis and Chris). I watched with a mixture of relief and astonishment as he spooned greyish-pink mush into the eager mouth of his nine-month-old girlfriend. He managed it almost without looking, and without ever breaking off in mid-sentence.

He'd already changed a nappy without flinching, which was a long way away from my idea of getting the day off to a good start.

I remember when northern men would have died rather than admit they knew how Pampers worked. Now, they pin you to the wall in café bars and tell you it's possible for men to produce tiny amounts of breast milk. Certainly, Jay's arrival had already achieved the seemingly impossible task of ending the superficial hostilities between Alexis and Richard. Before Jay, Alexis maintained she was a real journo and Richard a sycophant; Richard that he was a real journo and Alexis a police lackey. Work never entered their conversations any more.

As he did about once a week, Richard had taken Jay for the night to give Chris a chance at a straight eight hours. Oddly, when Jay spent the night with him, she slept through till seven in the morning. When Chris was within earshot, Jay would invariably pierce the night with her cries at two, four and six o'clock. I could see she was going to grow up into the kind of clever manipulator I wouldn't mind having on the staff. Never mind putting her name down for Eton, I was putting her name down for Brannigan & Co.

'So what are your plans for today?' Richard asked as we sat in the conservatory watching wet snow cascading from the sky.

'I've got Donovan minding Gloria, so I probably

don't need to go over there. I've told him she's to stay indoors, but looking at the weather, I don't think there'll be much temptation to leave the fireside. I'm going to do some background research in the *Chronicle* library so I can start asking sensible questions about Dorothea Dawson.'

'Great,' he said enthusiastically. 'You can take Jay in with you. I was supposed to drop her at the *Chronicle* crèche so Alexis can pick her up, but if you're going in anyway, I can stay home and get on with some writing.'

Time for the application of the Kate Brannigan irregular verb theory of life. In this case, 'I am diplomatic, you are economical with the truth, s/he is a lying little gobshite.' 'No problem,' I said. Why should I mind drumming my fingers on the table while Richard finished feeding her, changing her, swaddling her for the outside world, swapping the baby seat from his car to mine then strapping her in? It wasn't as if I had anything important like a murder to solve, after all.

I eventually tracked Alexis down in the office canteen. 'Your daughter is in the crèche,' I told her. 'So's her car seat.'

'That's great,' she said. 'I'll bob along in a minute and say hello. We really appreciate it, you know. It's the only time we get a decent night's sleep. She been OK?'

'As far as I know. She screamed her socks off when I got home last night, but that's just because she can't stand any competition for Richard's attention. So I left them to it. She probably had a better night's sleep than I did.'

Alexis shook her head, smiling. 'I know you love her really.'

She knew more than I did. I smiled vacantly and said, 'Dorothea Dawson.'

'She didn't see that coming, did she?'

I love journalistic black humour. It always comforts me to know there are people more cynical than me around. 'What's this morning's story?'

'What's your interest?' she asked, instantly on the alert. Her cigarettes came out and she lit one for real.

'I found the body.'

Alexis ran her free hand through her hair so it stood up in a punk crest. 'Shit,' she said. 'The bizzies never said anything about that at the press conference. They said the body had been discovered by a member of staff, the lying gets.'

'You're surprised?'

'No. Cliff Jackson would superglue his gob shut before he let the name "Brannigan" pass his lips. Unless the sentence also contained the words, "has been charged with". So give, KB. A first-person colour piece, that's just what I need for the city final.' Her notebook had appeared on the table.

'What are they saying?'

'That she was killed in her camper van in the car park of the NPTV compound by a blow to the head around six last night. And that's about all. What can you give me?'

I sighed. 'It isn't exactly something I want to dwell on. I needed to talk to Dorothea about the warning she'd given Gloria the last time she'd done a reading for her. I'd arranged to see her after her final client of the day. When I got there, I knocked but there was no reply. I knew she was expecting me, so I opened the door and walked in. She was lying face down on the table with her head caved in. It was obvious she was dead. Her crystal ball was lying on the carpet at the end of a track of blood. It looked to me as if that's what the killer used. It's much bigger than the usual crystal ball. It must be nine, ten inches across.'

Alexis nodded as she took notes. 'She was famous for it. Claimed it came from some mystical mountain mine. Me, I reckon it came from Pilkington Glass at St Helens.' She gave me an apologetic grin. 'Sorry about this but . . . How did you feel?'

'Sick. Can we talk about something else?'

'What, like Cliff Jackson's marital problems?'

'He's got marital problems?'

Alexis nodded, a grim little smile on her face. 'In spades. His wife's run off with another bloke.'

'What took her so long?'

'She probably couldn't find the key to the handcuffs. The best bit, though, is who she's run off with.' Alexis paused for effect. I rotated my wrist in the classic 'get on with it' gesture. 'His oldest lad's in his second year at Liverpool University. His wife's only run off with the lad's best mate.'

'You're kidding!'

'Would I lie to you?'

'How long have you been sitting on this?' I demanded.

'I only found out this morning. I was trying to get a comment from Jackson and he was going totally ballistic. I know one of his DCs from way back, so I cornered her and asked why Jackson was being even more of a pain than usual and she told me. So don't expect any favours.'

'I'll bear that in mind.' I grinned. 'Couldn't happen to a nicer bloke, though. By the way, did you get anywhere in tracking down who was the source of your story about me minding Gloria?'

Alexis savoured her last mouthful of smoke and regretfully crushed the stub in the ashtray. 'One of those things. Every Friday, the news credits book goes up to accounts so the payments can be processed. It doesn't come back till Monday morning. I was too late getting to it yesterday. Sorry.'

'I'll just have to possess my soul in patience,' I complained.

'So who was Dorothea's last appointment with? Which member of the *Northerners* cast was the last person to see her alive?'

'You'll have to ask Jackson that one.' I didn't have much hope that I'd be able to keep Gloria's name out of the papers, but the longer I could, the better for her. 'Any chance I can pillage the library? I could use some background on Dorothea.'

'You digging into this, then?'

I shrugged. 'If he's not made an arrest overnight, the chances are Jackson's stuck. Which means he'll be wasting time making my life hell. The best way to get him out of my face is to give him something else to think about. I figured if I took a trawl through the cuttings, something might occur to me that I could slip to Linda Shaw.'

I could see from her eyes that Alexis didn't believe a word of it, but she knew better than to try to push me in a direction I didn't want to travel. 'You'll tell me when you're ready,' she said. 'Come on, I'll sort you out.'

Ten minutes later, I was beginning to wish I hadn't asked. A stack of manila files six inches deep contained the *Chronicle*'s archive on Dorothea Dawson, newly returned from the news reporters who had been writing the background feature for that day's paper. Another two ten-inch stacks contained the last year's cuttings about *Northerners*.

I tore a hole in the lid on the carton of coffee I'd brought up from the canteen, took the cap off my pen and began to explore Dorothea Dawson's past.

I'd got as far as her early TV appearances when Alexis burst in, a fresh cigarette clamped between her teeth. The librarian shouted, 'Crush that ash, shit-for-brains!' Alexis ignored him and grabbed my arm, hustling me out into the corridor.

'Where's the fire? What the hell's going on, Alexis?'

'Your mate Dennis has just been arrested for murder.'

I understood each of the words. But together they made no sense. 'They think Dennis killed Dorothea Dawson?' I asked uncomprehendingly.

'Who said anything about Dorothea?'

'Alexis, just explain in words of one syllable. Please?'

'Some villain called Pit Bull Kelly was found dead early doors in one of the underground units in the Arndale. The place was empty, but apparently it had been squatted. According to my contact, they had a tip-off that it'd been Dennis who'd been using the place, and when they checked his fingerprints with records, they found them all over the place. So they've arrested him.'

I still couldn't get my head round it. Dennis was a hard man, no stranger to violence. But for a long time, he'd not lifted a hand in anger to anyone. The crimes he'd committed had all been against property, not people. The notion of Dennis as a killer struck at the heart of everything I believed about him. Alexis's words were a blow that felled my confidence in my own judgement. 'I need to speak to Ruth,' I said, pushing past her and heading blindly down the corridor towards the lifts. I was halfway there when I had to turn back and collect my jacket and bag from the library.

'Calm down, KB,' Alexis said pointlessly as I passed her.

'I don't want to be calm,' I shouted over my shoulder. 'Sometimes I get fed up with calm.' I half ran down the corridor and, too wound up to wait for the lift, started down the stairs. I could hear Alexis's feet pounding down behind me. 'He's not a killer, Alexis,' I shouted up at her. 'He loves his wife, he loves his daughter too much. He wouldn't do this to them.'

Her footsteps stopped. I could hear her gasping for breath. 'Phone me,' she managed to get out.

I didn't bother to reply. I was too agitated. Alexis would forgive me, I knew that. Specifically, she'd forgive me when she got the inside story. At the bottom of the stairwell, I pushed open the door to the car park and got into my car. My breath was coming in deep gulps and my hands were shaking. I realized it was probably delayed shock from the night before kicking in as soon as my defences were down. I was close to Dennis, but not that close, I told myself.

When my pulse was back within the normal range, I took my phone out and dialled the number of Ruth Hunter's moby. If being hated by the police and the judiciary is a measure of success in criminal defence work, Ruth must be one of the best solicitors in the North West. Behind her back, they call her firm Hunter, Killer & Co. A big woman in every sense of the word, she sails into court in her bespoke tailoring like an outsize catwalk queen and rips the Crown Prosecution case to rags. If she didn't have clients, I suspect she'd do it anyway, just for the hell of it. She drives Officer Dibble wild by turning up to cop shops in the middle of the night in her millionaire husband's Bentley Mulsanne turbo. She can park that car in streets where my Rover would be stripped to the chassis in ten minutes and know it'll be there unscathed when she comes back. If she wasn't one of my closest friends, I'd string garlic round my neck just to walk past her office.

'Ruth Hunter,' the voice said briskly.

'It's Kate. I heard about Dennis.'

'What took you so long?' she asked drily. 'It's at least three hours since they lifted him.'

'Are they charging him?'

'I can't talk now as I'm sure you'll appreciate.'

That meant she was in a police station, probably with a custody sergeant breathing down her neck. 'When can we talk?'

'Your office, three o'clock.'

'I'll be there. Should I go and see his wife?'

'I'd leave it for now. Maybe tomorrow. Things are a little . . . volatile at the moment. I'll see you later.' The line went dead.

I could imagine. Most of the contents of the glass cupboard were probably in bits. Debbie's never had a problem expressing her emotions and Dennis was on his final warning following the twelve-month stretch he'd recently done. She'd told him then, one more serious nicking and she'd file for divorce. She'd probably started shredding his suits by now, unless she was saving that for when they charged him.

The clock said half past eleven. I couldn't face sitting in the *Chronicle* library for another three hours, and I didn't want to kick my heels at home. It's ironic. I spend half my life complaining that I never have time to do my washing or ironing, then when I get a couple of hours to myself, I'm too wound up to do anything constructive. I needed to find something that would make me feel like I was being effective. Then I remembered Cassandra Cliff. Cassie had once been one of the household names among the stars of *Northerners*. Then some creepy hack had left no stone unturned to find the slug who revealed that years before she'd been cast as Maggie Grimshaw, the bitch goddess gossip queen of *Northerners*, Cassie had been Kevin.

In the teeth of the hurricane of publicity, NPTV pointed out that they had an equal opportunities policy that protected transsexuals and that Cassie's job was safe with them. They were using 'safe' with that particular meaning Margaret Thatcher inaugurated when she claimed the National Health Service was safe in her hands. Within months, Maggie Grimshaw had been killed off and Cassie was not only unemployed but unemployable.

She didn't run weeping into the wilderness. She sold the inside story of life on *Northerners* to the highest bidder, and there were no holds barred. Cassie never featured in any of the show's regular anniversary celebrations, but I suspected that didn't keep her awake at night. She'd chosen not to be bitter and instead of frittering away the money she made from her exposé, she set up a shop, magazine and social organization for transvestites and transsexuals.

Cassie had been a key source for Alexis for years, and we'd met following the death of a transvestite lawyer I'd been investigating. I'd met her a couple of times since then, most recently at Alexis and Chris's housewarming party. I knew she still kept in touch with a couple of people from *Northerners*. She might well know things Gloria didn't. More to the point, she might well tell me things Gloria wouldn't.

Energized by the thought of action, I started the car and headed for Oldham. Cassie's shop, Trances, was in one of those weary side streets just off the main town centre where some businesses survive against all the odds and the rest sink without trace, simply failing to raise the metal shutters one morning with no advance warning. There was little traffic and fewer pedestrians that afternoon; the wet snow that was melting away in Manchester was making half-hearted attempts at lying in Oldham, and ripples of slush were spreading across the pavements under the lash of a bitter wind. Anyone with any sense was sitting in front of the fire watching a black and white Bette Davis movie.

The interior of Trances never seemed to change.

There were racks of dresses in large sizes, big hair on wig stands, open shelves of shoes so big I could have got both feet in one without a struggle, racks of garish magazines that no one was ever going to read on the tram. The key giveaway that this was the land of the truly different was the display case of foam and silicone prostheses – breasts, hips, buttocks. The assistant serving behind the counter took one look at me and I could see her contemptuously classifying me as a tourist. 'Hi,' I said. 'Is Cassie about?'

'Have you an appointment?'

I shook my head. 'I was passing.'

'Are you a journalist? Because if you are, you're wasting your time. She's got nothing to say to anybody about *Northerners*,' she said, her Adam's apple bobbing uncontrollably.

'I'm not a journalist,' I said. 'I know Cassie. Can you tell her Kate Brannigan's here?'

She looked doubtful, but picked up the phone anyway. 'Cassandra? There's someone here called Kate Brannigan who wants to see you.' There was a pause, then she said, 'Fine. I'll send her up.' The smile she gave me as she replaced the receiver was apologetic. 'I'm sorry. The phone hasn't stopped ringing all day. It's always the same when there's some big *Northerners* story. If it's not that, it's Channel Four researchers doing documentaries about TSs and TVs.'

I nodded and made for the door at the back of the shop that I knew led to Cassie's office and, beyond that, to her private domain. Cassie was waiting for me at the top of the stairs, immaculate as ever in a superbly tailored cream suit over a hyacinth-blue silk T-shirt. I'd never seen her in anything other than fabulous clothes. Her ash-blonde hair was cut in a spiky urchin style, her make-up subtle. From below, her jawline was so taut I had to suspect the surgeon's knife. If I earned my living from looking as convincing as Cassie, even I'd have submitted to plastic surgery. 'Kate,' she greeted me. 'You've survived, then.'

I followed her down the hallway and into her office, a symphony in limed wood and grey leather. She'd replaced the dusty-pink fabric of the curtains and cushions with midnight-blue and upgraded the computer systems since I'd last been there. She'd obviously tapped a significantly profitable niche in the market. 'Survived?' I echoed.

Cassie sat on one of the low sofas and crossed legs that could still give any of her former colleagues a run for their money. 'I saw the story in the *Chronicle*. My idea of hell would be running interference for Gloria Kendal,' she said.

'Why do you say that?' I sat down opposite her.

'Unless she's changed dramatically, she's got a schedule that makes being Prime Minister look like a part-time job, she's about as docile as a Doberman and she thinks if she's hired you, she's bought you.'

I grinned. 'Sounds about right.'

'At least you're not a bloke, so you're relatively safe,' Cassie added archly.

I hoped Donovan was. 'I expect you can guess why I'm here?'

'It's got to be Dorothea. Except that I can't think why you'd be investigating her murder when it's Gloria you've been working for.'

I pulled a face. 'It's possible that the person who killed Dorothea is the same one who is threatening Gloria. I'm just nosing around to see what I can dig up.'

Cassie smiled, shaking her head slightly. 'You'll never make an actress until you stop pulling your earlobe when you're stretching the truth.'

My mouth fell open. I'd never realized what my giveaway body language was, but now Cassie had pointed that out, I became instantly self-conscious. 'I can't believe you spotted that,' I complained.

She shrugged. 'My business depends on being able to spot deception. I've got good at it. It's all right, Kate, I don't need to know the real reason you're interested in who killed Dorothea. I'm happy to tell you whatever I know. I liked Dorothea. She was a worker, like me.'

'How did the connection with *Northerners* begin?'

Cassie frowned in concentration. 'I've got a feeling it was Edna Mercer who first discovered her. You remember Edna? Ma Pickersgill?'

'She's dead now, isn't she?'

Cassie's smile was sardonic. 'Ma Pickersgill died of a heart attack when her house was burgled five years ago. Edna's still alive, though you'll never see her at an NPTV function.'

'She left under a cloud?'

'Alzheimer's. Towards the end, it was touch and go whether she'd stay lucid long enough for them to get her made up and on set. As for learning lines, forget it. Anyway, I'm pretty sure it was Edna who brought Dorothea to the studios. She'd come across her in some dead-end seaside town and Dorothea had hit a couple of nails on the head. So Edna, who was a woman given to enthusiasms, persuaded enough of us to sign up for sessions with Dorothea to make it worth her while coming over for the day. I was impressed, in spite of myself.'

'You surprise me,' I said. 'I'd have thought your feet were too firmly planted on the ground to care what's written in the stars.'

Cassie smiled wryly. 'Dorothea was very good. Whether you believed in it or not when you went in to see her, by the time you came out you were convinced she'd got something. After that first visit, we were all eating out of her hand. So it became a regular thing. The word spread through the cast, and soon she was coming more or less every week.'

'What kind of stuff did she tell you?'

'She'd cast your horoscope, and she'd kick off every session by explaining some little thing in your chart. That was one of the clever things about the way she operated – you had to keep going to see her if you wanted her insight into every element of your personal horoscope. Then she'd talk about the current relationships between the planets and how they might affect you.

'She did phenomenal research, you know. She knew everything there was to know about everybody she had dealings with. Dorothea made a habit of gathering every snippet, no matter how insignificant it seemed. You know how these things go – Edna would say something in passing about Rita's son, then three months later Dorothea would say something to Rita about her son, knowing full well that Rita knows she's never mentioned the boy to Dorothea. It all contributed to the myth of omniscience.'

'Making a virtue out of being a know-all. That is clever,' I acknowledged. 'So was that it?'

Cassie shook her head. 'She'd finish off by asking if there was anything bothering you that you wanted guidance with. You'd tell her and she'd gaze into her crystal ball and give you advice. She didn't go in for the riddle of the Sphinx stuff – she'd say things like, "You're never going to have emotional support from your husband while you're married to an Aries with Capricorn rising. You either have to get out of the marriage or find what you're lacking in your friendships."'

'More therapy than prediction, then?'

'A mixture of both. And actors are very gullible people.' Her smile reminded me that she'd once been an actor, and not just on the screen.

'So why would anyone have it in for her?' I asked.

'I haven't a clue. I hadn't heard that anybody had fallen out with her. She could be irritating when she was trying to impress you with how mystical and spiritual she was, but that's no reason to kill somebody.'

Changing tack, I said, 'What about Gloria? Has anybody from *Northerners* got it in for her?'

Cassie chuckled, a warm, throaty sound. 'How long have you got? The only surprising thing about Gloria is that she's still alive.'

11

She can feel insecure socially because she tends to find herself in conflict with conventional norms. She will construct a world of her own where she can be herself, but will maintain the pretence of being tough and self-sufficient to the outside world. She does not express emotion readily, but nevertheless will often choose a caring or self-sacrificing role in life.

From *Written in the Stars*, by Dorothea Dawson

It was the first time anybody had even hinted that Gloria wasn't the most popular girl in the school. I leaned forward and said as calmly as I could manage, 'And there was me thinking everybody loved Gloria.'

'They do. That's why she provokes thoughts of murder on a regular basis. Or at least, she always used to. It drives you insane to be around somebody who's always kind, always generous, always doing charity work, always making time for the fans. There are people in the cast of *Northerners* who have a permanent inferiority complex thanks to Gloria.' Cassie's voice was light, but there was an edge of something harder in her eyes.

'But like you just said, that's no reason to kill somebody.'

Cassie raised her perfectly shaped eyebrows. 'No? Well, you have more experience in these matters than I do. I tell you what people would kill for, though, and that's their roles in *Northerners*. Gloria's hot right now. The public adore her, and the management knows it. Granted, nobody's bigger than the show, but when actors are riding the crest of the wave, they do get a certain amount of input into the storylines. If somebody in the cast knew Gloria was suggesting a storyline that would see them written out, that'd be a strong enough motive for some of the idiots in the cast to put her out of the picture. But then, it's not Gloria who's been murdered, is it?'

I sighed. 'No. But one way or another, Dorothea's death has rebounded quite nastily on Gloria's life. She was the one who was in the room when Dorothea talked about the presence of death. She never said anything similar to anyone else, as far as I've been able to find out.'

Cassie suddenly jumped to her feet. 'Stay there a minute,' she said, crossing to a door in the far wall. 'I'll be right back.'

The minute stretched into two, then five. The more I thought about what she'd suggested, the more uneasy I became. I pulled out my phone and rang Gloria's number. 'Hiya, chuck,' she greeted me.

'Everything OK?' I asked.

'Grand as owt. We're watching a Bette Davis video and having a lovely time.'

All right for some. 'Can I speak to Donovan?' I waited while she summoned him. He came on the line almost immediately. 'Don? How's things?'

'Nothing except endless phone calls from the papers. Gloria just tells them she's too devastated to talk and puts the phone down. It's a class act.' He sounded both admiring and cautious.

'I've got something to do in town, but I'll be over in a couple of hours to relieve you. Is that OK?'

'Great.' I wasn't imagining the relief in his voice. Considering they've grown up in the inner city, Shelley's kids have led remarkably sheltered lives. There was no way Donovan had the sophistication to deal with a demanding woman like Gloria indefinitely. If I didn't rescue him before nightfall, his mother almost certainly would, and then we'd have another corpse on our hands. And I'm still too young to die.

Cassie returned just as I finished the call, carrying a paperback. She held it up so I could see the cover, a misty head-and-shoulders shot of Dorothea looking significantly younger than when I'd met her. *If I'd Known Then, by Dorothea Dawson. The Life of a Stargazer*, was emblazoned top and bottom across the cover. 'It was published about four years ago,' Cassie said, handing it to me. 'Bestseller list for four weeks, then the remainder pile, I suspect.'

I opened it. The title page had an inscription. *To my darling Cassie. Fire and water make for a steamy combination! Where you are is better for you than where you were. Go in peace. Love, Dorothea Dawson.* 'She seemed to know you well,' I remarked.

'Not as well as she liked to think,' Cassie said drily. 'Like most people, she thought anyone whose sexuality or gender was expressed differently from the mainstream had to be obsessed with sex. Anyway, you're welcome to borrow it. It's life with all the edges smoothed down, but it does show you a bit of what the woman herself was like.'

I pocketed the book and thanked her. It was clear from the way she was still standing that as far as Cassie was concerned, there was no more to be said. But before I left, I had to ask her one thing. 'You know they've got a mole,' I said. 'Any ideas who it might be?'

An indefinable bitterness crept into Cassie's face. She knew all about the damage that moles could do to the foundations of a life. 'John Turpin must be biting the carpet,' she said. 'There's nothing the management hates more than storyline leaks.'

'This isn't just storyline leaks,' I pointed out. 'It's the kind of stuff that ruined your career.'

She sighed. 'I know. I try not to think about it because it reminds me of what was probably the worst point in my life. When I was splashed all over the tabloids, I think I was actually more depressed than I ever was when I was still trapped inside a male shape. So when I see other people's lives being trashed in the same way, I just try to tune out and remind myself that it turned into the best thing that could have happened to me. But I don't know who's ratting on the *Northerners* cast any more than I know who gave me up.'

'You never found out?'

'I never found out. There were so few people who knew, you see, and I trusted them all with my life. I always thought someone from the Amsterdam clinic where I had my surgery must have been over here on holiday or on business or something and seen me on the TV.'

I got to my feet. 'Was Ross Grant doing the outside catering when you were on the show?'

'Ross? Big cuddly Scotsman? Wife with eyes like a hawk? Yeah, he took over the contract about a year before I was demolished. Wait a minute . . . You're not suggesting Ross is the mole?'

'I'm not, but Turpin seems determined to give it a whirl.'

Cassie laughed scornfully. 'Ross hasn't got the malice to do it or the brains to cover his tracks.'

'What about his wife?'

'Why should she? Why risk the goose that lays the golden eggs?'

'Greed?'

Cassie looked sceptical. 'I can't see her going in for that kind of short-term thinking.'

'Not even if she thought they were going to lose the contract? That way she kills two birds with one stone. She gets her revenge on Turpin for dumping them and she earns a nice little nest egg to cushion the blow while they look for other work.'

'They already have other work,' Cassie objected. 'Or they used to, at any rate. *Northerners* is their most regular source of income, but they do cater for other people's location shoots. So it wouldn't be the end of the world if they did lose the contract. And if she was discovered, it would mean the end of their business altogether. I just don't see it.'

As I walked back to my car, I pondered what Cassie had said. For it to be worth the mole's while, he or she had to be indifferent to the outcome of being found out. That meant it was either someone sufficiently skilled to overcome the stigma of being known in the TV business as the *Northerners* mole, or someone who was prepared to risk their career to vent their venom against the programme or its makers.

However I cut it, it didn't sound like a cast member to me.

I was back in my office by three. I wasn't alone; Gizmo was in the computer room in weekend uniform of jeans, Converse baseball boots with holes in the toes, and three shirts. When I'd stuck my head round the door, he'd lifted his head long enough to tell me he was working on some new computer security sub-routines for a local mail order company that had started direct selling via the Internet. Who was I to doubt him? Even if he had gone pink around the ears?

As soon as I had five minutes that I didn't need for sleeping, I was going to have to do some digging.

Ruth walked through the door with ten seconds to spare. She's the only person I know who's even more punctual than me. One of the mysteries of the universe for both of us is how we ended up hitched to men who think if you get to the cinema in time to see the British Board of Film Censors certificate, you're far too early. If I could change one thing about Richard, that's what it would be.

She pulled me into her arms and gave me the kind of hug that always makes me feel five years old. It was exaggerated today because she was swathed in a vast silver-grey fake fur that felt like the best fluffy toy a child ever held. 'You look like the Snow Queen,' I said, disentangling myself and giving her an admiring look from the perfectly pleated blonde hair to the soft leather boots that clung to her well-shaped calves.

'I was aiming for the scary-monster effect,' she said, shrugging out of her fur and dropping into a chair.

'Did it work?'

She pulled a face. 'Dennis is still in custody, so it rather looks as if I failed.'

'What's the score?' I asked, switching on the

cappuccino machine that was one of the few permanent reminders of my former business partner Bill Mortensen.

Ruth shook her head wearily. 'It's really not looking good for him. Especially with a record that includes burglary, robbery and GBH.'

'GBH? I didn't know about that.'

'He was twenty-two and he'd just come out of the Paras after a tour in Northern Ireland where his best friend was shot by a sniper in front of his eyes. Post-traumatic shock hadn't been invented then, otherwise a good brief would have walked him out of the door on that set of circumstances. He hasn't been convicted of a violent offence since, but it's still sitting there among his previous convictions like a great fat toad. Any battered body found in the vicinity of his fingerprints is always going to point to Dennis.'

I passed her a cup of frothy coffee and perched with my own on the corner of the desk. 'What exactly happened?'

Ruth filled me in succinctly. Patrick 'Pit Bull' Kelly was one of a gang of eight brothers from the unappetizing redbrick terraces of Cheetham Hill in North Manchester. They were all small-time criminals, good only at getting caught. Pit Bull had been running a shop-squat scam like Dennis, but since he lacked Dennis's nerve or imagination, he'd steered clear of the city centre and worked his own familiar turf with its restricted numbers of punters, none of whom had much cash to spare.

When he'd heard about Dennis's operation, he'd decided he wanted a slice so last night he'd told two of his brothers he was going into town to 'take that scumbag O'Brien's shop off him'.

The next anyone had seen of Pit Bull Kelly had been early that morning. The manager of the cut-price butcher's shop next door to Dennis's squat got more than he'd bargained for when he went to open up. He'd opened the door to the service corridor that ran behind the six-unit section. Facing him was a brindle-and-white pit bull terrier, the bulges of muscle making the hair on its shoulders and ribs stand out like a bristly halo. Its teeth were bared in a rictus that would have made Jaws look friendly, but instead of growling, it was whimpering. The poor bloke froze in his tracks, but the dog showed no signs of attacking him. Instead, it had backed up to Dennis's back door and started howling. According to Ruth, the witness claimed it sounded like the hound from hell.

He didn't know what to do, so he shut the door and called the mall security. Grateful for something more interesting than teenage trouble-makers, two uniformed guards had arrived within minutes. They had the local beat bobby in tow, less than thrilled at having his illicit tea break with the security men broken up. When they opened the corridor, the same thing happened. The dog showed its teeth, backed off and started howling outside the door to Dennis's shop.

The bobby decided they should take a look

inside. The door obviously wasn't locked, but there was something heavy behind it. A bit of brute force got the door far enough open for the copper to stick his head inside and check out the obstruction. Which happened to be the corpse of Pit Bull Kelly.

How he'd died was far from obvious. There was no blood, no visible wound. But the bobby was sensible enough to realize that somebody who looked as dodgy as Pit Bull Kelly probably hadn't dropped down dead with a heart attack. He'd radioed for back-up. By mid-morning, the finger-print team had matched Dennis's prints with the ones all over the curiously empty shop. And the pathologist had given them the tentative information that he thought Pit Bull Kelly had died from a sub-arachnoid haemorrhage.

'What's a sub-arachnoid haemorrhage?' I asked, my first interruption. Ordinarily I'm not that restrained, but, unusually in lawyers, Ruth actually tells a story with all the pertinent details in place.

Ruth tilted her head sharply to one side and pressed her fingers under the angle of her jaw. 'Just behind the jawbone here, there's a very vulnerable blood vessel. Rupture that and you're brain-dead in seconds. Normally it's protected by the jaw. And by the way we instinctively duck our heads when any threat approaches. It's almost impossible to hit accidentally, but it could be caused by, for example, a stiff-fingered karate blow to the neck.'

'And Dennis was a Para,' I said hollowly.

'Dennis was indeed a Para. He says he never learned any karate in the service, but we both know what a bugger it is to try proving a negative.'

'So the police are saying that Dennis was there, Dennis had good reason to get into a ruck with Pit Bull Kelly, so Dennis must have murdered him then emptied his stock out of the shop to cover his tracks?'

Ruth nodded. 'That's about the size of it. That, or Dennis caught Pit Bull Kelly in the act of stealing all his stock.'

'What's Dennis's version?'

'Perfectly plausible, as you'd expect. According to him, the landlord turned up yesterday with a couple of heavies who were even bigger than Keith. He gave Dennis twenty-four hours to get out or suffer the consequences. Dennis thought this was a not unreasonable proposition, so he spent yesterday evening with Keith and a couple of the lads, loading the stock into a van. Keith and the others went off with the van around half past nine, and Dennis went home, where he spent the rest of the evening watching a video with Debbie. They then went to bed, together, and woke up, again together, at around eight this morning.'

'That's his alibi? The blonde with no brain?'

'The blonde with no brain who has previously been caught out giving him false alibis,' Ruth said drily.

'Wasn't Christie home?' I asked. Dennis's daughter obviously couldn't testify that he'd been in bed all night, but at least she'd have been a more credible witness to his TV viewing.

'She stayed overnight with a friend.' Ruth carefully placed her empty cup on the side table. 'I won't deny it's looking bad, Kate.'

I nodded. 'I'll do what I can.'

Ruth stood up and enveloped herself in the fake fur. 'I know Dennis will appreciate it. I think they'll probably charge him tomorrow and bring him before the Mags on Monday. Once he's remanded, you'll be able to visit him and see if there's anything he can tell you that he'd prefer me not to know. If you need anything, you know where to find me.'

We hugged, the silken fur stroking my face. 'Just leave the coat,' I said. 'I've got to go to Saddleworth.'

Ruth groaned. 'It's not the coat you'll need, it's a team of huskies and a sled. You're surely not going there for pleasure, are you?'

I laughed. 'They do pleasure in Saddleworth? A place where their idea of a good time is brass bands, Morris dancing and the annual Ducking of the Greenfield Trollop? I don't think so.'

'So, strictly business,' Ruth said, adjusting her pelt so not a breath of chill air could penetrate. 'No fun Saturday night with Richard, then.'

'He's probably babysitting,' I said, more of an edge in my voice than I'd intended.

Ruth's eyebrows rose. 'The boy getting broody, is he?'

'If he is, he's wasting his energy,' I told her firmly.

'I'd keep an eye on that, if I were you,' Ruth said ominously as she swept out.

Where would we be if it wasn't for the love and support of our friends?

12

MERCURY SQUARES THE ASCENDANT

*She is inclined to keep her own counsel, but can't
resist poking her nose into everybody else's business.
She's never quite got to grips with the idea that there
are times when it's tactful to keep her advice to herself.
She is a quick worker, energetic and inventive. She
tends to be a chameleon, appearing all things to
all people.*

From *Written in the Stars*, by Dorothea Dawson

It's not often I feel sorry for journalists. But I
had to admit my heart went out to the handful
of hacks still staking out the entrance to Gloria's
enclave. The temperature was already below zero,
and the interiors of their cars were no match for a
winter's night on the edge of Saddleworth Moor.
They perked up momentarily when I swung into
the narrow lane, a couple of them even getting
out and trotting through the freezing slush in
my wake.

But I was through the gate and gone long before they caught up. I hadn't had to use the intercom; I'd phoned Donovan just as I was approaching precisely so I wouldn't have to run the gutter-press gauntlet. As I got out of the car, Gloria appeared in her doorway. She was wearing a high-necked, sparkling, midnight-blue evening dress that hung straight down from her bosom in an elegant fall. On her feet were glittering gold strappy sandals. She looked ready for the Oscars on a balmy California evening, not a charity auction in a Manchester hotel on the coldest night of the year. My charcoal wool crepe suit that doubles up for evening wear and impressing the hell out of clients left me feeling seriously underdressed. Gloria clearly agreed.

'You do know this is a black-tie affair?' she asked.

'I'm a minder, not a model,' I snapped, forcing her to step backwards as I hurried inside. Donovan was looming in the living room, a certain tension noticeable around his deep-set eyes. 'Any problems, Don?'

'Everything under control,' he reported, thrusting his big hands into the pockets of his jeans, which made his shoulders look even more like an American footballer's padding. 'Are you going to drop me off in town, or what?'

Gloria swept past me and slipped her arm through one of Donovan's. His eyes widened like a startled Bambi. 'Kate, don't you think it would be better if

Donovan escorted me tonight? All I'm thinking is that you've been splashed all over the papers, and I don't want you to have to spend your evening fending off nosy parkers.'

She didn't want anyone stealing her limelight, more like. Besides, women like Gloria like to impress people. What better fashion accessory than a drop-dead-gorgeous toy boy like Donovan? That would take everyone's mind off death threats and on to prurient scandal. 'I thought you just said it was black tie,' I said sourly.

Gloria gazed up at Donovan. 'Have you not got a dinner jacket, chuck?'

'Sorry, no.' Relief relaxed his features into a smile.

'Never mind,' Gloria said. 'Harry Gershon the tailor's on the committee for tonight's do. I'll give him a bell and you can tell him your measurements and he'll bring a suit along.'

'Oh,' Donovan croaked. 'But . . .'

Gloria gave him the hundred-watt smile. I could see sweat on his upper lip and it was nothing to do with the central heating. 'We'll have a great time, Donovan. I promise you.' Her throaty chuckle left almost nothing to the imagination.

'That might not be such a bad idea,' I said slowly, an idea beginning to form.

'But Kate,' Donovan protested, apprehension and betrayal in his voice.

'If I take Gloria's car and shove a Brenda wig over my hair, I can act as a decoy and pull the press off. Then you'll get a clear run into town. I've got some work to do digging into Dorothea's past, so I can get on with that while you two are out enjoying yourselves.'

Donovan looked like I'd just given him life with a recommendation for twenty-five years. 'You mean you want me to carry on bodyguarding Gloria?' he asked desperately.

'At least, chuck,' Gloria purred, delighted to be getting her own way.

'And I'll pick Gloria up later at the hotel and bring her back here,' I said sweetly, enjoying the irritation that flashed in her eyes as she watched her bubble burst.

Donovan grinned with relief. 'That's great. I don't think I can do tomorrow, Kate, because I've got to finish an essay for Monday.'

And I am Marie of Romania, I thought to myself. 'No problem. I'll handle it. OK?' I asked Gloria.

'You're the boss,' she pouted. 'I'll get you my spare Brenda wig.' She disentangled her arm from Donovan, gave him a little pat on his iron-hard gluteus maximus and sashayed out of the room.

Donovan moved to my side and stooped close to my ear. 'I thought you were going to make me spend another night here,' he whispered. I thought only the prospect of his mother's anger had the power to make him that twitchy.

'You survived last night intact, didn't you?' I asked sweetly.

He straightened up and scowled. 'Only just,' he muttered. 'What's the polite way to tell somebody ten years older than your mum to take her hand off your thigh?'

'You obviously found one,' I said drily.

'I went to the toilet a lot,' he said bitterly. 'And the spare bedroom's got a bloody big chest of drawers that fits nicely behind the door. It took me all my time to get it shifted, and it's just as well I did because I swear I woke up to the sound of the door handle turning.'

I stifled a snort of laughter. 'Sorry, Don,' I giggled. 'I know it's not funny. What happened?'

'I did snoring. Loudly. Eventually she went away. She must think I'm a pretty crap bodyguard if I can sleep through that.'

I grinned. 'Somehow I don't think it's the guarding capabilities of your body that she's interested in. Don't worry, I'll come and rescue you in good time tonight.'

We shut up and moved apart as we heard Gloria's approach. She came in twirling a rigid platinum-blonde beehive on the end of her finger. 'There you go, chuck. One Brenda Barrowclough barnet.' She tossed it in my direction. Donovan stretched out a long arm and intercepted it, then handed it ceremoniously to me.

'Let's see what you look like,' he said, a mischievous grin lighting up his eyes.

I pulled the wig over my head. It wasn't a bad fit, and in the poor light of the streetlamps

I reckoned it would be good enough to fool anyone expecting Gloria. Five minutes later and I was proving myself right, always a feeling I enjoy. At the end of the narrow lane leading to Gloria's, I slowed to turn on to the main road. To either side, headlights snapped on and engines coughed into life. 'Gotcha,' I said under my breath as I led the cavalcade down the road towards Oldham. As far as I could see, they were all nailed to my tail. I was just grateful there were no tunnels between Saddleworth and Manchester. And that it was too cold for riding motorbikes.

I drove to the office, not particularly wanting to invite the rat pack back to my own doorstep. I managed to find a parking space that wasn't illegal enough to earn a ticket on a Saturday night, aware of the four press cars hovering nearby, trying to find nonexistent spaces where they could abandon ship and follow 'Gloria'. I got out of the car, pulled the wig off and ran my hand through my hair. I wiggled my fingers at the hacks and walked round the corner to my office. Nobody followed me. Like private eyes, journos always know when they've just been had over by an expert. One humiliation was enough for one evening.

The office was dark and empty, Gizmo having finally remembered he had a home to go to. I brewed myself a cappuccino and stretched out on the clients' sofa to skim the authorized version of Dorothea's life. The two hundred and fifty pages of largish print left a lot of scope for the imagination.

The rosy glow of a happy Lancashire childhood in a poor but honest family, followed by an adolescence troubled only by the upheavals surrounding the discovery of her psychic powers and the difficulties of coming to terms with a 'gift' that set her apart from her contemporaries.

She had married at twenty to a man eight years older than her, referred to only as Harry. The marriage lasted less than a chapter. If Dorothea's cursory dismissal was anything to go by, the real thing hadn't endured much longer. Because she'd needed to support herself, she'd started charging for astrological consultations. By the time Edna Mercer had stumbled across her, she'd graduated from her front room to her own booth on a seaside pier.

Northerners had changed everything. Within months of becoming the personal astrologer to a handful of cast members, she was the most sought-after stargazer in the country. A year after Edna Mercer had plucked her from relative obscurity, she had a monthly slot on daytime TV, syndicated weekly newspaper columns and pre-recorded local radio horoscopes. Now, a few years after her book had appeared, she had been edged from pole position among astrologers by the high-profile appearances of Mystic Meg on the national lottery broadcasts, but Dorothea Dawson was still Seer to the Stars in the public's mind. The amazing thing, the one fact that had kept her going through the tough times, was the certain knowledge that once she reached a particular point in her astrological cycle, she would be a star herself. And the moon is made of green cheese.

Bored by the book's relentless tabloid prose and frustrated by its deliberate superficiality, I gave up on it after an hour or so. I knew that compared to the police, my chances of uncovering Dorothea's killer were slim. They had forensic evidence and teams of trained officers who could question everybody who'd ever crossed the threshold of the NPTV compound. All I had going for me was the chance that my informal networks could produce information that was denied to the police. Cassie had been some help, but I needed a lot more.

There was one source that I suspected wouldn't occur to Cliff Jackson if he thought from now till next Christmas. Even if it did, a private operator like me was always going to get a far better response from the anarchic community of the Internet than a copper ever would. Even the straightest suit turns into a bit of a rebel when he – or she – ventures into cyberspace.

Reluctantly abandoning the comfort of the sofa, I slouched in front of my PC and got on-line. I went straight to one of the search engines that act as the nearest thing the ever-expanding web has to a road map. Within minutes, I had a list of addresses for websites and newsgroups that might be useful sources of information. I posted a message in a dozen places – the technological equivalent of the personal column of the newspaper, with considerably faster and better results. While I was on-line, I posted a couple of other inquiries, to see if something I'd half remembered was the truth or just wishful thinking. Finally, I checked my own e-mail and printed out a couple of requests for information from investigators abroad. They were after routine background checks that would take them days or weeks but which I could polish off in a matter of hours thanks to my local knowledge. It used to be a lot easier for people to disappear abroad. Now it's really true that you can run but you can't hide.

I switched off the computer and checked the time. Way too early to pick up Gloria. There was no chance of Richard being home on a Saturday night, at least not before *Match of the Day*. But I knew someone who would be.

As I parked outside the O'Briens' house, a couple of pairs of curtains in the deeply suburban close twitched open, shards of light sparking on their frosted lawns like glitter on Christmas cards. Even thick middle managers know that nobody as small as me gets into the police, so the pale stripes of curtain gaps soon disappeared. Debbie answered the door with a defiant glower that turned her beauty into a threat. 'Oh, it's you,' she said. 'I thought it was the Old Bill come back for another run through the laundry basket. Bastards. Come on in.'

It was hardly a gracious invitation, but I don't

suppose I'd have been any better behaved in the circumstances. I followed her into the immaculate and characterless kitchen. I'd been right about the glasses. The cabinet was empty. I didn't think that was because Debbie was secretly having a party in the next room. 'Want a drink?' she asked.

When I started working in Manchester, the first time someone had asked me that I'd said, 'No thanks, I'm driving.' He'd given me a very strange look. It took me about six months and a lot of thirsty encounters to realize that when you're offered a drink around here, they mean tea or coffee. 'Coffee,' I said. 'White, no sugar.'

The silence grew thick between us while Debbie brewed up, the hiss as boiling water exploded coffee granules perfectly audible. She's never quite sure what to make of me. Being a woman whose IQ is around the same as her continental shoe size, she can't quite make herself believe that any woman would prefer to go out to work to support herself from choice. She also finds it hard to get her head round the notion that any heterosexual woman could spend serious time with her husband without having designs on his body. Every now and again Dennis or I or their teenage daughter Christie convinces her that our relationship is purely platonic. Then she forgets what platonic means and we have to start all over again. Sometimes I think it would just be easier if I told her I was a lesbian.

On second thoughts, perhaps not.

'Ruth says you're going to help him,' Debbie said flatly as she plonked the mug in front of me.

'I'll do what I can. But I'm not sure what I can usefully do. It's not like I can track down missing alibi witnesses or anything.'

Debbie bristled. 'That's because he was here with me all night.'

'You're sure he didn't pop out for a packet of fags or anything?' I asked.

Debbie glared at me. 'Whose side are you on? You sound like the bloody bizzies. Look, he didn't pop out for a packet of fags because I buy his fags at the supermarket, right?' She swung away from me and yanked open one of the tall kitchen units. The cupboard contained an unbroached carton of Dennis's brand and a half-full wrap of hers. 'Even Dennis can't smoke two hundred fags a night.'

'I'm just checking, Debbie,' I said calmly. 'I'm on Dennis's side. I only asked because if he did bob out for ten minutes, you can bet the dibble are going to find out and use that to make you look like a liar.'

She lit a cigarette, then gripped her right elbow with her left hand in a classic defensive gesture. 'Look, I know I gave him a moody alibi one time. But you've got to when it's your man. And I'm not lying this time. He really was here all night. Him and Keith and the lads had been loading up the stock. He was too knackered even to go out for a pint.'

I held my hands up in a placatory gesture.

'I believe you. The problem I've got is that I'm not up to speed with who hates who among the Cheetham Hill villains. Until I can speak to Dennis, I haven't a clue whose doors I should be kicking in.'

Debbie sighed a long ribbon of smoke. 'No point in asking me. I've always kept my nose out. There is one thing, though,' she added, frowning as she thought. The absence of permanent lines on her forehead demonstrated what a rare event I was witnessing.

'What's that?' I had little hope of a result, but my mother brought me up to be polite.

'The dog. I can't understand how come the dog was in the corridor and Pit Bull Kelly was in the shop.'

'Pit Bull must have been attacked as he walked in the door.'

'So how did whoever killed him get out past the dog? That's a killer dog, that. It wouldn't let Pit Bull's killer walk. It'd rip his throat out.'

She had a point. I sipped my coffee and thought about it. 'A bit of a puzzle, that,' I said.

'Plus,' she added with a triumphant air, 'if Pit Bull went down the shop to front up Dennis, he'd never have moved an inch without the dog. If Dennis had been in the shop, it would have been the dog that went through the door first, not that gutless wonder Pit Bull. Plus, if Dennis had still been using the shop, his night watchman would have been inside.'

'Of course,' I breathed.

'So the dog being in the corridor proves Dennis wasn't there.'

Somehow, I thought a jury might need a bit more convincing than the dog that didn't rip a throat out in the night. But at least it gave me somewhere to start.

Traditionally, the serious players in Manchester's drug wars have been the black gangs of Moss Side and the white gangs of Cheetham Hill. The Cheetham Hill lads have been around longer, their criminal roots deep in the cracks between the paving stones of the narrow terraced streets north of the wholesale district of Strangeways, their horizons bisected by the central tower of the Victorian prison and the slender black chimney of Boddingtons Brewery. Most of them are descended from long lines of gangsters and scam artists; it's a mark of status in Cheetham Hill to reveal your great-granddad did time for black marketeering during the war.

The Kellys were one of the oldest families, and most of them stuck to the old ways. Protection rackets and schneid sports gear, long firm frauds and small-time thieving, that was the Kellys' style. The team of brothers had always had contempt for the drug lords, which was about the only good thing you could say for them.

I had to endure three boozers where I drank beer straight from the bottle because I wasn't prepared to risk the glasses before I found a pair of grieving Kelly brothers. The Dog and Brewer was the kind of dump where your feet stick to the carpet and the fag ash forms a paste on the bottom of ashtrays that nobody has bothered to dry after rinsing them under the tap. Most of the punters had the blurred jawlines and bleary eyes of people who have smoked and drunk so much for so long change seems pointless. The women wore clothes that might have flattered them fifteen years before but now insulted them even more than the flabby men in ill-fitting casual clothes who were buying them drinks. Tom Jones was rejoicing loudly that again he'd touch the green, green grass of home.

I brazened out the eyes on me and bought a bottle of Carlsberg. 'Any of the Kelly boys in?' I asked the barman, my fingers resting lightly on the fiver on the bar.

He looked at the money and gave me the once-over. I obviously didn't look like a cop, for he jerked his head towards two shaggy-haired men in padded flannel work shirts at the far end of the bar. Before I could turn back, the fiver was gone. One good thing about lowlife dives is that the information comes cheap.

I picked up my bottle and pushed through the crowd until I was standing next to the two men. Their blue eyes were bloodshot, their stubbled cheeks scarlet with the stout and whisky they were pouring down their throats. 'I'm sorry for your loss, gentlemen,' I said. 'Will you let the *Evening Chronicle* buy you a drink?'

The taller of the two managed a half-hearted leer. 'I'll let you buy me a drink any time, darling.'

I signalled the barman and blew a tenner on drink. 'Hell of a shock,' I said, raising my bottle to clink against their glasses.

'I told him he was a dickhead, going up against Dennis O'Brien. Hard bastard, that one,' the smaller brother slurred.

'I heard the dog was supposed to be good protection,' I said. 'Bit of a handful, I heard. They say he gave the Old Bill a hard time.'

The taller one grinned. 'Thank fuck for that. I'm Paul, by the way, and this is Little Joe.'

I shook the outstretched paw. 'I'm Kate. How come Patrick went to see O'Brien on his own? If the guy's so tough?'

Little Joe snorted. 'Because he was a big girl's blouse. He was always trying to prove he was a hard man, our Patrick, but he was about as hard as Angel Delight. He was complaining that Dennis O'Brien had muscled in on his racket, and we all got so fucked off with listening we told him to go and sort O'Brien out if he was so pissed off.'

'And he'd had enough to drink to think he was man enough to take on that South Manchester scumbag.' Paul shook his head. 'He was an eejit, Patrick.'

'Especially when he had a drink in him.' Little Joe shook his head too.

'And a draw,' Paul concluded.

'So he'd been drinking and smoking dope before he went off to the Arndale to front up O'Brien?' I asked.

'That's right,' Little Joe confirmed. 'I mean, what kind of bastard has to top some drunken tosser just to make a point? O'Brien could just have broken a few bones and chucked Patrick out on his ear. He didn't have to go and kill him. Anybody could see Patrick was an eejit.'

'What about the dog, though?' I persisted.

Paul gave a contemptuous bark of laughter. 'Yeah, well, even a hard nut like O'Brien might have thought twice about taking on that mad bastard dog. I can't figure out how the dog didn't rip his throat out.'

Suddenly, Little Joe's eyes were full of tears. 'He didn't have to kill him, though, did he? The bastard didn't have to kill my baby brother.' His hand snaked out and grabbed my lapel. 'You tell them that in your paper. My baby brother was a big soft lump. Even with a drink and a draw in him, he wouldn't have done to O'Brien what that shit O'Brien done to him. You tell them, d'you hear? You tell them.'

I promised I'd tell them. I promised several times. I listened to the Kelly boys telling me the same things a few more times, then made my excuses and left. I carried my own haze of stale smoke and spilled drink into the car and made for the city centre.

I virtually had to drag Gloria off Donovan in the end. She'd been ~~taking advantage of having~~ a driver to attack the champagne with the brio of an operatic tenor. As she slid from happy to drunk to absolutely arseholed, so her amorousness had grown, according to Donovan, who I found with a slew of red lipstick below one ear and one shirt-tail hanging down the front of his trousers. He was keeping Gloria upright by pure strength, lurking in a corner near the revolving doors.

'Why didn't you sit her down in a quiet corner of the bar?' I hissed as we steered her into the street. It was like manipulating one of those wooden articulated models artists use, only life-sized and heavy as waterlogged mahogany.

'Every time I sat down she climbed on my lap,' he growled as we poured Gloria into the passenger seat of her car.

'Fair enough.' I slammed the door and handed him my car keys. 'Thanks, Don. You did a good job in very trying circumstances.'

He scratched his head. 'I expect it'll be reflected in my pay packet.'

Like mother, like son. 'It would be nice to find my car outside my house sometime tomorrow, keys through the letterbox. I'll talk to you soon.' I patted his arm. It was like making friends with one of the Trafalgar Square lions.

Gloria was snoring gently when I got behind the wheel. The engine turning over woke her up. She rolled towards me, hand blindly groping for my knee. 'I don't think so,' I said firmly, returning it to her own lap.

Her eyes snapped open and she looked at me in astonishment. 'Hiya, chuck,' she said blearily. 'Where did Donovan go?'

'Home to bed.'

She gurgled. I hoped it was a chuckle and not the overture to a technicolour yawn. 'Lucky girl,' she slurred. 'Poor old Glo. Whatchou been up to, then? Bit of nookie with the boyfriend?'

We turned into Albert Square where the giant inflatable red and white figure of Santa Claus clutched the steeple that rises out of the middle of the town hall roof. It looked vaguely obscene in the garish glare of the Christmas lights. I jerked my thumb upwards. 'He's seen more action than I have tonight. I've been trying to find out about Dorothea's past,' I said, more to fill the space than in any hope of a sensible response.

'Bloody tragic, that's what it was. Tragic,' Gloria mumbled.

'Murder always is.'

'No, you daft get, not the murder, her life. It was tragic.' Gloria gave me one of those punches to the shoulder that drunks think are affectionate. The car swerved across two lanes and narrowly missed a bus. Gloria giggled as I wrestled with the wheel.

'What was tragic?' I asked, my jaw clenched so tight the muscles hurt.

'She never got over losing him.' She groped in her evening purse for a cigarette and lit up.

'Losing who? Her husband?'

'Flamin' Nora, Kate. When did a woman ever regret losing a no-good waste of space like her old man?' she reproached me. 'Her son, of course. She never got over losing her son.'

'I didn't know she'd had a son.'

'Not a lot of people know that,' Gloria intoned in a very bad impersonation of Michael Caine. 'She had a son and then she had post-natal depression.'

'And the baby died?'

''Course he didn't die,' she said scornfully. 'He got taken off her. When she got put away.'

This was beginning to feel like one of those terrible black and white Northern kitchen sink dramas scripted by men with names like Arnold and Stanley. 'When you say "put away", do you mean sectioned, Gloria?' I asked as sweetly as I could manage.

'Tha's right,' she said. 'Put away in the loony bin. He did that to her. Her old man had her put away because having the baby had sent her a bit off her rocker. Christ, every woman goes a bit off her rocker when she's had a littl'un. If they put us all away just because we went a bit daft, there'd be a hell of a lot of men changing nappies. Right bastard he must have been.'

'So Dorothea's baby was adopted then, is that what you're saying?'

'Aye. Taken off her and given to somebody else. And they gave her electric shocks and cold showers and more drugs than Boots the Chemist and wondered why it took her so bloody long to get better. Bastards.' She spat the last word vehemently, as if it was personal, her eyes on the swirl of pinprick snowflakes tumbling thinly in the cones of sulphur-yellow street-lights.

'Did Dorothea tell you about this?'

'Who else? It were when I asked her to do a horoscope for my granddaughter. We'd gone out for a meal and we ended up back at my place, pissed as farts. And she started on about how she could be a grandmother half a dozen times over and she'd never be any the wiser. When she sobered up, she made me swear not to tell another living soul. And I haven't, not until now. Tragic, that's what it was. Tragic.'

I came at the subject half a dozen different ways before we finally arrived back at the deserted alley leading to her fortification. Each time I got the same version. No details added, no details different. Dorothea might have been lying to Gloria, but Gloria was telling me the truth.

I helped her out of the car and across cobbles covered in feathery white powder to her front door. I wasn't in the mood to go any further. I wanted home and bed and the sleep that would make sense of the jumbled jigsaw pieces of information that were drifting through my head like the snow across the windscreen. And not a snowplough in sight.

God, I hate the country.

13

SUN CONJUNCTION WITH PLUTO

Compromise is not in her vocabulary. She is not afraid of initiating confrontations and is a great strategist. She enjoys conflict with authority, she will not stand for personal or professional interference, but she is capable of transforming her own life and the world around her. People can be nervous of her, but this is a splendid aspect for a detective.

From *Written in the Stars*, by Dorothea Dawson

I woke up with that muffled feeling. It didn't go away when I stuck my head out from under the duvet. Richard only grunted when I slipped out of bed and pulled on my dressing gown before I died of hypothermia. The central heating had obviously been and gone while I was still sleeping, which made it sometime after nine. I lifted the curtain and looked out at a world gone white. 'Bugger,' I said.

Richard mumbled something. 'Whazza?' it sounded like.

'It's been snowing. Properly.'

He pushed himself up on one elbow and reached for his glasses. 'Lessee,' he slurred. I opened one side of the curtain. 'Fabulous,' he said. 'We can make a snowman.'

'And what about Gloria? I'm supposed to be minding her.'

'Not even a mad axeman would be daft enough to go on a killing spree in Saddleworth in this weather,' he pointed out, not unreasonably. 'It'll be chaos on the roads out there. And if Gloria's got the hangover she deserves, she won't be thinking about going anywhere. Come back to bed, Brannigan. I need a cuddle.'

I didn't need asking twice. 'I obey, o master,' I said ironically, slipping out of my dressing gown and into his arms.

The second time we woke, the phone was to blame. I noted the clock as I grabbed the handset. I couldn't believe it was nearly noon. I'd obviously needed the sleep. Or something. 'Yes?' I said.

'It's me, chuck.' It was the voice of a ghost. It sounded like Gloria had died and somehow missed the pearly gates.

''Morning, Gloria,' I said cheerfully, upping the volume in revenge for her attempt at groping my knee. 'How are you today?'

'Don't,' she said. 'Just don't. For some reason, I seem to have a bit of a migraine this morning. I thought I'd just spend the day in bed with the phone turned off, so you don't have to worry about coming over.'

'Are you sure? I could always send Donovan,' I said sadistically.

I sensed the shudder. 'I'll be fine,' she said. 'I'll see you tomorrow, usual time.' Click. I didn't even get the chance to say goodbye.

Richard emerged, blinking at the snow-light. 'Gloria?' he asked.

'I'm reprieved for the day. She sounds like the walking dead.'

'Told you,' he said triumphantly. 'Shall we make a snowman, then?'

By the time we'd made the snowman, then had a bath to restore our circulation, then done some more vigorous horizontal exercises to raise our core body temperatures, it was late afternoon and neither of us could put off work any longer. He had some copy to write for an Australian magazine fascinated by Britpop. Personally, I'd rather have cleaned the U-bend, but I'm the woman who thinks the best place for Oasis is in the bottom of a flower arrangement. I settled down at my computer and trawled the Net for responses to last night's queries.

I downloaded everything, then started reading my way through. I immediately junked the tranche from people who thought it must be cool to be a private eye, would I give them a work-experience placement? I also quickly dumped the ones that were no more than a rehash of what had been in the papers and on the radio. That left me with half a dozen that revealed Dorothea had had a breakdown back in the 1950s. There were two that seemed to have some real credibility. The first came from someone who lived in the picturesque Lancashire town where Dorothea had grown up.

Dear Kate Brannigan, it read, I am a sixteen-year-old girl and I live in Halton-on-Lune where Dorothea Dawson came from. My grandmother was at school with Dorothea, so when I saw your query in the astrology newsgroup, I asked her what she remembered about her.

She said Dorothea was always a bit of a loner at school, she was an only child, but there was nothing weird or spooky about her when she was growing up, she was just like everybody else. My gran says Dorothea got married to this bloke Harry Thompson who worked in the bank. She says he was a real cold fish which I think means he didn't know how to have a good time, except I don't know what they did then to have a good time because they didn't have clubs or decent music or anything like that.

Anyway, Gran says Dorothea had this baby and then she went mad and had to go into the loony bin (Gran calls it that, but she really means a mental hospital). Anyway, her husband went away and was never seen again, and when Dorothea came out of the hospital after a couple of years, she only came back to pack her bags and get the next bus out.

I don't know what happened to the baby, Gran says it probably got put in a home, which is not a good place to be brought up even if your mum is a bit barking.

I hope this helps.

Yours sincerely

Megan Hall

The other was better written. I didn't much care; literary style wasn't what I was after.

Dear Ms Brannigan

It may come as a surprise that a man of my age knows how to <surf the Internet>, but I am a contemporary of Dorothea Dawson. I was a year younger than her, but my sister was in the same class at school, and was the nearest Dorothea had to a close friend. Dorothea used regularly to come to our house for tea, and the two girls often played together.

That all changed when Dorothea met Harry Thompson. He was a bank clerk, good-looking in a rather grim sort of way, and he was drawn to girls inappropriately young. When they met, Dorothea was, I think, a rather young 17, and he must have been 25 or 26. He was what I think we would now call a control freak and Dorothea was always on pins lest she upset him.

Quite why she agreed to marry him none of us ever knew, though it may well have been the only route she could see by which she could escape the equally oppressive regime of her stepmother. They were married and within eighteen months Dorothea was confined to the cheerless Victorian world of the local mental hospital following an appalling experience with what we now term post-natal depression.

Harry resolutely refused to have anything to do with the child, claiming that the baby was tainted with the same madness that had claimed the mother. An ignorant and cruel man, he sought and gained a transfer to a branch of the bank in the Home Counties, handing the child over to an adoption agency. What became of the baby, I have no knowledge. This far on, I am ashamed to say that neither my sister nor I can remember if the child were a boy or girl; in my sister's defence, I would say that by that time, thanks to Harry, there was little contact between her and Dorothea.

When she finally was allowed to leave the mental hospital, Dorothea was very bitter and wanted to cast her past entirely from her. My sister was saddened by this, but not surprised. We were delighted to see her rise to celebrity, though both horrified by the news of her death.

I do hope this is of some assistance. Should you wish to talk to me, you will find me in the Wakefield telephone book under my parish of St Barnabas-next-the-Wall.

With best wishes

Rev. Tom Harvey

I wasn't surprised that Gloria had called the whole sorry business tragic. I couldn't help wondering where Harry Thompson was now and what he was doing. Not to mention the mysterious baby. I kept having visions of a swaddling-wrapped infant abandoned on the doorstep of the local orphanage. I think I saw too many BBC classic serials when I was a child.

It was time for some serious digging, the kind that is well beyond my limited capabilities with electronic systems. I copied the two key e-mails to Gizmo, with a covering note explaining that I needed him to use his less advertised skills to unearth all he could about Harry Thompson and the riddle of the adopted child. Then I started accessing what legitimate data sources were available on a Sunday evening to answer the queries that had come in from the two foreign agencies.

When the doorbell rang, I exited the database I'd been in and severed my connection. Those on-line services charge by the minute and I wasn't prepared to put myself in hock if it took me five minutes to dislodge a Jehovah's Witness or a local opportunist offering to dig my car out of snow that would probably be gone by morning. To my astonishment, it was Gizmo. 'I just sent you an e-mail,' I said.

'I know, I got it.' He marched in without waiting to be asked, stamping slush into my hall carpet. On the way to the spare room that doubles as my home office, he shed a parka that looked like it had accompanied Scott to the Antarctic and had only just made it home again. By the time I'd hung it up, he was ensconced in front of my computer. 'Gotta beer?'

I was shocked. I didn't think I'd ever seen Gizmo with any kind of liquid within three feet of a keyboard. Same with food. If it wasn't for thirst and hunger and bodily functions, I've often thought he would spend twenty-four hours a day in front of a screen. 'I'll get one,' I said faintly. I raided Richard's fridge and came back with some elderberry beer made to an old English recipe, a grand cru wheat beer and a smoked rye ale. I swear to God the beer drinkers are getting even more pretentious than the winos and foodies. I mean, how can you have a grand cru beer? It's like going into McDonald's and asking for one of their gourmet burgers.

Gizmo went for the elderberry beer. Judging by the look on his face as it hit his taste buds, he'd have preferred a can of supermarket own-brand lager. I sat on the edge of the bed and sipped the Stoly and grapefruit juice I'd sensibly sorted for myself. 'You were about to tell me what was in my e-mail that made you rush round,' I lied.

Gizmo shifted in his seat and wrapped his legs around each other. I'd seen it done in cartoons, but I'd always thought until then it was artistic licence. 'I felt like some fresh air.' Lie number one. I shook my head. 'I was a bit worried about discussing hacking in e-mail that wasn't encrypted.' Lie number two. I shook my head again. 'I wanted to check what virus protection you've got running on this machine because I've not looked at it for a while and there's all sorts of clever new shit out there.'

I shook my head sadly. 'Strike three, Giz. Look, you're here now. You've made the effort. You might as well tell me what you came to tell me because we're both so busy it could be weeks before there's another window of opportunity.' I felt like a detective inspector pushing for a confession. I hoped it wasn't going to be another murder.

Gizmo ran a finger up and down the side of the beer bottle, his eyes following its movement. 'There's this . . .' He stopped. He looked up at me like dogs do when they're trying to tell you where it hurts. 'I've met . . . well, not actually met . . .'

Light dawned. 'The flowers,' I said.

The blush climbed from the polo neck of his

black sweater, rising unevenly like the level of poured champagne in a glass. He nodded.

'"www gets real." The cyberbabe,' I said, trying to sound sensitive and supportive. The effort nearly killed me.

'Don't call her that,' Gizmo said, a plea on his face. 'She's not some bimbo. And she's not a saddo Nethead who hasn't got a life. She's really interesting. I've never met a woman who can talk about computer code, politics, sociology, music, all of those things.'

All of those things I never knew Gizmo knew anything about. Except computer code, of course. 'You've never met this one,' I said drily.

'That's kind of what I wanted to talk to you about.'

'A meeting? Getting together for real?' I checked my voice for scepticism and thought I'd probably got away with it.

'What do you think?'

What did I think? What I really thought was that Gizmo was probably typical of the people who spent their nights chattering to strangers in Siberia and Sao Paolo and Salinas, weird computer geeks telling lies about themselves in a pathetic attempt to appear interesting. A blind date with Gizmo would probably have turned me celibate at sixteen. On the other hand, if I'd been a geek too – and there were one or two female nerds out there, most of them inevitably working for Microsoft – I might have been charmed, especially since my efforts at grooming had rendered Gizmo almost indistinguishable from the human species. 'Does she work for Microsoft?' I asked.

He gave me a very peculiar look. 'That's sick. That's like asking a member of CND if he fancies someone who works for MOD procurement.'

'Has she got a name?'

His smile was curiously tender. 'Jan,' he said. 'She has her own consultancy business. She does training packages for the computer industry.'

'So how did you . . . meet?'

'Remember when Gianni Versace got shot? Well, there was a lot of discussion on the Net about it, how the FBI were using the on-line community to warn people about the suspect, and how far the federal agencies should go in trying to exploit the Net to catch criminals. I was checking out one of the newsgroups and I saw Jan had said some interesting things, and we started exchanging private mail.' Oh great, I thought. A mutual interest in serial killers. Always a good place to start a relationship. 'Then we found out we both hung out in quite a few of the same newsgroups,' Gizmo continued. 'We'd just never crossed paths before.' He stopped dead and took a deep swig of beer. It was possibly the longest speech I'd heard Gizmo make.

'And?'

'And we really hit it off. Loads of stuff in common. Lately, it's been getting more and more intense between us. I . . . I don't think I've ever felt like this before,' he mumbled.

'And now you want to do a reality check by getting together in the flesh?'

He nodded. 'Why not? Pen friends have been doing it for years.'

This wasn't the time to remind him that pen friends had one or two little safeguards like knowing where each other lived. It also wasn't the time to remind him that it was somehow easier to lie in cyberspace than in meatspace, since right from the beginning the hackers and computer freaks who had hung out on the very first bulletin boards had always hidden behind nicknames. The first time I'd been confronted with Gizmo's real name was years into our acquaintance, when he'd signed his initial consultancy contract with Brannigan & Co. I sipped my drink and raised my eyebrows. 'And sometimes it's a big disappointment. Why is it so important that you meet? If things are so excellent between you, maybe it's better to keep it cyber.'

He squirmed in his seat. 'Sometimes it's too slow, the Net. Even in a private conference room in a newsgroup, you can still only communicate as fast as you can type, so it's never as spontaneous as conversation.'

'I thought that was the charm.'

'It is, to an extent. You can structure your dialogue much more than you can in a meatspace conversation where you tend to go off at tangents. But we've been doing this for a while now. We need to move on to the next stage, and that's got to be a face-to-face. Hasn't it?'

206

I wasn't cut out for this. If I'd been an agony aunt, my column would have invariably read, 'For God's sake, get a grip.' But Gizmo was more than just another contractor. Less than a friend, admittedly, but somebody I cared about, much as I'd cared about Polly the cocker spaniel I'd grown up with. So I took a deep breath and said, 'Where does she live?'

'London. But she comes up to Manchester every two or three weeks on business. I was thinking about suggesting we got together for a beer next time she's up.'

It would be a beer, too. Somehow I didn't have this woman pegged as a white-wine-spritzer drinker. 'You don't think it might destroy what you've already built up?'

He shrugged, a difficult feat given that he was impersonating a human pretzel. 'Better we find that out now, don't you think?'

'I honestly don't know. Maybe the cyber relationship is the shape of things to come. Communication with strangers, all of us hiding behind a façade, having virtual sex in front of our terminals. Not as replacement for face-to-face stuff, but as another dimension. Adultery without the guilt, maybe?' I hazarded.

'No,' Gizmo said, unravelling his limbs and straightening up. 'I think it's just another kind of courtship. If you don't take it out of virtuality into reality, it's ultimately sterile because you've no objective standards to measure it against.'

Profound stuff from a man I'd never suspected of being capable of love for a sentient being without microchips. 'Sounds to me like you've already made your decision,' I said gently.

He took a deep breath. His shoulders dropped from round his ears. 'I suppose I have.'

'So go with your instincts.'

I'd said what he wanted to hear. The relief flowed off him like radiation. 'Thanks for listening, Kate. I really appreciate it.'

'So show me how much, and dig me some dirt on Harry Thompson and the mystery baby.'

14

JUPITER TRINE SATURN

Cheerful Jupiter tempers the stern, hard-working nature of Saturn. She is a visionary, but one firmly rooted in the practicalities. She is a good organizer and seldom feels overwhelmed by her responsibilities. She is good at coordinating people to collaborate with her. She has the self-discipline to achieve her goals without getting wound up about it.

From *Written in the Stars*, by Dorothea Dawson

I'd set off early enough to follow the snow-plough down the main road from Oldham through Greenfield. Getting down Gloria's alley was out of the question, but the hacks had moved on to the next big thing, so the only threat to Gloria's wellbeing was the possibility of wet feet. I should have known better.

She emerged in knee-high snow boots and a scarlet ski suit with royal-blue chevrons and matching earmuffs. 'Hiya, chuck,' she greeted me.

'I've never been skiing in my life, but they do great gear, don't they?' she enthused. As usual, I felt underdressed. Wellies over jeans topped with my favourite leather jacket had seemed fine in Ardwick, but somehow they just didn't cut it in the country.

'Got over your hangover?'

'I'll thank you to remember it was a migraine, young lady.' She wasn't entirely joking. 'By the way,' she said as she settled into the car, 'there's been a change of schedule. Somebody got excited about the snow, so we're going to do some location shooting instead of studio filming.' Gloria explained that because of the weather, cast members involved in the location shooting had been told to go directly to Heaton Park on the outskirts of the city rather than to the NPTV compound. The park was easier to reach than the studios since it was just off the main motorway network and on a major road. There were various nearby locations that would be used in the course of the day, but we'd be based in the main car park with the catering truck, make-up and wardrobe. And the snow. I could feel myself growing almost wistful about being a lawyer, cocooned in a nice warm courtroom with nothing more taxing to do than get a client off a murder charge.

The one good thing about being away from NPTV was that we seemed to have escaped the delights of Cliff Jackson's company. According to Rita, Jackson and his team had been interviewing cast members in their homes over the weekend, but they were concentrating on office and production staff at the studios now. Also according to Rita, who had clearly elected herself gossip liaison officer, they were no closer to an arrest than they had been on Friday night. She had managed to get Linda Shaw to admit that neither Gloria nor I were serious suspects; Gloria because there were no spatters of blood on the flowing white top she'd been wearing, me because Linda thought it was one of the daftest ideas she'd ever heard. I thought she'd probably been telling the truth about me, but suspected she might have had her fingers crossed when she exonerated Gloria. In her shoes, I would have.

Gloria went off with Ted so Freddie Littlewood could work his magic on their faces. I let them go alone since I could see the short gap between the two vehicles from where I was sitting in a corner of the cast bus with Rita and Clive. I settled down, ready to soak up whatever they were prepared to spill. 'So who had it in for Dorothea?' I asked. Some people just don't respond to the subtle approach. Anyone with an Equity card, for example.

Clive looked at Rita, who shrugged like someone auditioning for 'Allo, 'Allo. 'It can't have been to do with her professional life, surely,' he said. 'Nobody murders their astrologer because they don't like what she's predicted.'

'But nobody here really knew anything about

her private life,' Rita objected. 'Out of all the cast, I was one of her first regulars, and I know almost nothing about her. I've even been to her house for a consultation, but all I found out from that was that she must have been doing very nicely. A thatched cottage between Alderley Edge and Wilmslow, if you please.'

'Did she live alone?' I asked.

'Search me,' Rita said. 'She never said a dicky bird about a boyfriend or a husband. The papers all said she lived alone, and they probably know more than the rest of us because they'll have been chatting up the locals.'

Clive scratched his chin. 'She knew a lot about us, though. I don't know if she was psychic or just bloody good at snapping up every little scrap of information she could get her hands on, but if she'd written a book about *Northerners*, it would have been dynamite. Maybe she went too far with somebody. Maybe she found something out that she wasn't prepared to keep quiet about.'

The notion that there was any secret black enough for a *Northerners* star to feel squeamish about using for publicity was hard for me to get my head round. Then I remembered Cassie. Not only what had happened to her, but what she'd said about the prospect of losing a plum role being motive enough for some desperate people. 'If that's the case, then the dark secret probably died with her,' I said despondently.

'I'm afraid so,' Clive said. 'Unless she kept the

details on her computer along with our horoscope details.'

My ears pricked up. 'You think that's likely?'

Rita's eyes were sparkling with excitement. 'That'll be why the police have taken her computer off to analyse what's on it,' she said. 'That nice Linda said they'd got someone working on it already, but they've got to call in an expert who knows about astrology because a lot of it's in symbols and abbreviations they can't make head nor tail of.'

Another alley closed off to me. Out of the corner of my eye, I saw Ted emerge from the make-up caravan. Time for action, I thought. I didn't want Gloria left alone with anybody connected to *Northerners*, even someone as seemingly innocuous as Freddie from make-up. He was just finishing off painting Gloria's lips with Brenda's trademark pillar-box-red gloss as I walked in. 'Don't say a word,' he cautioned Gloria. 'I won't be a minute,' he added, frowning as he concentrated on getting the lipline just right. I closed the door behind me and leaned against the wall. 'There,' he said with a satisfied sigh. 'All done.'

Gloria surveyed herself critically in the mirror and said, 'Bloody hell, Freddie, that's the most you've said all morning.'

'We're all a bit subdued today, Gloria,' he said, sounding exhausted. 'It's hard not to think about what happened to Dorothea.'

Gloria sighed. 'I know what you mean, chuck.'

She leaned forward and patted his hand. 'It does you credit.'

'It's scary, though,' Freddie said, turning away with a tired smile and repacking his make-up box. 'I mean, chances are it's somebody we know who killed her. Outsiders don't wander around inside the NPTV compound. It's hard to imagine any of us killing someone who was more or less one of us.'

'The trouble is,' Gloria said, getting to her feet and pulling her coat on, 'that half of us are actors. Who the hell knows what goes on in our heads?'

Neither Freddie nor I could think of anything to say to that one. I followed her out the door and caught up with her and Ted at the edge of the car park. The director was explaining how he wanted them to circle round so that they could walk down the virgin snow of the path towards the camera. It looked like they were set for a while, but I didn't want to go back to the bus and leave Gloria exposed. It wasn't as if I could prevent an attack on her; but I hoped my presence would be enough to give her menacer pause.

I walked over to the catering bus, where Ross was working with a teenage lad I'd not seen before. 'I suppose a bacon butty would be out of the question?' I asked. 'I left the house too early for breakfast.'

Ross served me himself, piling crispy rashers into a soft floury roll. 'There you go. Coffee?' I nodded and he poured me a carton. 'Mind the shop a wee minute, son,' he said, coming out of the side door and beckoning me to join him. 'You got anything for me?' he asked.

I shook my head, my mouth full of food. 'I'm working on it,' I managed to mumble. 'Irons in the fire.'

'I was doing some thinking myself. You know, nobody knows more about what goes on behind the scenes of *Northerners* than Dorothea did. She had the inside track on everybody. She'd have been perfectly placed to be the mole,' he said eagerly.

'Handy for you,' I said cynically. 'What better way to get yourself off the hook than to blame a dead woman?'

His mouth turned down at the corners and his bright blue eyes looked baffled. 'That's a wee bit uncalled for. You know I liked Dorothea fine. It's just with her being in the news this weekend, I couldn't help remembering how she always had everybody's particulars at her fingertips. And she was never backwards about taking advantage of the press for her own purposes. That's all I was getting at.'

'I'm sorry,' I said. 'You might have a point. The only problem I can see is that Dorothea didn't have access to scripts, so she wouldn't have known the details of the future storylines, would she?'

Ross looked crestfallen, his shaggy red hair falling unheeded over his forehead. 'I suppose,' he said. 'I wasn't really thinking it through. My wife says I never do.'

Before I could say anything more, the bleat of my moby vibrated in my armpit. I unzipped my jacket and pulled it out. 'Hello?'

'All right, KB? Where are you?' It was Alexis, far brighter than she had any right to be on a Monday morning when she was the co-parent of a teething baby.

'Why?'

'I'm out and about making some calls and I thought we could link up. I've got a juicy bit of info for you, and you know how insecure the airwaves are these days. We've probably got half the world's press listening in at your end and the bizzies at mine. Are you down at NPTV?' she asked, her voice all innocence.

'Security be buggered,' I said. 'You just want to get alongside the *Northerners* cast to see how many exclusives you can dig up about Dorothea.'

A throaty chuckle turned into a cough. 'You got me bang to rights. Call it the quid pro quo.'

I wiggled my fingers at Ross. He took the hint and shambled back inside. 'I'm not actually at NPTV.' I told her where to find me. 'They've got some very basic security on the main entrance, but a devious old bag like you should have no problem with that.'

'They'll be laying out the red carpet for me, girl, just you wait and see. I won't be long, I'm only down the road in Salford.'

I cut across the car park at an angle, ploughing my feet through the dirty slush. It's just as much fun at thirty-one as it is at five. I ended up over near the entrance, but still in a line of sight to Gloria. I was pretty certain by now that she was at no real risk, but being visible was what I was being paid for, so visible I'd be.

Alexis was as good as her word. Within ten minutes of our phone call, she drove authoritatively into the car park. The two elderly security men made a few futile gestures in a bid to get her to stop, but it's hard to argue with something as big as the Range Rover her and Chris had bought to combat the wild weather on the Pennines. Nobody else was interested. I'd soon realized that in a TV production unit, everybody's too busy with their own job to pay attention to anything else short of a significant thermonuclear explosion. That would make Cliff Jackson's job a lot harder. I couldn't resist a shiver of *schadenfreude* at the thought.

Alexis jumped down into the slush and took a few steps towards the security men. 'I'm with her,' I heard as her arm waved in my general direction. There was nothing wrong with her eyesight. 'Brannigan and Co,' she added, veering off towards me.

'You really are a lying get,' I said when she was close enough for them not to hear.

'Only technically,' she said. 'I am, after all, here on a mission on your behalf.'

'No, you're not, you're here entirely on a fishing expedition to net you tomorrow's front page. So what's this momentous news you have to impart?'

I glanced over my shoulder to make absolutely sure we couldn't be overheard.

'Does F. Littlewood mean anything to you? F. Littlewood of fifty-nine, Hartley Grove, Chorlton?'

I tried not to show that more bells were ringing and lights flashing inside my head than on the average pinball machine. The address was unfamiliar, but I had no trouble recognizing the name. Why was Freddie Littlewood the make-up artist betraying his colleagues so viciously and comprehensively? What could he possibly have to gain? And how did he obtain the intimate details of people's past secrets? I'd already seen how casually Gloria let slip information to the charming Freddie, but I couldn't believe her fellow stars would have readily revealed most of the *Northerners* scandals. Alexis had done me a favour, but in the process she'd given me a headache.

I found a pen and notepad in my bag and got Alexis to write down Freddie's address. 'You're sure this is the mole?' I asked.

'This is the person who got paid for the story about you bodyguarding Gloria,' she said cautiously. 'More likely than not, that's your mole. I finally got my hands on the credits book this morning, and that didn't take me a whole lot further forward. What it is, you see, sometimes we need to make irregular payments to regular sources who need to be protected. So then we use code names. The very fact that this Littlewood person has a code name means he or she has done this before.'

'So how did you get from the code name to the identity?' I asked. It wasn't important, but I'm a sucker for other people's methods. I'm not such an old dog that I can't learn new tricks.

Alexis winked. 'There's this cute little baby dyke in accounts. She thinks being a reporter is seriously the business. She thinks my new haircut is really cool.'

I groaned. Forget the new tricks. 'And does she also know you're happily married?'

'Let the girl have her dreams. Besides, it made her day to tell me that The Mask is F. Littlewood. Whoever he or she is?'

I shook my head. 'That's for me to know and you to find out.'

'Oh, I will, believe me. This isn't soft news any more. It's crime, and that's my business. If the newsdesk won't share, I'll just have to help myself.' Alexis cupped her hands round a cigarette and lit it. She breathed a smoky sigh of satisfaction. 'God, I love the first cigarette of the day. If you need more leverage, by the way, we've paid F. Littlewood five times in the last year. I checked out the back numbers and they were all *Northerners* stories. I'd bet it's the same mole selling the stories to the nationals, because all the ones we've had have either been local interest only or time sensitive. Except for the one about you and Gloria, interestingly enough.' Alexis's eyes were flickering round the car park and over towards the distant shrubberies. She'd done her duty and now she was sniffing the air for her story. 'You going to tell me who this Littlewood character is?' she asked, not really expecting an answer.

'Just be grateful I've not shopped you. Thanks, Alexis.'

'No problem.' She was already on the move. 'Hang in there, KB. Jackson's so busy getting his knickers in a twist about his missus that he's not got a fucking clue who to arrest. So there's plenty of room for glory.'

I watched her trudge through the snow, the ultimate bulldog when it came to stories. Which reminded me that I had to see a woman about a dog. I checked my watch. Chances were that Ruth would be in court. I decided to call her mobile and leave a message with the answering service. 'Ruth, it's Kate,' I said. 'Can you check for me if Dennis shows any signs of having been in a ruck with Pit Bull's pit bull? Or if the pit bull shows any signs of having been in a ruck with person or persons unknown? I'm ashamed to say it was Debbie's idea rather than mine, but it's worth pursuing.'

The second call was to Detective Chief Inspector Della Prentice of the Regional Crime Squad's fraud task force. She should have been Detective Superintendent by now, but a sting I'd set up with her had gone according to someone else's script and Della was still scraping the egg off her face. I knew she didn't blame me, but if anything, that made it worse. Sometimes I looked round the table on our girls' nights out and wondered how Alexis,

Ruth, Della and two or three of the others put up with the fact that one way or another I'd exploited each and every one of them and managed to drop most of them in the shit along the way. Must be my natural charm.

I tracked her down in a building society office in Blackpool. She sounded genuinely pleased to hear me, but then she was working her way through a balance sheet at the time. 'I doubt you're having a more pleasant time than I am,' she said. 'I see from the papers that you and Cliff Jackson are too close for comfort again.'

'Being on the same land mass as Jackson is too close for comfort. Especially at the moment. Did you hear about his wife?'

'Even in Blackpool,' she said drily.

'You should rescue that Linda Shaw from his clutches. She's got the makings of a good copper, but he gives her the shit work every time and sooner or later she's going to get bored with that.'

'We'll see. My sources tell me that my promotion's likely to come through soon,' Della said. It sounded like a nonsequitur, but I figured she was trying to tell me that she was slated for a senior post in the Greater Manchester force. And that Linda might not be Jackson's gofer much longer.

'I can't tell you how relieved that makes me feel. I'm buying the champagne that night.'

'I know,' Della said without bitterness. 'So what's the favour?'

'Does there have to be a favour,' I asked, wounded.

'In working hours, yes. You never ring up for a gossip between nine and five.'

'You know about Dennis?'

'What about Dennis? I've been stuck in Blackpool since Thursday. I'm praying the snow keeps off so I can get home tonight. What's Dennis done this time?'

'For once, it's what he's not done.' I gave her a brief rundown. 'I've got a hunch that's so far off the wall I'm not even prepared to tell you what it is,' I said.

'What is it you need?'

'A look at the scene-of-crime photos. I don't know any of the team working the case, otherwise I'd ask. The boss cop's a DI Tucker.'

'I know Tucker's bagman. He did a stint with me at fraud before he was made up to sergeant. I expect I can persuade him he owes me one. I'll try and sort something out this evening, provided I can get back to Manchester,' she promised. I grovelled, she took the piss, we said goodbye.

I automatically scanned the car park, clocking Alexis over by the chuck wagon. She was leaning on the counter, steam rising from the cup of coffee in her hand, deep in conversation with Ross and a couple of the younger cast members who had braved the cold in search of a free bacon butty. I didn't envy their chances of escaping the front page of the next day's *Chronicle*.

I drifted back across the churned-up slush to where Ted and Gloria were rounding some bushes and walking into shot, their body language shouting 'argument' at the top of its voice. At the same moment, I heard a commotion behind me. I swung round to see Cliff Jackson loudly lecturing a PA that he was a police officer and this was a public car park and she was in no position to tell him where to stand.

The director's head swung round. 'Jesus Christ!' she yelled. 'And cut. Who the fuck do you think you are?' she demanded.

'Detective Chief Inspector Jackson of Greater Manchester Police. I'm here to interview Ms Gloria Kendal.'

'Are you blind? She's working.'

Nothing was calculated to make Jackson's hackles rise faster than anyone who thought the law didn't apply to them. 'You can't seriously imagine that your television programme takes precedence over a murder investigation? I need to talk to Ms Kendal, so, if you don't mind, you'll just have to rearrange your filming schedule to accommodate that.'

Gloria and Ted had reached us by now. 'Accommodate what?' she demanded crossly. She was clearly not thrilled with the prospect of shooting the snow scene again.

'As I've just explained to your director here, I'd be obliged if you would accompany me to the police station for a further interview,' Jackson barked. He clearly wasn't star struck like Linda Shaw.

Gloria gave me a panic-stricken look. 'I don't want to,' she protested.

Time for my tuppenceworth. 'You don't have to. Not unless he's arresting you. If you want him to interview you here, that's your right.'

Jackson rounded on me. 'You're still here? I thought I told you to butt out of this investigation?'

'When you pay my wages you can give me orders,' I said mutinously. 'My client does not wish to accompany you to the police station, as is her right. She is willing to talk to you here, however. Do you have a problem with that, Inspector?'

Jackson looked around him. 'There's nowhere here to conduct an interview,' he said contemptuously.

Seemingly out of nowhere, Alexis loomed up at his elbow. 'I wouldn't say that, Mr Jackson. I've been doing interviews all over the place. Is there some kind of problem here? Is somebody being arrested?'

'What the hell is the press doing here?' Jackson exploded.

'Press?' the director yelped. 'Suffering Jesus, this is supposed to be a closed set. Security!' she bellowed. She pointed at Alexis. 'You, out of here.' Then she turned to Jackson. 'The same goes for you. Look, we've got a people carrier over there.

Plenty of room in that. All of you, just fuck off out of my sight, will you?'

Gloria started walking towards the big eight-seater van as two uniformed security guards appeared to escort an unprotesting Alexis back to her car. 'Come on, Kate,' Gloria called over her shoulder. 'I'm not talking to him without you there.'

'She's got no right,' Jackson protested. 'You're not a lawyer, Brannigan.'

I shrugged. 'Looks like you get to talk to Gloria with me present, or you don't get to talk to Gloria at all. She is one determined woman, let me tell you.'

I watched Jackson's blood pressure rise. Then he turned abruptly on his heel and stalked past Gloria towards the people carrier. She followed more slowly and I brought up the rear with Linda Shaw. 'I thought Gloria was off the hook,' I said mildly.

Linda pursed her lips. Then, so quietly I could have believed I was imagining things, she said, 'That was before we knew about the motive.'

15

PLUTO IN VIRGO IN THE 5TH HOUSE

She is critical, both of herself and others. She is driven to seek the answers to the world's problems and has an analytical mind which she uses in her pitched battles against injustice. She has a great appetite for life, enjoying a vigorous lust in her sexual relationships.

From *Written in the Stars*, by Dorothea Dawson

I'd barely absorbed the impact of Linda Shaw's bombshell when she delivered the double whammy. 'Or the fingerprints on the murder weapon,' she added. There was no time for me to find out more; we'd reached the people carrier by then. Funny, I'd never suspected her of sadism before.

Gloria had already climbed into the front row of rear seats and Jackson, predictably, was in the driving seat. I went to sit next to Gloria, but Linda put a hand on my arm and motioned me into the back row before she slid into place next to my client. 'I've already told you everything I know,' Gloria started before the doors were even closed. Bad move.

'I don't think so,' Jackson said brusquely, twisting round to face us. I had a moment's satisfaction at the sight of a painful razor rash along the line of his collar. Couldn't happen to a nicer bloke.

'I didn't kill her. She was still alive when I left her.'

'You had reason to want her dead, though.' Jackson's words seemed to materialize in the cold air, hanging in front of us like a macabre mobile.

'I beg your pardon, I never did,' Gloria protested, her shoulders squaring in outrage.

Jackson nodded to Linda, who took out her notebook and flipped it open. 'We've had a statement from a Mr Tony Satterthwaite –'

'That vicious scumbag?' Gloria interrupted. 'You're not telling me you wasted your time listening to that no-good lying pig?'

'Your ex-husband has been extremely helpful,' Jackson said smoothly, nodding again at Linda.

'Mr Satterthwaite was distressed by Ms Dawson's death, not least because, according to him, it was his affair with her that precipitated the end of your marriage.'

I remembered that line about backbenchers resembling mushrooms because they get kept in the dark except when someone opens the door to shovel shit on them. I knew just how they felt. I glared at Gloria. She stared open-mouthed at Linda. It was the first time I'd ever seen her stuck for something to say.

'He suggested that you had never really forgiven Ms Dawson for the affair, and that you were, and I quote, "the sort of devious bitch who would wait years to get her own back". We'd be very interested in your comments, Ms Kendal,' Linda said coolly.

'You don't have to say a thing, Gloria,' I said hurriedly.

'What? And let them go on thinking there's a word of truth in what that money-grubbing moron says? My God,' she said, anger building in her voice, 'you lot are gullible. I dumped Tony Satterthwaite because he was an idle leech. He couldn't even be bothered to look further than his own secretary when he decided to have a bit on the side. Even though she looked like Walter Matthau. He never even met Dorothea, never mind had an affair with her. I'd kicked him out a good six months before she first turned up at *Northerners*.'

'So why would he tell us a pack of lies?' Jackson sneered.

'Because if he saw a chance to give me a bad time, he'd not let it go past him,' Gloria said bitterly. 'Especially if he could see a way of turning it into a moneyspinner. You can bet your bottom dollar that the next call he made after he spoke to you was to the *Sun* or the *Mirror*. You've been had, the both of you. What you don't realize is that if he had been having an affair with Dorothea, I'd have bought her a magnum of champagne for giving me a twenty-four-carat reason for ditching the sod. Ask my daughter. Ask anybody that was around me then. They'll tell you the same.' She snorted. 'Tony Satterthwaite and Dorothea? Don't make me laugh. Apart from anything else, Dorothea had a hell of a lot more taste than to get between the sheets with a snake like Tony.'

'You married the man,' Jackson pointed out.

'Everybody's entitled to one mistake,' Gloria snapped back. 'He were mine. Let me tell you, you'll not find a single person can back up his tale and there's a good reason for that.'

Linda and Jackson exchanged a look that said they both knew they were backing a loser here. I wasn't so sure. I'd seen how well Gloria acted off screen. But even if the tale of the affair was true, I couldn't see Gloria nursing her bitterness for all those years. She was far too upfront for that. If she'd had a bone to pick with Dorothea, it would have been lying bleached in the sun a long time since.

'At the end of the day, we don't have to prove motive in a court of law,' Jackson pointed out. 'Most people think detectives have to prove means, motive and opportunity. But we don't. All we need is evidence. And we've got evidence against you. There's circumstance – you're the last person known to have seen her alive, and more often than not the last person to see a victim alive is also the first person to see them dead.'

229

I opened my mouth to speak and he waved a hand at me. 'You'll get your say in a minute. Let me finish first. But we've got more than that, Gloria. We've got fingerprints. To be precise, we've got your fingerprints on the murder weapon.'

There was a long silence. Gloria stared impassively at Jackson, then lit a cigarette with a hand that showed no tremor. 'The crystal ball?' she asked.

His smile was as thin as the line of the new moon. 'The crystal ball,' he confirmed.

It was obviously my week for fingerprints. All I needed now was for one of DI Tucker's merry band to find Gloria's prints inside Dennis's shop and then I could swap client for buddy behind bars. Then something occurred to me. 'Excuse me, but I don't remember anyone taking my client's fingerprints. Where exactly has the comparison set come from?' I asked belligerently.

Linda's eyes widened and I could see her forcing her body not to react. Jackson scowled. 'That's neither here nor there. Take my word for it, the prints on the murder weapon are a perfect match for Gloria's here.'

I shook my head. 'You'll have to do better than that.' I glanced at my watch. 'Otherwise I'm going to call Ruth Hunter and get this whole shooting match on the record. And I don't have to tell you how much Ruth hates having her lunch interrupted.' I knew the last thing Jackson wanted now was to get to the 'lawyers at dawn' stage. He was relying on Gloria being confident enough to think she could handle this alone, and even with me along to stick a spoke in his wheel, he still thought he was the one holding all the cards. You'd think he'd have known by now. 'So where did you get a verified set of my client's prints?' I demanded again.

'You gave her a glass of water in the green room on Friday night when we had our initial interview,' Linda said. Jackson glared at her, but he must have known they'd reached the point of put up or shut up.

'And you helped yourself to it after we left,' I said, shaking my head in a pretence of sorrow at their deviousness. 'So how do you know it's not my prints on the murder weapon?'

Linda allowed herself a small moment of triumph. 'Because you were still wearing your leather gloves.'

OK, so I'd forgotten. I didn't think Gloria was going to sue me. At least the conversation had provided enough of a diversion for my client to pull herself together. 'Of course my fingerprints were on the crystal ball,' she said. All three of us turned to stare at her.

'Gloria,' I warned, stifling a momentary panic that she was about to confess.

'It's all right, chuck. There's a simple explanation.'

My favourite kind.

'I'd just had a consultation, hadn't I? I'd been sat opposite Dorothea, with my fingertips touching the crystal ball. That's what we always did. I suppose she did it with everybody, but she must have buffed it up between times because it was always sparkling, that crystal. She'd lay her fingertips on one side and I'd match her on the other side. To form a psychic bond,' she added, as if stating the obvious.

I grinned. Usually when I'd been present to watch Jackson get shafted, I was the one doing the shafting, which meant the pleasure was always tinged with a degree of apprehension. This time, the delight was entirely unadulterated. Jackson looked like a man whose cat just ate his prize canary.

'I bet it was just my fingertips on that crystal ball, wasn't it? Not my whole hand,' Gloria said. She sounded as if she was half teasing, half scolding a naughty schoolboy. 'You've been trying to get me going, haven't you? You've been stretching the truth to try and get me to confess.' She wagged her finger at him. 'I don't like people that think they're smart enough to get clever with me. Brenda Barrowclough might have come up the ship canal on a bike, but I'm not so daft. I'm not talking to you again, Mr Jackson, not without I've got my solicitor with me.'

'I can't believe you tried that on, Jackson,' I said. 'Wait till Ruth Hunter hears about this. You better thank your lucky stars that you didn't drag us down the nick for this bag of crap.'

Jackson turned dark red, his eyes narrowing as I'd seen them do too many times before. Just before the geyser of his rage erupted over us, the door behind him jerked open, nearly tipping him backwards towards the slushy car park.

John Turpin stepped back, not prepared to stand between Jackson and a nasty fall. At the last minute, Jackson grabbed the steering wheel and hauled himself back into the seat. 'Jesus,' he exclaimed. 'You nearly had me on the floor there, Mr Turpin.'

Turpin's broad face was wearing a scowl that matched most of the tales I'd heard about him. 'I'm very disappointed in you,' he said, his voice as sharply clipped as a topiary peacock. 'I had thought we'd reached an accommodation. We've bent over backwards for you and your team. We've given you space to work in, we've offered you full access to our site and to all NPTV staff. The one thing I asked was that you didn't disrupt filming.' He shook his head sorrowfully.

Jackson was at a major disadvantage, stuck in the van seat well below Turpin's superior height. 'I'm conducting a murder inquiry,' he retorted, pushing himself clear of the steering wheel and out into the car park. He was still four inches shorter than Turpin, but that didn't seem to worry him. 'When evidence presents itself, I have to act on it. I said we'd do our best not to disrupt your filming schedules, but as far as I'm concerned, better your film crew stands about idle than a murder suspect slips through the net.'

Turpin snorted and jerked his thumb at Gloria. 'That's your murder suspect?' he said, his voice a suppressed laugh. 'My God, man, you must be grasping at straws. This is the woman who's so timid she's hired a private detective because she's had some hysterical hate mail. Even if she had the nerve to commit murder, I don't think she'd be doing it when she's got a minder on her tail. Unless of course you think Gloria hired Brannigan and Co to commit murder for her?' I couldn't repress my smile. Linda broke into a spasm of tactical coughing, but Jackson couldn't see the funny side. He probably thought Turpin's sarcastic suggestion was a promising line of inquiry. 'It wouldn't have hurt to have waited for a natural break in filming. I mean, she's hardly dressed to go on the run, wearing Brenda Barrowclough's wig,' the TV executive continued with genial sarcasm. 'Did you think she was going to take a cameraman hostage with her handbag?'

'This is a police inquiry,' Jackson said obstinately. 'Only the case dictates the timetable I work to.'

Turpin gave Jackson a thoughtful look. When he spoke, his voice had a kindly tone at odds with his words. 'The press is always interested in anything that affects *Northerners* and this company is a noto-riously leaky sieve. You might think your murder investigation is the most important thing in this city, but there are far more people interested in the outcome of Monday night's episode of *Northerners* than in who killed some stargazing charlatan. You might want to think about how dumb you could be made to look by some news-hungry journalist.'

Without waiting for a reply, Turpin bent forward, head and shoulders into the van, forcing Jackson to step hastily aside, with the cavalier lack of concern most big men display.

'Gloria, my dear,' he said coldly. 'Time to earn your grossly inflated salary. Mustn't keep Helen waiting, must we?'

Gloria squared her shoulders, gathered her coat around her and made a nimble exit. 'Ta-ra, Linda, chuck,' she said, leaning back into the van. 'I won't be talking to you again without a lawyer, but I don't hold that sneaky trick with the glass against you. You were only doing your job, and we both know what it's like to work for complete shits, don't we?'

Turpin's stare was surprisingly malevolent. 'The people you have to deal with in this job,' he sighed, including us all in his comprehensive glower.

'Never mind,' I said sweetly. 'If NPTV sell out to cable or satellite, you'll be able to retire to the South of France on your profits.'

His calculating eyes made the snow look warm and welcoming. 'You really shouldn't believe actors' gossip,' he said. He turned on his heel, brushing past Jackson, and made for the catering truck. I didn't envy Ross if the coffee was stewed.

Jackson spun round to close the door, his face still scarlet with rage. It was clear he regarded my continued existence on the planet, never mind in his eyeshot, as pure provocation. Rather than wait to be arrested for behaviour likely to cause a breach of the peace, I slid along the seat and out of the opposite side of the van. Sometimes, bottling out is the sensible course of action.

I gave the catering van a wide berth too and trudged across to the knot of people round the director. Gloria and Ted were already heading back across the snow to begin their long tracking shot again. At this rate it was going to take all day to film one scene. I didn't have to be an account-ant to work out why that would piss Turpin off, especially if he was obsessed with making the balance sheet look good to possible bidders for the show.

I switched my phone to mute, not wanting to risk the rage of the director if it rang during another take. When the shot was finally in the bag, I followed Gloria back to the wardrobe truck. While she changed back into her own clothes, I checked for messages. To my surprise, Della had called back already. I found a quiet and sheltered corner behind the make-up trailer and dialled her number. 'Good news,' she said.

'I could use some.'

'I'm on my way back to Manchester now. I managed to get hold of my contact, and he's meeting me around three in La Tasca. If you

236

want to swing by there around half past three, I should have what you need.'

'And I can buy you both some tapas?' I said with resignation.

'Just me,' she said firmly. 'I'm not having you corrupting any more police officers.'

'As if. See you.' I hung up and checked my watch. If the roads were still as clear out in Saddleworth as they'd been earlier, I could get Gloria back home and still make it to the tapas bar in time for my meeting with Della.

Forty minutes later, outside my house, I handed Gloria's car keys to a nervous Donovan. 'Do I have to stay over?' he asked, glancing apprehensively at Gloria who was giving him flirtatious waves and winks through the windscreen.

'She's got no personal appearances this evening, but she wants to visit her daughter for dinner. I'd like you to drive her there and take her home afterwards. I've told her I think she's in no danger and she should pay us off, but she's adamant that she wants us to carry on.'

'She's after my body, more like,' he grumbled.

'You should be so lucky. I think pretending she's trying to get into your knickers is a more acceptable motive to her than admitting she's scared shitless. Just because she doesn't like doing vulnerable doesn't mean she's not afraid,' I told him. 'So it might not be a bad thing if you do stay over. It also saves me having to drive to Saddleworth in arctic conditions at the crack of sparrowfart, and if

I was you, I'd be happy to store up a few Brownie points with the boss.'

He grinned. 'You going to tell my mum, then?'

Suckered again. 'I'll tell her. At least you're not going to get arrested for taking care of Gloria.'

He didn't look as if he thought it was much of a consolation. I waved them off, then walked across to Upper Brook Street and caught a bus down to Deansgate. Even public transport was better than trying to get into town and parked legally when the snow was falling three weeks before Christmas. I ducked into the steamy warmth of La Tasca with five minutes to spare. I was glad Della had suggested it; with its wood panelling, nicotine-coloured paintwork and salsa music, it feels enough like the real thing to hold a Manchester winter in abeyance.

I spotted Della right away, sitting at a round table near the back. She was sitting with a young Asian bloke who I guessed was her former colleague, now DI Tucker's bagman. I helped myself to one of the tall wooden bar stools and ordered a Corona. It came with the obligatory slice of lime, which always made me feel like an amateur teenage drinker again, fourteen and down the pub with a half of lager and lime. These days, I need all the help I can get.

Ten minutes later, her companion left and I picked up my beer and threaded my way across the room. 'You look good,' I said, meaning it. Her copper hair had started to show a few silver strands, but somehow it only made it look richer. Her skin was still glowing from the month she'd just spent in Australia; the old shadows under her eyes hadn't reasserted themselves yet. A Cambridge-educated economist, Della had one of the most devious financial minds I'd ever encountered. Way too smart for the Serious Fraud Office, she'd carved out her own niche in the north, unrivalled when it came to unravelling the sordid chicanery of the sharks in sharp suits.

'You look knackered,' she said. 'Have some chorizo. I just ordered more prawns and the aubergine with grilled cheese.'

My mouth watered and I remembered how long it had been since breakfast. As I made uncouth sandwiches with French bread and the meltingly rich sausage, I filled Della in on my day. She winced at the encounter between Turpin and Jackson. 'I wouldn't like to be Linda Shaw this afternoon,' she said. She pushed a large manila envelope towards me as I finished the last of the chorizo. 'One set of crime-scene photographs. I've had a quick look myself, and I didn't see anything to excite me. But then, murder has never interested me much.'

I didn't bother opening them. There would be a better time and place soon. Besides, food was due any minute, and I didn't want to lose my appetite. 'Thanks.'

Della smiled. 'I said it might tie in with a long firm fraud I was working on, but I didn't want to go public on it yet, hence the unofficial request. I don't think he believed me, but I don't think he much cared. So, no big deal.'

'I owe you,' I said. I meant it; but what I owed Della was nothing compared to the debt Dennis would face if my hunch worked out. I couldn't wait to see his face when I told him he was in hock to a DCI.

16

SUN CONJUNCTION WITH URANUS

She has an independent, progressive and original mind, backed with a strong and forceful personality. Individuality is important to her and she thrives on breaking patterns. She can be a breath of fresh air or a devastating tornado. In the 5th house, friends will be important in helping her to secure success.

From *Written in the Stars*, by Dorothea Dawson

The gods had finally started to smile on me, I decided when I arrived at the office to find Shelley temporarily absent from her desk. Before she could emerge from the loo, I slipped into my old office where I found Gizmo hunched over one of the computers. I recognized the program he was running, a basic template for a computer-controlled security system for a medium-sized building split into a mix of large and small rooms. It looked like one of the privately owned stately homes whose owners had turned to us after we'd scored

241

a spectacular success in closing down a ring of specialist art thieves. It was a case that I didn't like thinking about, for all sorts of reasons, so I was more than happy to have Gizmo around to take care of that end of the business.

He grunted what I interpreted as a greeting. 'I've been thinking, Giz,' I said. 'I know you probably think I'm being paranoid, but if you're going ahead with a meeting with the cyberbabe . . .' I caught his warning look and hurriedly corrected myself. 'I mean Jan, sorry. If you're going to arrange a meeting with her, you should have somebody to cover your back. Just in case she turns out to be a nutter. Or the whole thing is some terrible set-up.'

He did that thing with his mouth that people use to indicate you might just have something. 'I guess,' he said. 'It'd have to be somebody I could trust. I don't want the piss taking out of me from now till next Christmas if it's a meltdown.'

'How about me?'

'You don't mind?'

I sat down and made meaningful eye contact. 'Gizmo, you need someone who can suss this woman out at a hundred yards. Your anorak friends would be about as much use as a cardboard barbecue. Besides, this is self-interest. The last thing I need right now is the human equivalent of the Pakistani Brain Virus eating up my computer genius. Just check the date and time with me, and I'm all yours.'

242

'Sound,' he said, his eyes already straying back to the screen.

'There is, of course, a price to pay,' I said.

He closed his eyes and raised his face towards the ceiling. 'Suckered,' he said.

I spread out the contents of the envelope Della had given me and explained what I wanted. 'It's a freebie,' I said. 'For Dennis. Can do?'

He scratched his chin. 'It won't be easy,' he said. 'I'll have to take it home with me. I don't have the software loaded here. But yeah, it should be doable. When do you need it for?'

'The sooner the better. The longer it takes you, the longer Dennis is going to be behind bars.'

He shuffled the photographs together, giving each one a glance as he fed them back into the envelope. 'I'm still working on the Dorothea information,' he said. 'I farmed one end of it out to a lad I know who's shit hot on adoption records. But there are some more avenues I can pursue myself. Which is the priority – this stuff or the Dorothea material?'

I had to think about it. All my instincts said that I should be pulling out all the stops to help Dennis. But whoever killed Dorothea might have other victims in mind so the sooner I got to the bottom of that can of worms, the better. Besides, I was being paid for finding out who had murdered the astrologer. If there had been only me to consider, the decision would have been easy. But being the boss isn't all about strutting your stuff in jackboots, especially with wages day approaching on horseback. 'Dorothea,' I said reluctantly.

Gizmo had the look kids get when they're told they can't play with the new bike until Christmas morning. 'OK,' he said. 'By the way, I think Shell wants a word.'

I bet she did. Short of abseiling out of the window, I didn't see how I was going to be able to avoid letting her have several. I took a deep breath and walked into the outer office. Shelley was sitting behind her desk. It looked as if she was balancing the cheque book, a manoeuvre I find slightly more daunting than walking the high wire. 'Hi, Shelley,' I said breezily. 'I'm glad you're back. I wanted to tell you Donovan will be doing an overnight, so you won't have to bother cooking for him tonight.'

If glares had been wishes, the genie would have been on overtime that day. 'I've been wanting to talk to you about my son,' Shelley informed me.

The words alone might not have seemed menacing, but the tone put them on a par with, 'Has the prisoner a last request?' Ever since she had her hair cut in a Grace Jones flat top, I've been expecting her to batter me. Sometimes when I'm alone, I practise responses to the verbal challenges I know she's storing up to use against me. It doesn't help.

I smiled and said brightly, 'Don's settling in really well, isn't he? You must be well proud of him.'

Her eyes darkened. I waited for the bolts of black lightning. 'I was proud of his A level results. I was proud when he made the North West schools basketball team. I was proud when he was accepted at Manchester University. But proud is not the word for how I feel when I find out my son's been arrested twice in the space of a week.'

'Ah. That.' I tried edging towards the door, but noticed in time that she'd picked up the paperknife.

'Yes, that. Kate, I've been against this right from the start, but I gave in because Donovan wanted so badly not to be dependent on me and not to get deep into debt like most of his student friends. And because you promised me you wouldn't expose him to danger. And what happens? My son, who has managed to avoid any confrontation with the police in spite of being black and looking like he can take care of himself, gets arrested twice.' She banged her fist on the desk three times, synchronizing with her last three words. I've watched enough natural history documentaries to understand the mother's passion for her young. I wondered whether I'd make it to the door before she could rip my throat out.

'You can't hold me responsible for police racism,' I tried.

'Suddenly it's a secret that the police are racist?' Shelley said sarcastically. 'I can hold you responsible for putting him in places where he's exposed to that racism.'

'We're working on a way to deal with that,' I

said, trying for conciliation. 'And the work he's doing tonight couldn't be less risky. He's protecting Gloria Kendal against a nonexistent stalker.'

Shelley snorted. 'And you don't think that's dangerous? I've seen Gloria Kendal, remember?'

Time for a different approach. 'Gimme a break here, Shelley. People pay money in encounter groups for the sort of experience Don's getting here. He's not complaining, and he's making good money. You've done a great job with him. He's solid as a rock. He can handle himself, he knows how to take responsibility, and it's all because he's your son. You should believe in him. And it's about time you let him go. He's a man now. A lot of lads his age are fathers. He's got more sense, and it's down to the way you've brought him up.'

Shelley looked astounded. I couldn't remember the last time I'd stood up to her like that either. We faced off for a good thirty seconds that felt more like minutes. 'His name's Donovan,' she said finally. 'Not Don.'

I nodded apologetically. 'I'm going home now,' I said. 'I need to have a bath and a think. I've done some background checks for Toronto and San Juan, I'll e-mail you the billing details.' I made for the door. On my way out, I turned back and said, 'Shelley – thanks.'

She shook her head and returned to the cheque book. We hadn't actually built a bridge, but the piers were just about in place.

*   *   *

I got home to two messages on the answering machine. Richard had called to tell me he'd be home around nine with a Chinese takeaway, which was more warning than I usually get from him. I'd been thinking about going round to Freddie Littlewood's to ask him why he was leaking such destructive stories to the press, but just for once, I was tempted to let pleasure beat business into second place. Richard and I hadn't had much time alone together lately, and the fact that he'd taken the trouble to phone ahead with his plans indicated he was missing it as much as I was. I decided to leave Littlewood until the morning.

The second message was from Cassie, asking me to call her when I could. She sounded concerned but not panicky, so I fixed myself a drink and ran a hot bath that filled the air with the heady perfume of ylang-ylang and neroli essential oils. I was determined to make the most of a night in with Richard. I slid into the soothing water and reached for the phone. Cassie picked up on the second ring.

'Thanks for getting back to me, Kate,' she said.

I could feel the water soothing me already. 'No problem. How can I help?'

'Well . . .' She paused. 'It could be something and nothing. Just a coincidence. But I thought you might be interested.'

'Fire away,' I said. 'I'm always interested in coincidence.'

'I've just had a reporter round. A freelance that

does a lot for the national tabloids. She was waving the cheque book, trying to get me to dish the dirt on Dorothea and the *Northerners* cast. Scraping the bottom of the barrel, I thought, but I suppose everybody who's still on the show has closed ranks. They'll have been warned, reminded that their contracts forbid them to talk to the press without the agreement of NPTV. So the hacks have to dredge through their contacts books to see if they can find anybody who might talk.'

'And because you sold your story at the time, they think you might be tempted to spill some more beans?'

'Exactly. But I said everything I was ever going to say back then. And that's what I told this reporter. The thing is, though, I recognized her name. Tina Marshall. It's her by-line that's been on most of the really big *Northerners* scandal stories. She's obviously somebody that has a direct relationship with the mole.'

'That's certainly worth knowing,' I said, trying to sound interested. I couldn't figure out why Cassie felt the need to phone me up to tell me something I could have worked out for myself. Discovering who the mole was talking to wasn't going to get me any further forward, not even if this Tina Marshall and Alexis went way back. No journalist, especially not a freelance, was going to give up a source who was the fountainhead of her bank balance.

'But that's not all I recognized,' Cassie continued. 'I recognized her face, too. A couple of months back, a friend of mine took me to dinner at the Normandie. Do you know it?'

I knew the name. Alexis and Chris always went there for their anniversary dinners. Alexis claimed it was one of the best restaurants in the region, but I wasn't likely to be able to verify that for myself as long as I stayed with a man who believes if it hasn't come from a wok it can't be food. 'Not personally,' I sighed.

'Well, it's not cheap, that's for sure. Anyway, when I went to the loo, I noticed this woman. I didn't know then that she was Tina Marshall, of course.'

I was sceptical. A quick glance in a restaurant a couple of months previously wasn't the sort of identification I'd want to base anything on. 'Are you sure?' I asked. The fragrant warmth had clearly activated my politeness circuit.

'Oh, I'm sure. You see, the reason I noticed her in the first place was her companion. She was dining with John Turpin.' Cassie mistook my silence for incredulity rather than stupefaction. 'I wouldn't make any mistake about Turpin,' she added. 'He's the bastard who gave me the bullet, after all. So seeing him wining and dining some woman in the kind of sophisticated restaurant where he's not likely to run into *Northerners* regulars was a bit like a red rag to a bull. I paid attention to the woman he was with. When she turned up this afternoon on my doorstep, I knew her right away.'

'Turpin?' I said, puzzled. The man had no possible motive for leaking stories about *Northerners* to the press, least of all to the woman who had plastered scandal after scandal over the nation's tabloids. I pushed myself up into a sitting position, trying not to drop the phone.

'Turpin. And Tina Marshall,' Cassie confirmed.

'Unless . . . he was trying to get her to reveal her source?' I wondered.

'It didn't look like a confrontation,' Cassie said. 'It was far too relaxed for that. It didn't have the feel of a lovers' tryst, either. More businesslike than that. But friendly, familiar.'

'You got all this from a quick glimpse on the way to the loo?' I asked doubtfully.

'Oh no,' Cassie said hastily. 'Turpin had been sitting with his back to me, but once I realized it was him, I kept half an eye on their table.' She gave a rueful laugh. 'Much to the annoyance of my companion. He wasn't very pleased that I was so interested in another man, even though I explained who Turpin was.'

'Did Turpin see you?' I asked.

'I don't think so. He was far too absorbed in his conversation.'

'I'm surprised Tina Marshall didn't clock you. Women check out other women, and you must have been familiar to her,' I pointed out.

'I look very different from my Maggie Grimshaw days,' Cassie said. 'Nobody stops me in the street any more. Thank God. And like I said, the Normandie isn't the sort of place you'd expect the *Northerners* cast to be eating. It's not owned by a footballer or a rock star,' she added cynically. 'So, do you think there's something going on between them?'

I groaned. 'I don't know, Cassie. Nothing makes sense to me.'

'It's very odd, though.'

I was about to tell her exactly how odd I thought it was when my doorbell rang. Not the tentative, well-mannered ring of a charity collector, but the insistent, demanding, lean-on-the-bell ring that only a close friend or someone who'd never met me would risk. 'I don't believe it,' I moaned. 'Cassie, I'm going to have to go.' I stood up. It must have sounded like a whale surfacing at the other end of the phone.

'Are you OK?' she asked anxiously.

'Somebody at the door. Sorry. I'll call you when any of this makes sense. Thanks for letting me know.' As I talked, the phone tucked awkwardly between dripping jaw and wet shoulder, I was wrapping a bath sheet round me. I switched off the phone and drizzled my way down the hall.

I yanked the door open to find Gizmo on the doorstep. 'Hiya,' he said, not appearing to notice that I was wrapped in a bath sheet, my damp hair plastered to my head.

'What is *wrong* with the telephone, Gizmo?' I demanded. Remarkably restrained in the circumstances, I thought.

He shrugged. 'I was on my way home from

the office. You know, going home to sort out Dennis's little problem? And I thought you'd like to see what I found out about Dorothea's mysterious past.'

I shivered as a blast of wintry air made it past him. There goes snug, I thought. 'Inside,' I said, stepping back to let him pass. I followed him into the living room. 'This had better be good, Giz. I'd only just got in the bath.'

'Smells nice,' he said, sounding surprised to have noticed.

'It was,' I ground out.

'Any chance of a beer?' Spoken like a man who thinks 'considerate' is a prefix for 'done'.

'Why not?' I muttered. On the way, I collected my own glass and topped it up with the Polish lemon pepper vodka. I grabbed the first bottle that came to hand and relished the look of pained disgust that flashed across Gizmo's face when his taste buds made contact with chilli beer – ice-cold liquid with the breathtaking burn of the vengeful vindaloo that curry shops serve up to Saturday-night drunks. 'You were saying?' I asked sweetly, enjoying the sudden flush on his skin and the beads of sweat that popped out across his upper lip.

'Jesus, Mary and Joseph,' he gasped. 'What in the name of God was that?'

'I didn't know you'd been brought up Catholic,' I said. That should discourage him from the space-invading that was threatening to become a habit.

'It's a beer, like you asked for. Now, what did you want to tell me about?'

He fished inside his vast parka and produced a clear plastic wallet. Wordlessly, he handed it over. I took the few sheets of paper out of the sleeve and worked my way through them. By the time I reached the end, I knew when Dorothea had been born and who her parents were, when she'd married Harry Thompson and when they'd been divorced. I knew the date of Harry's death, and I knew the date of Dorothea's release from the mental hospital.

Most importantly, I knew who the mystery baby was. And I had more than the shadow of a notion why the relationship might have led to murder.

I opened my mouth to try out my idea on Gizmo. Of course, the phone rang. 'I don't believe this,' I exploded, grabbing the handset and hitting the 'talk' button. 'Hello?' I barked.

'It's me,' the familiar voice said. 'I'm in Oldham police station. I've been arrested.'

17

MOON TRINES MERCURY

She concentrates best on matters she's emotionally involved with. She expresses herself fluently and clearly and has a quick grasp of what is being said, easily picking up facts and drawing apt conclusions. Shrewd and intuitive, she sometimes lacks a sense of direction, shooting off in different directions at the same time. She has a good memory and is naturally inquisitive.

From *Written in the Stars,* by Dorothea Dawson

The desk sergeant at Oldham police station was obviously having about as good an evening as I was. His waiting area was clogged with hacks who'd heard there had been an arrest involving Gloria Kendal. Somewhere inside the station, the three photographers and two reporters were being treated as witnesses. Somewhere else, my part-time process-server and bodyguard was under arrest for breach of the peace and assault. Berserk student batters mob-handed team of journos. Yeah, right.

I pushed my way through the representatives of Her Majesty's gutter press, waving an ineffectual hand against the cigarette smoke and wondering if force of numbers was the only reason why they were allowed to ignore the 'no smoking' notices that everybody else was told to obey. 'You're holding an employee of mine,' I said to the sergeant, trying to keep my voice down. 'His solicitor is on her way. I wonder if I might have a word with the arresting officer?'

'And you are?'

'Kate Brannigan.' I pushed a business card across the counter. 'Donovan Carmichael works for me. I think we can clear all this up very easily if you could arrange for me to talk to the arresting officer.'

He picked up the card as if it contained a communicable disease. 'I don't think so,' he said dismissively. 'We're very busy tonight.'

'I was hoping to reduce the burden of work on your officers,' I said, still managing sweetness. 'I'm sure there has been some misunderstanding. I don't know about you, Sergeant, but I hate paperwork. And just thinking about the amount of paperwork that a racism case against GMP would generate gives me a headache. All I want to do is chat to the arresting officer, explain one or two elements of the background that might show the evening's events in a different light. I really don't want to spend the next two years running up legal bills that your Chief Constable will end up paying.' I could feel the smile rotting my molars. For some reason, the desk sergeant wasn't smiling.

'I'll see what I can do,' he said.

That was clearly my cue to go and sit down. I just carried on smiling and leaning on the counter. 'I'll wait,' I said.

He breathed heavily through his nose and disappeared through a door behind the counter. One of the hacks casually wandered across to me and offered his cigarettes. 'I don't do suicide,' I said. 'Quick or slow.'

'Sharp,' he said, slotting in beside me at the counter with a swagger designed to show off his narrow hips and expensive suit. 'What's a spice girl like you doing in a place like this?'

'Just a little local difficulty to sort out,' I said. 'What about you? You don't look like Oldham Man to me.'

He couldn't resist. 'I'm a reporter.'

'Ooh,' I said. 'That sounds exciting. Who do you work for?'

I got the full CV, ending with the most notorious national tabloid. He shrugged his shoulders in his jacket, just to make sure I hadn't missed how gorgeous he was. In his dreams.

'Wow,' I said. 'That's impressive. So what's the big story tonight?'

'Are you a *Northerners* fan?' I nodded. 'You'll have read about Dorothea Dawson getting murdered on the set, then?' I nodded again. 'Well, a couple of my colleagues got a tip-off from the police handling the murder inquiry that Gloria Kendal's fingerprints were plastered all over the murder weapon.'

I couldn't believe what I was hearing. I had no doubts where this particular leak had come from. That bastard Jackson was getting his own back for being made to look a pillock first by me and Gloria and then by John Turpin. 'No!' I gasped, struggling to keep up the pretence in the teeth of my anger.

'I'm telling you, that's what we heard. So we send out a pic man and a reporter to Gloria's place, out in Greenfield. She comes out in the car, and our lads are standing at the entrance to her lane, just doing their jobs, trying to get a picture or a story. Then this big black lad comes jumping out of the car and weighs into our lads. One of the reporters calls the police, Gloria shoots off God knows where in the car, and the rest is history.'

'The bodyguard started it?' I couldn't keep the scepticism out of my voice.

My new friend winked. 'Five words against one. Who do you think the cops will believe?'

Not if I had anything to do with it they wouldn't. But before I could let him know what I thought of the credibility of the press, the door to the station swung open and Ruth sailed in like a Valkyrie on ice, her blonde hair loose for once, falling in a cascade over the silver fake fur. At once, the journalist forgot all about chatting me up and scuttled towards her. 'Ruth,' came the cry from several throats. 'Tell us what's going on!'

She swept past them, a snow leopard scattering fleas in her wake. 'Later, boys and girls, later. Let me at least speak to my client. Kate,' she greeted me, putting one arm round my shoulders and turning me so that we formed an impenetrable wall of backs as she pressed the button for the desk officer. 'You know I can't take you in with me?' she said, her voice low but audible against the clamour behind us.

'I know. But I want to talk to the arresting officer first, before you all get embroiled in interviews. I want him to know that if they charge Don, I'm filing a racial harassment suit first thing in the morning. I told you about their antics last week, didn't I?'

'Oh yes. I'm sure we're not going to have a problem with them.'

'It's Jackson that's behind this.' I told her briefly what I'd just learned. There was no time to discuss it further, for the desk officer reappeared.

'I'm Ruth Hunter,' she said. 'Here to see my client, Donovan Carmichael. His employer also has some relevant information to place before the arresting officer if you would be so good as to get him here?'

The desk man nodded to a door at the side of the reception area. 'He'll be right out.'

The journalists were still hammering us with questions when the door opened moments later.

The uniformed sergeant who emerged looked harried and hassled, his short red hair sticking out at odd angles as if he'd been running a hand through it. His freckles stood out like a rash on skin pallid with tiredness. 'Ms Brannigan?' he asked, looking at Ruth.

'I'm Ruth Hunter, Donovan's solicitor,' she said. A gentle shove in the small of my back propelled me towards the door. 'This is his employer.' Ruth continued her forward movement, sweeping all three of us back through the door and neatly closing it behind us. 'A moment of your time before I see my client, Sergeant?'

He nodded and led us into an interview room that looked freshly decorated but still smelled inevitably of stale smoke, sweat and chips. I think they buy it in an aerosol spray. 'I'm Sergeant Mumby,' he said, dropping into a chair on one side of the table. 'I'm told Ms Brannigan wanted a word.'

'That's right,' I said, glad I'd had the chance to forearm myself with information from the smoothie outside. 'I don't want this to sound threatening, but if you charge Donovan tonight, Ms Hunter's firm will be making a complaint of racial harassment against GMP. He's already been arrested twice in the last week for nothing more than being black in the wrong place. Now he's facing serious charges because five white people who were blocking my client's private road wouldn't get out of the way and they didn't like being told what to do by a young black lad. That's about the size of it, isn't it?'

He sighed. 'I've got five witnesses saying he came at them like a madman, pushing them and shoving them, and that he punched one of them in the back. Believe me, I sympathize with your point of view. When we turned up, it was all over bar the shouting. But Mr Carmichael had made no effort to get away from the scene. And he's actually the only one with any visible injury.'

I caught my breath. 'What happened?'

'Just a split lip. He says one of the photographers swung his camera at him; the photographer says Mr Carmichael tried to head butt him and the camera got in the way.'

I shook my head incredulously. 'This is outrageous. Some scummy paparazzo smacks Donovan in the face with a camera then turns round and says he started on them? And Don's the one facing charges? What has Gloria got to say about all this?'

The sergeant's lips compressed in a thin line. 'We've not been able to contact her yet.'

'I bet she'll have plenty to say. Not least about the fact that this whole thing happened because one of your colleagues decided to leak confidential evidence in a murder inquiry to the press. Evidence which has already been totally discredited,' I said bitterly.

Ruth leaned forward. 'There is, of course, one way to make all of this go away. You can let my client go without charge. Give him police bail if you must. He's not going anywhere. He's a student at Manchester University, he lives at home with his mother and sister, he has no criminal record and he has a part-time job with Ms Brannigan. I'm certain that once Ms Kendal has outlined the real course of events you'll realize the only charge that should be brought is one of wasting police time, and not against my client. What do you say, Sergeant? Shall we all have an early night?'

He rubbed a hand over his chin and cocked his head on one side. 'And if I do what you suggest, it'll be all over the papers that we let a black mugger walk free.'

'Probably,' Ruth agreed. 'But that's a story that will be history by the weekend, whereas a racial harassment action will rumble on for a very long time. Especially one that's supported by Gloria Kendal.'

'And the *Manchester Evening Chronicle*,' I added. 'Donovan's mother is a very close friend of the *Chronicle*'s crime correspondent, Alexis Lee. They love a good campaign at the *Chron*.'

He smiled, a genuine look of relief in his eyes. 'You talked me into it, ladies. Between ourselves, I never saw it the way the journalists were telling it. For one thing, a lad built like your client would have done a hell of a lot more damage if he'd had a serious go. But what can you do? You've got witnesses saying one thing and not much evidence pointing the other way. At least now I can let you take Mr Carmichael home secure in the knowledge that I've got good reasons to put in front of my inspector.' He got to his feet. 'If you'd just wait there a minute, I'll get it sorted.'

He left us alone to exchange gobsmacked looks. 'I'd always heard the police out here were a law unto themselves, but I didn't think that'd ever work in my favour,' I said faintly.

'I know,' Ruth said, sounding somewhat baffled. 'I must tell all my clients to make a point of getting arrested in Oldham.'

'I can't believe that scumbag Jackson,' I said.

'You'll never nail him on it. He'll have got one of his minions to do the dirty work. Go after Jackson and you'll probably end up with Linda Shaw's head on a stick.' Ruth leaned back in her seat and lit one of her long slim cigarettes. 'By the way, I made those inquiries you suggested about Pit Bull Kelly's dog. Dennis has no marks anywhere on his body that correspond to dog bites. And the dog himself showed no signs of having been in a fight. Care to tell me where this is going?'

'I've got Gizmo working on something. An idea I had. It came from a case I read about on the Internet a while back. An American case. I'd rather wait till I've got something concrete to show you, because it sounds so totally off the wall.'

Ruth gave me the hard stare, but she could see I wasn't going to budge. 'How long?'

'Probably tomorrow? I'll need you to set up a

meeting with DI Tucker. Preferably at my office. I'll let you know when I'm ready. Is that OK?'

'The sooner the better,' Ruth said. 'Normally, Dennis takes custody in his stride, but this time he's not handling it well. Probably because he's genuinely innocent,' she added drily.

The door opened and Sergeant Mumby stuck his head into the room. 'Your client's ready to leave now. I think the back way would be better, in the circumstances.'

I left Donovan climbing reverently into the Bentley, Ruth promising to drop him at his girl-friend's so we could avoid letting his mother know about his latest brush with the law. I looked at the dashboard clock and realized there was no point in going home. Richard would have eaten the Chinese; it takes more than irritation at being stood up to disturb his appetite. Then, if habit held, he'd have decided to show me how little he needed me by jumping a taxi back into town and partying the night away. I couldn't honestly blame him.

I sat in my car and rang the number Gloria had given me for her daughter's house. The voice that answered was familiar in its inflexions, but twenty years younger in its tones. 'I'm looking for Gloria,' I said. 'Can you tell her it's Kate?'

'Hang on, love, I'll just get her.'

Moments later, I heard the real thing. 'All right, chuck?'

'I am now,' I said severely. 'Now I've got Donovan out of jail.'

She chuckled. 'That poor lad's having a proper education, working for you. I knew you'd have it sorted in no time. Whereas if I'd hung around, it would just have got more and more complicated.'

'He got a smack in the mouth from a journalist's camera,' I said coldly.

There was a short pause, then, serious, she said, 'I'm really sorry about that. Is the lad OK?'

'He'll live. But the police need a statement from you, otherwise they're going to have to believe that bunch of scumbag hacks claiming Donovan set about them without any provocation.'

She gasped. 'Is that what they're saying?'

'What else do you expect paparazzi to be saying, Gloria? The truth?' I demanded sarcastically. 'They've got bosses on the newsdesk who aren't going to be well impressed if they tell them they didn't get a story or pictures because a teenage lad told them to bugger off. If they don't get a proper story, they make one up.'

'Aye well, at least you got it sorted,' she said, sounding chastened for once.

'It'll be sorted once you've given Sergeant Mumby a statement and half his colleagues an autograph. Now, are you staying at your daughter's tonight?'

'I better had, I suppose. And I'm not filming tomorrow, so I'll probably take her shopping.'

'Not in town,' I said firmly.

'Harvey Nicks, chuck,' she said. 'In Leeds. I'll bell you in the morning once we've decided what's what. Thanks for sorting it all out, Kate.'

The line went dead. Nothing like a grateful client. Given that the wheels were well and truly off my evening, I figured I might as well go for broke and see what Dorothea Dawson's child had to say about her murder. It was, after all, what I was being paid for. I drove through the virtually deserted streets of Oldham, south through Ashton, Audenshaw and Denton, past rows of local shops with peeling paint, sagging strings of dirty Christmas lights, sad window displays and desperate signs trying to lure customers inside; past the narrow mouths of terraced streets where people sprawled in front of gas fires denying the winter by watching movies filled with California sunshine; past down-at-heel pubs advertising karaoke and quiz nights; past artificial Christmas trees defiant in old people's homes; past churches promising something better than all of this next time round in exchange for the abandonment of logic.

It was a relief to hit the motorway, hermetically sealed against the poverty of the lives I'd driven past. Tony Blair said a lot about new Labour giving new Britain new hope before he was elected; funny how nothing's changed now he's in power. It's still, 'get tough on single mums, strip the benefit from the long-term unemployed, close the mines and make the students pay for their education.'

I cruised past Stockport, admiring the huge glass pyramid of the Co-op Bank, glowing neon green and indigo against the looming redbrick of the old mills and factories behind it. It had stood empty for years, built on spec in the boom of the Thatcher years before the Co-op had rescued it from the indignity of emptiness. I bet they'd got a great deal on the rent; wish I'd thought of it.

I took the Princess Parkway exit, almost the only car on the road now. Anyone with any sense was behind closed doors, either home writing Christmas cards or partying till they didn't notice how cold it was outside while they waited for the taxi home. Me, I was sitting in my car opposite the other deadheads in the vast expanse of the Southern Cemetery. Only one of us was using the *A-to-Z*, though.

The street I was searching for was inevitably in the less seedy end of Chorlton, one of those pleasant streets of 1930s semis near the primary school whose main claim to fame is the number of lesbian parents whose children it educates. To live comfortably in Chorlton, you need to have a social conscience, left-of-centre politics and an unconventional relationship. Insurance salesmen married to building society clerks with two children and a Ford Mondeo are harder to find around there than hen's teeth.

The house in question was beautifully maintained. Even in the dead of winter, the garden was neat, the roses pruned into symmetrical shapes, the lawn lacking the shaggy uneven look that comes from neglecting the last cut of autumn. The stucco on the upper storey and the gable gleamed in the streetlight, and the stained glass in the top sections of the bay window was a perfect match for the panel in the door. Even the curtain linings matched. I walked up the path with a degree of reluctance, knowing only too well the kind of mayhem I was bringing to this orderliness.

Sometimes I wish I could just walk away, that I wasn't driven by this compelling desire for unpicking subterfuge and digging like an auger into people's lives. Then I realize that almost every person I care about suffers from the same affliction: Richard and Alexis are journalists, Della's a detective, Ruth's a lawyer, Gizmo's a hacker, Shelley's never taken a thing at face value in all the years I've worked with her. Even Dennis subjects the world around him to careful scrutiny before he decides how to scam it.

The need to know was obviously too deeply rooted in me to ignore. Sometimes it even seemed stronger than the urge for self-preservation. Driven as I was by the prospect of finding out what lay behind the string of recent strange events, I had to remind myself that I might be knocking on the door of a murderer. It wasn't a comfortable thought.

I took a deep breath and pressed the bell. A light went on in the hall, illuminating me with green and scarlet patterns from the stained glass. I saw a dark shape descend the stairs and loom towards me. The door opened and Dorothea Dawson's genetic inheritance stood in front of me. I should have seen it, really. The features were so similar.

'Hi,' I said. 'I've come for a chat about your mum.'

18

SATURN OPPOSES URANUS

Whenever she seems about to carve out a destiny or even a destination, Uranus steps in to force her to kick over the traces and express her individuality. Something always disrupts her best-laid plans; she is forever having to include new elements in her arrangements. The rest of her chart indicates capability; she will succeed in a conventional world by unconventional means.

From *Written in the Stars,* by Dorothea Dawson

Freddie Littlewood blinked rapidly, dark eyes glittering. His thin lips twitched. It was hard to tell if he was furious or on the point of tears. I figured he was deciding whether to brazen it out or to deny all knowledge of what I was talking about. It was possible, after all, that I was only guessing. 'My private life is no concern of yours,' he said eventually, sitting firmly on the fence.

I sighed. 'That's where you're wrong, Freddie.

I'm very concerned with the relationship between you and Dorothea. The nature of my concern rather depends on whether you killed her or not. If you did, it puts my client in the clear and it probably means Gloria isn't the next target of a killer. If you didn't, you can probably tell me things that would help me to protect her. Either from false accusation or from murder. So my concern is legitimate.'

'I've nothing to say to you,' he said, closing the door in my face.

I hate bad manners. Especially when it's late and there are almost certainly more interesting things I could be doing with my time. I took out my mobile phone and pushed open the letterbox. 'The police don't know Dorothea was your mother.' I started to press numbers on the phone, hoping the beeping was evident on the other side of the door. 'Want me to tell them now?'

Before I could have pressed the 'send' button if I'd been serious, the door opened again. 'There's no need for this,' Freddie snapped. 'I didn't kill Dorothea. That's all you need to know. And it's all you're getting from me. I don't care if you tell the police she was my birth mother. It's not like it was news to me. I've known for ages, and I can prove it. Even the police aren't stupid enough to take that as a motive for murder.' He was probably right. The bitterness in his voice spelled motive to me, but acrimony's never been grounds for arresting someone.

I leaned against the doorjamb and smiled. 'Maybe so. But if you factor in the stories you've been selling to the papers, the picture looks very different. Intimate details that people have revealed to Dorothea, spiced with the snippets you've picked up, that's what's been tarted up in the tabloids. Maybe Dorothea decided she didn't need a partner any more?'

His eyes widened and he flashed a panicky glance to either side of me, as if checking whether I was alone. 'You're talking rubbish,' he said, his voice venomous.

I smiled. 'Have it your own way. But you didn't get paid in cash. Somewhere there's a paper trail. And one thing the stupid old plod is very good at is following a paper trail. Freddie, if what you're saying is true, and you didn't kill Dorothea, I've got no axe to grind with you. John Turpin isn't paying me to find out who the *Northerners* mole is.' I refrained from mentioning that Ross Grant might be. There was no point in complicating things that were already difficult. 'All I'm interested in is protecting Gloria. You *like* Gloria, for God's sake, I know you do. I've seen the way you are with her. Can we not just sit down and talk about this? Or do I have to blow your life out of the water with NPTV as well as the cops?'

One side of his mouth lifted in a sneer. 'Gloria said you were smart,' he said, opening the door wide enough to let me enter. He shooed me ahead of him into a small square dining room. There was an oak table with four matching chairs, all stripped back to the bare wood, oiled and polished till they gleamed in the soft glow of opalescent wall lights. A narrow sideboard in darker oak sat against the far wall. The only decoration came from the vibrant colours of the Clarice Cliff pottery ranged along a shelf that ran round the room at head height. If it was genuine, selling the collection would have bought him a year off work. Freddie waved me to a chair and sat down with his back to the door.

'How did you find out she was my birth mother?' he asked.

I raised one shoulder in a shrug. 'There's not much a good hacker can't find out these days. How did you find out?'

He ran his thumb along the sharp line of his jaw in a curious stropping gesture. 'A mixture of luck and hard work,' he said. 'The first time I got into a serious relationship, when I was in my twenties, I decided I wanted to know where I'd come from. It hadn't seemed important before, but the idea of being with someone long term, maybe even having kids with them, made me curious. I searched the records, and found out my father was already dead. Killed by a heart attack.' He gave a bitter cough of laughter. 'Not bad for a heartless bastard. I carried on looking and I discovered my mother was Dorothea Thompson, née Dawson. But the trail went cold.' His eyes were alert, never leaving my face. I suspected he was watching for any signs that he was breaking new ground, revealing things I didn't already know.

'I know about the breakdown,' I said. 'Was that where the trail petered out?'

He nodded. 'She was released from the hospital still using her married name, and she disappeared without trace. I found a cousin, the only other member of the family still alive, but he had no idea what had happened to her. The only useful thing I got from him was a copy of her wedding picture. I even hired one of your lot, but he never found her. Then one day I was sitting in the staff canteen at NPTV and Edna Mercer walked in with her latest fad. It was like someone took my stomach in their fist and squeezed it tight. I didn't need to hear her name to know who she was. That was just confirmation of what I knew the minute I saw her face. All those years later, she was still the spitting image of her wedding picture.'

'But you didn't rush across the room and reveal you were her long-lost son.'

He gave a twisted smile. 'When I started out looking for my past, I don't think I'd thought it through. In a way, it was almost a relief not to have found her. You see, I blamed her. My childhood was a nightmare. I never knew what it was to be held with love. I was bullied because I was small. I was beaten black and blue by one sadistic bitch of a foster mother because I was still wetting the bed when I was seven. I was gang-raped in a children's home when I was eleven by three older boys and

273

a so-called care worker. I never got to choose my own clothes or my own toys. I was supposed to be grateful for what I was given. I never even got to keep my own name. My father changed it by deed poll before he dumped me.' He stopped, apparently choking on the bile of memory.

I couldn't think of anything to say that wasn't offensively trite. My childhood was breathtaking in its comforting and confident normality. When I'd fallen over, there had been someone there to pick me up and stick a plaster on my knee. I'd fallen asleep with stories, not nightmares. There had always been arms to hold me and faces to reflect pride in my achievement. I could barely imagine the yawning gap of such an absence, never mind the agony of having it filled with such poisonous viciousness. 'You must have come to hate her,' I said, surprised by the huskiness of my voice.

He shifted in his chair so his face was obscured by shadow, his spiky hair emphasized in a dark fragmented halo. With his black polo neck and black trousers, he looked like a satanic ghost. 'I wanted to make her life a misery too,' he said. 'I wanted her to understand something about the pain and misery she'd given me.'

'I don't think she had a lot of choice in the matter.'

'More choice than I did,' he blazed back at me. 'She could have come looking for me. It couldn't have been that hard to find a child in care. But she made the decision to leave me in whatever hell I happened to be in.'

In the silence that swallowed his outburst, I thought of how it must have been for Dorothea. Tainted with the stigma of mental illness, abandoned by her husband, wrenched from her child, without resources. She couldn't go home for she had no home to go to. The village where she'd grown up was the one place she'd never be allowed to forget or escape. She had no formal training, no professional skills to fall back on, yet she had to find a way to scrabble together enough to live on in a town where she had not one friend to turn to. It must have taken every ounce of guts she had just to survive. She probably saw it as a kindness to her son to leave him be. 'Maybe she did try,' I suggested. 'Maybe they wouldn't give you back to her.'

'*She* tried to get me to fall for that line,' he said scornfully. 'No way. She never came after me. She left me to it. And my problem is that I'm not stupid. I know I'm fucked up. And I know exactly how and why. I'm fucked up because she left me to rot, to be abused, to be fucked over. And that's why I didn't murder her. I hated her far too much to give her the easy way out. I wanted her to go on suffering a whole lot longer. She still had years to pay for.'

Strangely, I believed him. The vitriol in his voice was the real thing, so strong it made the air tremble. 'So you didn't let on when you realized Edna Mercer's latest discovery was your mother?'

He shook his head. 'I didn't say a word. I just watched her, every chance I got. I listened to the actors talking about her when I made them up. At first, I was confused. It was like part of me desperately wanted to love her and be loved back. And another part of me wanted revenge. I just sat it out, waited to see which side would win.' Freddie shifted in his chair, folding his arms across his stomach and bending forward. Lit from above, his eyes were impenetrable pools in shadowy sockets. 'It was no contest, not really. The more they went on about how lovely she was, the more I resented what she'd deprived me of. I wanted revenge.'

'But you ended up in business with her. Earning money together,' I said, trying not to show how baffled I was by that. I suspected that he still harboured a determination not to tell me any more than I already knew.

He looked up then and stared into my face. He gave a strange barking cough of laughter. 'Don't you get it? That was my revenge. One night, I waited till her last client had gone and I walked into the van. I told her my date, time and place of birth and watched the colour drain out of her face. I didn't have to tell her who I was. Sure, she'd seen me around the place, but now it was like she was looking at me for the first time. But even then, her head was right in control of her heart. Nearly the first thing she said to me was, "Who have you told about this?"

'You see, if she revealed that I was her son, it

wouldn't just be another happy tabloid reunion story. She'd have to explain how she came to give me up in the first place. She'd have to tell the world she was a nutter. Most people find mental illness frightening. She was convinced that she'd lose her contracts, lose her clients at *Northerners* and end up back where she was all those years ago when she came out of the mental hospital. I think she was wrong, but it suited me that she believed it. That way, I had leverage. I made her tell me people's secrets and then I sold them. She had this phoney reverence thing about her psychic gift. She was always going on about being like a priest or a doctor, the repository of people's confidences.' His contemptuous impersonation was frighteningly accurate; if I'd been the superstitious type, I'd have sworn I could see Dorothea's ghost rising up before me.

'In that case, why did she tell you?'

'I was her son,' he said simply. 'She wanted to please me. It helped that she was desperate to keep our relationship secret, so she needed to keep me sweet.'

'So you put together what she winkled out from her clients with what people let slip in the make-up chair, and with the overlap between two sources you were able to expose all those people who probably think of you as a friend?' I said.

'Don't make me laugh,' he said bitterly. 'I'm not a friend to them. I'm a servant, a convenience. Oh sure, they treat me like I'm their best buddy, but if

I died tonight I doubt if more than three of them would make it to the funeral, and then only if they knew the photographers were going to be there. The programme's last publicist, he made the mistake of thinking they were his friends. He had a breakdown – too much stress. One cast member sent him a get-well card. One sent him a bunch of flowers. And that was it. He'd been working his socks off to cover their backs for the best part of five years, and the day he went sick, it was as if he'd never existed. So don't do the betrayal number on me. The only person I betrayed was my mother, and that was deliberate. And she knew it.'

'Wasn't it a bit of a risk, revealing secrets people knew they'd told Dorothea? Didn't anybody put two and two together?'

He shook his head, a smirk on his narrow mouth. 'I always waited a few months. I used the time to do a bit more digging, see if I could come up with extra information, stuff my mother hadn't been told about. Once you know where to look, it's amazing what you can find out.'

Tell me about it, I thought, feeling a strange pity for this damaged man who'd subverted the tricks of my trade and used them to generate misery. 'I suppose leaking the storylines as well helped to cover your tracks.'

He frowned. 'Storylines? That wasn't me. I never really know the storylines in advance. Just bits and pieces I pick up from what people say. I'd heard it's supposed to be somebody in the location catering company doing that. Turpin's giving them the heave, and they're getting their own back. That's what I'd heard.'

I couldn't help believing him. He'd been so honest about the other stuff, and that painted him in a far worse light. Besides, he was completely off-hand on the subject. I'd begun to realize that Freddie Littlewood was intense about the things at the heart of his life. Anything else was insignificant. 'Did you make her take some of the money too?' I asked.

'I tried. But she wouldn't cash the cheques. I even paid cash into her bank account once. The next week, she gave me a receipt from Save the Children for the exact same amount.'

It would have been so simple if I could have persuaded myself Freddie had killed his mother. All the pieces were there; a racket selling stories to the press that worked primarily because their relationship remained secret; a falling out among thieves, aggravated by the emotional charge of their relationship; a spur of the moment act of shocking violence. The only problem was that it wasn't true. And if I gave Cliff Jackson the pieces, he'd force them to fit the pattern his closed mind would impose.

But if it wasn't Freddie, who else? Who else would benefit from Dorothea's death? Whose purpose would be served? 'I don't suppose you know what was in her will?' I asked.

'I know I wasn't,' he said decisively. 'When I told her I was going to start selling the stories to the papers, she said that if I needed money, all I had to do was ask. She said that as soon as she'd satisfied herself that I really was her son, she'd changed her will in my favour. She said I might as well have the money now, while she was still alive and we could enjoy it together. I told her I didn't want her money, that wasn't the point. I wasn't selling the stories to make a few bob. I was doing it to hurt her. The money was just a bonus. She told me if I went ahead with it, she'd change her will back again and leave all her money to mental health charities.'

'I bet she didn't do it,' I said.

He moved his head almost imperceptibly from side to side, rubbing his thumb along his jaw again. 'You didn't know Dorothea. The week after the first story was published, she sent me a photocopy of her new will. Dated, signed, witnessed. Apart from a few small legacies to friends, everything she owns goes to charity.'

'It could have been a bluff. She might also have made a second will leaving it all to you.'

He shook his head. 'I don't think so. If she had, I think the police would have been round. Either that or the solicitor would have been on the phone. No, she meant it. I don't mind, you know. I've never expected anything good from life. That way, you're not disappointed.' Freddie pushed his chair back, the legs squeaking on the parquet floor.

He looked down anxiously, checking the polished surface wasn't scarred.

I stood up. 'I'm sorry,' I said.

His wary look was back. 'Why? I wasn't part of her life. I don't know who her friends were outside *Northerners*. I don't even know if she had any lovers.' He sighed. 'In all the ways that count, we were strangers, Kate.' It was the first time he'd used my name.

I followed him to the door. As we emerged into the hall, a woman was coming downstairs wrapped in a fluffy towelling dressing gown. I don't know who looked more startled, me or her. I hadn't registered any sounds to indicate there was anyone else home. She looked uncertainly from me to Freddie, her soft features concerned rather than suspicious. 'This is Kate,' Freddie said. 'She's from work. She just bobbed round to tell me about a change of schedule for tomorrow's filming. Kate, this is Stacey, my fiancée.'

I took my cue from Freddie and grinned inanely at the woman who continued down the stairs and gave me a trusting smile. She had a disturbing resemblance to Thumper the rabbit but with none of his street smarts. 'Hello and goodbye, Stacey,' I said, noticing that she looked a good ten years younger than Freddie.

'Maybe see you another time, eh?' she said, standing back to let me reach the front door.

'Maybe,' I lied, suddenly feeling claustrophobic.

I turned the knob on the lock and let the night in. 'See you, Freddie.'

'Thanks, Kate.'

I looked back once, as I turned out of the gate. His slim frame was silhouetted dark against the light spilling out of the hallway, Stacey a white blob beside him. I didn't fancy her job one little bit.

My stomach hurt. Not because of the nagging sense of failure but because it was a very long time since I'd last eaten. I stopped at the first chippie I came to and sat in the car eating very fishy cod and soggy chips, watching tiny stutters of snow struggling to turn into a blizzard. They were getting nowhere fast, just like me. So far, I had no idea who'd been sending hate mail to Gloria Kendal, or why. I had no idea who had killed Dorothea Dawson, or why, or whether they posed a threat to Gloria or anybody else. I couldn't even clear my sort-of other client, Ross Grant, because the only mole I could substitute for him in Turpin's firing line was someone who had even more to lose. My assistant had been arrested more times than I'd had hot dinners all week, my computer specialist was in love with somebody who might not even exist and one of my best friends was in jail.

It was just as well none of the women's magazines were thinking about profiling me as an example of Britain's thrusting new business-women.

I scrunched up the chip papers and tossed them into the passenger footwell. I hoped I'd remember to dump them when I got home, otherwise the car would smell of fish and vinegar until the first sunroof day of spring. Home seemed even less appetizing, somehow. The idea of an empty house and an empty bed felt too much like film noir for my taste.

I had a reasonably good idea where Richard might have gone. Since he'd planned a romantic night in, he wouldn't have made any plans to listen to a live band. That meant he'd have chosen somewhere he could sit in a corner with a beer and a joint and listen to techno music so loud it would make his vertebrae do the cha-cha. I knew he wouldn't have ventured further afield than the city centre when the roads were so treacherous and there was no one to drive him home. There were only a couple of places that fitted the bill.

I gave the matter careful thought. Frash was the most likely. He'd been raving about the new midweek DJ there. The way my luck was running, that meant he was almost certainly not grooving in Frash. It had to be the O-Pit, a renovated die-cast works down by the canal that still smelled of iron filings and grease. To add insult to injury, there was a queue and I didn't have enough energy left to jump it. I leaned against the spalled brickwork, shoulders hunched, hands stuffed deep into my pockets. I might not be dressed for the club, but

I was the only one in the queue who stood a chance against hypothermia. Eventually, I made it inside.

It was wall to wall kids, fuelled with whizz and E, pale faces gleaming with sweat, clothes sticking to them so tight they appeared to be wearing body paint. I could spot the dealers, tense eyes never still, always at the heart of a tight little knot of punters. Nobody was paying them any mind, least of all the bar staff who could barely keep pace with the constant demand for carbonated pop.

I found Richard where I'd expected, in the acoustic centre of the club, the point where the music could be heard at maximum quality and volume. Unlike the dancers, he went for the drug that slowed down rather than speeded up. His eyes had the gently spaced look of the benevolently stoned. A half-litre bottle of Czech Bud hung from his right hand, a joint from his left. A copper-haired teenager wearing a lot of stripy Lycra and young enough to be his daughter was giving him covert come-on glances. I could have told her she was wasting her time. He was lost in the music.

I moved into his line of vision and tried an apologetic smile. Instead of a bollocking, he gave me that slow, cute smile that had first reeled me in, then drew me into his arms and gently kissed the top of my head. 'I love you, Brannigan,' he shouted.

Nobody but me heard. 'Let's go home,' he yelled in my ear.

I shook my head and took a long swig of his beer, leading him to the dance floor. Sometimes sex just isn't enough.

19

NEPTUNE IN SCORPIO IN THE 6TH HOUSE
*She loves research and investigation, particularly if
it is done secretly. She uses her discoveries to assert
her power in the workplace. She is subtle, fascinated
by secrets and their revelation and loves to expose
hidden wickedness, especially if they feed her sense
of social justice.*

From *Written in the Stars*, by Dorothea Dawson

I remember a Monty Python sketch where a
character complains, 'My brain hurts. I've got
my head stuck in the cupboard.' I knew just
how he felt when the opening chords of Free's
'All Right Now' crashed through my head. It felt
like the middle of the night. It was still dark. Mind
you, in Manchester in December, that could make
it mid-morning. I dug Richard in the ribs. It was
his house, after all. He made a noise like a sleeping
triceratops, rolled over and started snoring.

I stumbled out of bed, wincing as my aching

feet hit the ground and gasping at the stiffness in my hips as I straightened up. Richard's 'Twenty Great Rock Riffs' doorbell blasted out again as I rubber-legged my way down the hall, wrapping my dressing gown around me, managing to tie the belt at the third fumbling attempt. I knew I shouldn't have had that last treble Polish hunter's vodka on the rocks. I yanked the door open and Gizmo practically fell in the door, accompanied by half a snowdrift.

'I've done it,' he said without preamble.

I wiggled my jaw in various directions, trying to get my mouth to work. 'Oh God,' I finally groaned through parched lips. I leaned against the wall and closed my eyes while the floor and ceiling rearranged themselves in their normal configuration.

'You look like shit,' Gizmo observed from the living-room doorway.

'Bastard,' I said, gingerly pushing myself away from the wall to test whether I could stand upright. Nothing seemed to collapse, so I put one foot in front of the other until I made it to the living room. 'My place,' I croaked, leading the way through the conservatory to the life support system in my kitchen.

'It's not that early,' Gizmo said defensively. 'You said it was important.'

The clock on the microwave said 07:49. 'Early's relative,' I told him, opening the fridge and reaching for the milk. 'So's important.' I poured a glass with shaking hand and got the vitamins out. Four grams of C, two B-complex tablets and two extra-strength paracetamol. I had a feeling it was going to be one of those days when ibuprofen and paracetamol count as two of the four main food groups. I washed the pills down with the milk, shuddered like a medieval peasant with the ague and wished I'd remembered to drink more water when we'd finally got home the wrong side of four o'clock.

'Did you come on the bus?' I asked. Gizmo has the same affection for public transport as most obsessives. He's the sort who writes to TV drama producers to complain that they had the hero catching the wrong bus on his way to his rendezvous with the killer.

'The one-nine-two,' he said. 'Single decker.'

'Do me a favour? I left my car at the O-Pit. If you get a cab round there and pick it up for me, by the time you come back I'll be able to listen to whatever you've got to say.'

His mouth showed his discontent. 'Do I have to?' he asked like a ten-year-old.

'Yes,' I said, pointing to the door. 'Call a cab, Giz.'

Half an hour later, I'd kick-started my system with a mixture of hot and cold showers followed by four slices of peanut-buttered toast from a loaf that had been lurking in the freezer longer than I liked to think about. I even managed a smile for Gizmo when he returned twirling my car keys round his trigger finger.

'Thanks,' I said, settling us both down in my home office with a pot of coffee. 'Sorry if I was a bit off. Rough night, you know?'

'I could tell,' he said. 'You looked like you needed a new motherboard and a few more RAM chips.'

'It's not just the brain, it's the chassis,' I complained. 'This last year I've been starting to think something terrible happens to your body when you hit your thirties. I'm sure my joints never used to seize up from a night's clubbing.'

'It's downhill all the way,' he said cheerfully. 'It'll be arthritis next. And then you'll start losing nouns.'

'Losing nouns?'

'Yeah. Forgetting what things are called. You watch. Any day now, you'll start calling everything wossnames, or thingumajigs, or whatchamacallits.' He looked solemn. It took me a few seconds to realize I was experiencing what passed for a joke on his planet. I shook my head very slowly to avoid killing off any more neurones and groaned softly.

Gizmo reached past me and switched on my computer. 'You've got Video Translator on this machine, haven't you?'

'It's on the external hard disk, the E drive,' I told him.

He nodded and started doing things to my computer keyboard and peripherals too quickly for my hungover synapses to keep up. After a few minutes of tinkering and muttering, he sat back and said, 'There. It's a bit clunky in places, not enough polygons in the program to keep it smooth. The rendering's definitely not going to win any awards. But it's what you asked for. I think.'

I managed to get my bleary eyes to focus on the screen. Somehow, the colours looked brighter than they had on the original crime-scene photographs. If I'd been alone, I'd have been reaching for the sunglasses, but my staff has little enough respect for me as it is. I leaned forward and concentrated on what Gizmo had put together.

We both sat in silence as his work unfolded before us. At the end, I clapped him on the shoulder. 'That's brilliant,' I enthused. 'That must have taken you hours.'

He tilted his head while shrugging, regressing to awkward adolescent. 'I started soon as I got home. I finished about two. But I did have a little break to talk to Jan. So it wasn't like I blew the whole night on it or anything.' He scuffed his feet on the carpet. 'Anyway, Dennis is your mate.'

'He owes you,' I said. 'Don't let him forget it. There must be somebody out there you want menacing.'

Gizmo looked shocked. 'I don't think so. Unless he knows where to find the moron who sent me that virus that ate all my .DLL files.'

I said nothing. It wasn't the time to point out that if the lovely Jan was a hoax, he might want Dennis's talent for terror sooner than he thought. 'I'm going to be half an hour or so on the phone. You can either wait or head on into the office.'

'I've got my Docs on. I'll walk over,' he said. 'I like it in the snow. I'll let myself out.'

I reached for the phone and called Ruth. Within ten minutes, she'd rung back to tell me she'd set up a meeting with DI Tucker at our office later that morning. 'He's not keen,' she warned me. 'I think your fame has spread before you. He did ask if you were the PI involved with the Dorothea Dawson case.'

'Did you lie?'

'No, I told him to check you out with Della. Apparently his bagman used to work for her, so it's a name that meant something to him.'

'Ah.'

'Is that a problem?'

'Not for me, but it might be for the bagman,' I said. Tucker wouldn't have to be much of a detective to work out where I'd gained my access to the crime-scene photographs. 'My fault. I should have warned you.'

'I don't like the sound of this,' Ruth said warily.

'Don't worry. I'll see you later.'

It took another twenty minutes to sort out Donovan and Gloria. We finally fixed that he would pick up her and her daughter, take them to the police station and hang on while Gloria gave the statement that would get him off the hook. Then he'd take them shopping. I hoped they'd stick to the plan of going a very long way away from anywhere policed by the Greater Manchester force. If they were going to be arrested for shoplifting, I didn't want to be involved.

I took a fresh pot of coffee out into the conservatory. The sun had come back from wherever it had been taking its winter holiday. The reflection on the snow was a killer. I fished a pair of sunglasses out of the magazine rack and stared at the blank white of the garden. Some days I could do with being a Zen master. The sound of one hand clapping was about all my tender nerve endings could cope with, but I still had a murder to solve and no apparent prospects for the role of First Murderer. Somebody must have wanted to murder Dorothea, because what had happened to her definitely hadn't been suicide. But I still couldn't figure out who or why.

I wasn't any nearer a solution by the time I had to leave for my meeting with Tucker and Ruth. Richard was still asleep, flat on his back, arms in the crucifixion position. I considered nails but settled for sticking an adhesive note to his chest suggesting lunch. When all else fails, I've found it helps to enlist another brain. Failing that, I'd make do with Richard and his hangover.

If Shelley had heard about the previous night's debacle, the atmosphere in the office was going to be frostier than it was outside. I stopped off at the florist on the way in and bought the biggest poinsettia they had. It would act both as peace offering and office decoration. There were three weeks to Christmas, and even with my chlorophyll-killer touch the plant had to stand a good chance of making it into the New Year.

I placed the poinsettia on her desk, a tentative smile nailed on. She looked up briefly, surveyed the plant and savaged me with fashion folk wisdom. 'Red and green are never seen except upon a fool,' she said. 'Gizmo was right. You do look like shit.'

'And a merry Christmas to you too, Scrooge,' I muttered.

'I don't have to work here,' she sniffed.

'Nobody else would put up with you now the war's over,' I told her sweetly and swept into my office. Gizmo had already set everything up. All I needed now was a cop with an open mind. If they could get miracles on 34th Street, I didn't see why we couldn't have them on Oxford Road.

Ruth was first to arrive. 'I hate surprises,' she grumbled, dropping her fake fur in a heap in the corner. Maybe Tucker would take it for a timber wolf and be cowed into submission.

'Nice outfit,' I said, trying to change the subject.

'Mmm,' she said, preening her perfectly proportioned but extremely large body in its tailored kingfisher-blue jacket and severe black trousers. 'You don't think it's a bit Cheshire Wife?'

'Sweetheart, you *are* a Cheshire Wife.'

She bared her teeth in a snarl. If she'd still been wearing the coat I'd have dived out of the window. 'Only geographically,' she said. 'I thought you needed me on your side this morning?'

Before we could get too deeply into the banter, the intercom buzzed. 'I have a Detective Inspector Tucker for you,' the human icicle announced. I made a big production of crossing my fingers and opened the door.

If the man standing by Shelley's desk had been any taller, we could have dipped his head in emulsion and repainted the ceiling. He was so skinny I bet he had to make a fist when he walked over cattle grids. He had a thick mop of salt and pepper hair, skin cratered from teenage acne and a thousand-watt smile that lit up the kind of grey eyes that can resemble granite or rabbit fur. 'I'm Kate Brannigan,' I said. 'Thanks for coming. Would you like to come through?'

Close up, my eyes were on a level with the breast pocket of his jacket. I flashed Ruth a 'why didn't you tell me?' look and ushered him in. He exchanged ritual greetings with Ruth and folded himself into the chair I pointed him towards. I swung the monitor screen round till it was facing them both. 'I'm sorry I was so mysterious about this,' I said. 'But if I'd told you what I had in mind, you'd have laughed in my face. You certainly wouldn't have taken it seriously enough to come and see for yourself.'

'I'm here now, so let's cut to the chase. We're all busy people,' he said, with no trace of hostility. He obviously didn't go to the same Masonic dinners as Cliff Jackson.

'It's not a long preamble, I promise you. Last

week, you found Pit Bull Kelly dead inside a shop that had previously been squatted by Dennis O'Brien. Pit Bull had told his brothers he was going down to the shop to sort Dennis out and take over the pitch for himself. Next morning, Pit Bull was found dead from a sub-arachnoid haemorrhage, an unusual injury and one that's hard to inflict. You decided, not unreasonably given what you know about Dennis, that he'd used a commando karate blow to kill Pit Bull. But given what I know about Dennis, I know it couldn't have happened like that.' I held my hands up to ward off the objection I could see Tucker about to make.

'But putting prejudice aside, there's a key piece of evidence that tells me Dennis didn't kill Pit Bull. I've known Dennis a long time, and the one thing he won't have anything to do with is guard dogs. Back when he was burgling, he'd never touch a house that had a guard dog. If Pit Bull Kelly had turned up with his dog in tow, Dennis wouldn't even have opened the door. But just supposing he had, that dog is a trained killer. He was Pit Bull Kelly's private army, according to his brothers. If Dennis had lifted his hands above waist level, the dog would have gone for him. He'd never have got as far as laying a hand on the master without the dog ripping his throat out.'

Tucker nodded sympathetically. 'I've already heard this argument from Ms Hunter. And if this crime had taken place out in the open, I might have been forced to agree. But what you tell me about O'Brien's dislike of fierce dogs doesn't mean he didn't kill Patrick Kelly. I could make the argument that the fact the dog was separated from its master by the back door of the shop lends weight to the notion that O'Brien was in fact in the shop and agreed to talk to Kelly on the sole condition that the dog stayed in the service corridor.'

'If so, how did he escape? There's no way out through the front without being filmed by security cameras and breaking through a metal grille,' I pointed out.

Tucker shrugged. 'O'Brien's a professional burglar. If he put his mind to it, I'm sure he could find a way out that neither of us would come up with in a month of Sundays.'

'That's not an argument that will carry much weight with a jury in the absence of any evidence to the contrary,' Ruth chipped in drily. Tucker's eyebrows descended and his eyes darkened.

'What I want to show you,' I interrupted before the goodwill melted, 'is an alternative hypothesis that answers all the problems this case presents. It should be relatively easy to make the forensic tests that will demonstrate if I'm right or wrong. But for now, all I want the pair of you to do is to watch.'

I tapped a couple of keys and the screen saver dissolved. The corridor behind Dennis's squat appeared. A few seconds passed, then a jerky figure with Pit Bull Kelly's face and clothes walked towards us. Even with the limited resources of time and software that Gizmo had been working with, he managed to convey that Kelly was under the influence of the drink and cannabis that, according to his brothers, he'd indulged in before he had the courage to face Dennis. Beside Kelly, a boisterous pit bull terrier lurched, its movements twitchy and not very well coordinated. Every few steps, the dog would jump up towards its master's chest and Kelly would slap it down. Gizmo had even overlaid a soundtrack of a barking dog.

'Two of his brothers confirmed that the dog was always jumping up at Pit Bull. It's still not much more than a pup. It's full of energy,' I said, forestalling any protest from Tucker when he saw where this was heading.

'It's impressive,' was all he said.

We watched Kelly and the dog arrive at the door to Dennis's squat. He reached out a hand for the doorknob and clumsily turned it. Expecting it to be locked, he stumbled as it opened under his hand. As Kelly lurched forward, the dog yanked on its leash, jerking Kelly off balance and spinning him half around so that the vulnerable angle under his jaw cracked into the doorjamb, accompanied by a thud courtesy of Gizmo.

The screen went black momentarily. Then the point of view shifted. We were inside the shop, behind the door. Again, we saw Kelly topple into the doorjamb, the dog skittering back from his master. The leash dropped from Kelly's fingers and the dog scampered back into the service corridor as Kelly collapsed sideways to the floor, the weight of his body slamming the door shut as he fell. The final scene dissolved into the starkness of the crime-scene photograph that had been the starting point for the whole process.

I heard Tucker's breath leak from him, the first sign that he'd been taking seriously what he saw. 'I suppose I'd be wasting my time if I asked you where exactly your source material came from?'

I nodded. 'I'm afraid so. All I will say is that it wasn't the obvious route,' I added in an attempt to give Della's contact a little protection.

'I take it I can expect the immediate release of my client, in the light of this?' Ruth said, leaning back expansively and lighting a cigarette. Noel Coward would have loved her.

Tucker shook his head. 'A very convincing performance, Ms Brannigan, but you know as well as I do that it doesn't change anything.'

'It should, because it explains everything a damn sight better than any hypothesis you've been able to come up with,' I said. 'The door was unlocked because Dennis didn't want to be responsible for the landlord having to cause any damage getting into the premises. Dennis's alibi holds water. It also explains why the dog didn't get into a fight with the killer, because there was no killer. I know it's bad for your clear-up statistics, but this wasn't a murder, it was the purest of accidents.'

Tucker sucked his lower lip in between his teeth.

'You make a good case. But O'Brien's wife has given him false alibis before, and he did have a strong reason for falling out with the dead man.'

'You will be running full forensic checks on the doorjamb, won't you, Inspector?' Ruth said ominously.

'I'm not sure that's justified,' Tucker said cautiously. 'Besides, the crime scene has been released.'

'Because if you don't,' Ruth continued as if he hadn't spoken, 'I will. I'll be getting my own expert witness down there this afternoon. And when he finds fragments of skin and maybe even a bit of blood with Patrick Kelly's DNA all over that doorjamb at precisely the height where his jaw would have hit it, Mr O'Brien will be suing you for false imprisonment. Won't that be fun?'

'A lovely Christmas present for the Chief Constable,' I added. I was starting to get the hang of threatening the police. I could see why Ruth got such a buzz out of her job.

Tucker sighed then chewed his lower lip some more. 'I will get someone to take a look at the door,' he eventually said. 'And I will also have a word with the pathologist.' He stood up, his long body unfolding to its unnerving height. 'It's been an interesting experience, Ms Brannigan. I'm sure we'll meet again.'

Ruth extracted a promise that he'd call her as soon as he had any information, and I shepherded him out.

'Tell me, what set you off on this train of

thought?' Ruth demanded the moment the door closed.

'I wish I could say it was some brilliant intuitive leap. But it wasn't. I'm on the Internet mailing list of a forensic pathology newsgroup,' I said, feeling slightly sheepish. 'Mostly I'm too busy to do much more than skim it, but every now and again, some bizarre detail sticks in my mind. I read about a similar case and I remembered it because the reporting pathologist described it as, "Man's best friend and worst enemy".'

If Ruth had had four paws and a tail, her ears would have pricked up. Instead, she settled for leaning forward with an intent gaze. 'You've got a copy of this?'

I shook my head. 'I don't save the digests. But I could put out a request for whoever filed the original case report to get in touch with me. I've managed to track down a couple of references to it, and that should be enough to get me heading in the right direction.'

Ruth got to her feet, stubbing out her cigarette in the soil of the dying Christmas cactus on the windowsill. 'Do it,' she said decisively, reaching for her coat. 'You did a great job there,' she added. 'I shall tell Dennis he owes his freedom entirely to you. Send me a bill, will you?'

'I thought Dennis was on Legal Aid?'

'He is.'

'But the Legal Aid Board won't pay for this,' I protested.

Ruth's smile matched the timber-wolf coat. 'No, but Dennis will. You're running a business, not a charity. There's favours for friends, and there's charges for professional services. This is one he pays for.'

'But . . .'

'No buts. You're no use to either of us if you can't make this business pay. Send me a bill.'

I would have argued. But she's bigger than me. Besides, it always takes forever to argue with a lawyer. And I had a lunch appointment.

20

JUPITER TRINES NEPTUNE
*She is idealistic, and enjoys discussion on a theoretical
or philosophical level. She can be excessively generous
and will go out of her way to help others. She does not
always manage to meet her own high standards.*
From *Written in the Stars*, by Dorothea Dawson

The Yang Sing was Manchester's most famous
Chinese restaurant until it burned down, and it
suffered accordingly. Trying to get a table at a busy
time of day or night, especially near Christmas, was
about as rewarding as waiting for a night bus. What
the tourists didn't know was that just round the
corner is the sister restaurant, the Little Yang Sing,
where the cooking is at least as good and the decor
leans more towards the clean lines of sixties retro
than the traditional fish tanks and flock wallpaper
of most Chinese restaurants.

Richard was already there by the time I arrived.

So were a couple of bottles of Tsing Tao, a plate of salt and pepper ribs and a tidy little mound of prawn wontons. I dropped into my seat and reached for the beer. If the morning had taught me anything, it was that the only way to get through the day was going to be by topping up the alcohol level in my bloodstream at regular intervals. I didn't have time to suffer today; I'd have my hangover when I was asleep and not before.

As I swigged beer, I checked out Richard. Even allowing for the fact that he'd had four hours more sleep than me, he had no right to look so untouched by the excesses of the night before. His hazel eyes looked sleepy behind his new rimless glasses, but then they always have that fresh-from-the-bedroom look. The light dusting of stubble was sexy rather than scruffy, and his skin stretched tight over his broad cheekbones. I swear he looks no older than the night we first bumped into each other six years ago. I wish I could say the same, but one look in the mirrors that line the back wall of the restaurant and I knew it was a lie. The unforgiving light glinted on a couple of strands of what might have been silver in my dark-auburn hair. To dye or not to dye was a decision that was closer than I liked.

'How was your morning?' he asked just as I got a spare rib to my lips. Typical; he always asks questions when there's food to be fought over.

I shook my head and stripped the bone with my

teeth. 'Tough,' I said. 'But it looks as if Dennis is going to be back on the streets for Christmas.'

'That's one less thing for you to worry about, then. And Gloria? Has she had any more hate mail?'

'Nothing. I've got Donovan taking her and her daughter shopping today. I keep waiting for the phone call.'

Richard grinned. 'Switch the phone off. You need both hands for what I've ordered.'

He wasn't wrong. We ate our way through half a dozen dim sum and appetizers, a double helping of hot and sour soup and four main-course dishes. My capacity for food after a heavy night never ceases to astonish me. I'll probably need a stomach transplant when I'm forty. By then, they'll probably be able to give me one.

I picked up the last king prawn with my chopsticks then laid it regretfully back on the plate. 'I can't do it,' I said.

'Me neither,' Richard admitted. 'So where are you up to with this murder?'

I brought him up to speed on my meeting with Freddie Littlewood. It felt like half a lifetime ago, but it was only the night before. 'So I seem to have tracked down the source of most of the tabloid stories,' I said. 'At least, the ones involving personal scandal rather than storyline revelations. But I don't know how to use the information to clear Ross Grant without dropping Freddie in the shit. I don't really want to do that if I can help it, because, to be honest, he seems to have had a pretty raw deal from life anyway.'

'And you're sure he didn't kill his mother? He'd have had the opportunity, and he freely admits to hating her.'

'I just don't think he did it. Why should he? He was making a nice little earner out of their story selling, and he got the added bonus that it really upset her. Profitable revenge. There's not many of us manage that.'

Richard poured himself a cup of Chinese tea and stared into it consideringly. 'Maybe she'd had enough,' he said at last. 'Maybe she was going to blow the whistle on the whole racket and throw herself on the mercy of her clients.'

I snorted. 'She certainly wouldn't have got much change out of them. And even supposing the cast members were prepared to forgive and forget, John Turpin would never let her back on NPTV property again. Which reminds me . . .' I drifted off, remembering what Cassie had told me.

'I said,' Richard commented in the tones of a man repeating himself, 'who is John Turpin?'

'He's the Administration and Production Co-ordinator at NPTV,' I said absently. 'One of those typical telly executives. You know the kind. About as creative as a sea slug. They're great at counting beans and cutting expenses. You must have them in journalism.'

'Editorial managers,' he said glumly.

'And he's obsessed with uncovering the mole

who's leaking the *Northerners* stories. He's even threatening to end the location caterers' contract because he suspects one of them of being guilty.'

'Nice guy. So what is it about this Turpin that sent you off the air just now?' Richard asked.

'I was just remembering a conversation I had yesterday with Cassie Cliff.'

'Maggie Grimshaw as was?'

'The same.'

Richard smiled reminiscently. 'I loved Maggie Grimshaw. The woman who put the "her" in *Northerners*. The sex goddess of soap.' His smile slipped. 'Until the truth came slithering out. So what did Cassie have to say about John Turpin?'

I told him the tale about Turpin and Tina Marshall in the Normandie. 'I can't figure it out at all,' I said.

'He might have been wining and dining her on the off-chance that she'd let something slip about her mole.'

I pulled a face. 'I don't think he's that stupid.'

'He might be that vain,' Richard pointed out. 'Never underestimate a middle-aged executive's opinion of himself.'

I sighed. 'Well, if that's what he was after, he obviously didn't succeed, since he's still making a huge performance out of flushing out the mole.'

'Has he got shares in NPTV?' Richard asked.

'I think so. *Northerners* is up for contract renegotiation. One of the actors was talking about how much money Turpin would make if NPTV got into a bidding war between the terrestrial and the pay channels over *Northerners*. So I guess he must have some financial stake.'

Richard leaned back in his seat, looking pleased with himself. 'That's the answer. That's why Turpin was cosying up to Tina Marshall. John Turpin's the *Northerners* mole.' He signalled to a passing waiter that we wanted the bill.

Sometimes I wonder how someone who never listens makes such a good living as a journalist. 'Richard, pay attention. I already told you who the mole is. Freddie Littlewood was using Dorothea to dig the dirt then he was dishing it.'

'I *was* paying attention,' he said patiently. 'Freddie was pulling skeletons out of cupboards, courtesy of Dorothea's privileged information. What you didn't tell me was who's been selling out the storylines. From what you say, Turpin must have access to them.'

'But why? What does he gain by it?'

Richard shook his head in wonderment. 'I can't believe you're being so slow about this, Brannigan,' he said. 'You're normally so quick off the mark where money's concerned. It's viewing figures, isn't it? The more notorious *Northerners* becomes, the more people watch. The more people watch, the higher the value of the show when it comes to negotiating any satellite or cable deal because there are people who will shell out hundreds of pounds for satellite dishes and cable decoders and subscription charges rather than be parted from their regular fix of *Northerners*.'

'I know that,' I protested. 'But it's different with storylines that get leaked before transmission. That makes people turn off.'

The waiter dumped the bill on the table between us. Automatically, we both reached for our wallets. 'Says who?' Richard demanded as his plastic followed mine on to the plate.

'Says the actors. When the punters know what happens next, they don't mind missing it. And they get hooked on something else so they drop out altogether.'

The waiter removed the bill and the credit cards. 'Two receipts, please,' we chorused. He nodded. He'd served us enough times to know the routine of two self-employed people who liked to eat together. 'That's bollocks, you know,' Richard said. 'That might be what Turpin's telling them, but it's bollocks. If you leak upcoming storylines, what happens is you get a buzz going. First one paper breaks the story, then all the rest follow it up, then the TV magazines pick it up and run with it and before you know it, everybody's buzzing. Don't you remember the whole "Who shot JR?" thing back in the eighties? Or the furore over Deirdre Barlow and Mike Baldwin's affair on *Coronation Street*? The whole nation was watching. I bet Turpin got the idea when Freddie's exclusives started hitting the headlines and the viewing figures rose along with them.'

'He wouldn't dare,' I breathed.

'Where's the risk? He's in charge of hunting for the source of the *Northerners* stories. Turpin knows there's a real mole as well as himself, so if he does uncover anything, he can pin all the guilt on the other one. There's no way Tina Marshall is going to expose him, because he's the goose that lays the golden eggs. She's probably not even paying him much.'

I leaned across the table and thrust my hand through his thick butterscotch hair, pulling his head towards mine. I parted my lips and planted a warm kiss on his mouth. I could still taste lemon and ginger and garlic as I ran my tongue lightly between his teeth. I drew back for breath and said softly, 'Now I remember why I put up with you.'

The waiter cleared his throat. I released Richard's head and we sheepishly signed our credit card slips. Richard reached across the table and covered my hand with his. 'We've got some unfinished business from last night,' he said, his voice husky.

I ran my other thumbnail down the edge of his hand and revelled in the shiver that ran through him. 'Your place or mine?'

Just before we slipped under my duvet, I made a quick call to Gizmo, asking him to arrange for some background checks into the exact extent of John Turpin's financial involvement with NPTV. Then I switched the phone off.

Sometime afterwards, I was teetering on the edge of sleep, my face buried in the musky warmth of Richard's chest, when his voice swirled through my mind like a drift of snow. 'I'll tell you one thing, Brannigan. If a few juicy stories can push up the ratings, just think what murder must have done.'

Suddenly, I was wide awake.

Sandra McGovern, née Satterthwaite, had inherited her mother's flair for ostentation. The house where she lived with her husband Keith and their daughter Joanna had definite delusions of grandeur. Set just off Bury New Road in the smarter part of Prestwich, it looked like the one person at the party who'd been told it was fancy dress. The rest of the street consisted of plain but substantial redbrick detached houses built sometime in the 1960s. Chateau McGovern had gone for the Greek-temple makeover. The portico was supported by half a dozen ionic columns and topped with a few statues of goddesses in various stages of undress. Bas reliefs had been stuck on to the brick at regular intervals and a stucco frieze of Greek key design ran along the frontage just below the first-floor windows.

They might just have got away with it on a sunny summer day. But the McGoverns clearly took Christmas seriously. The whole house was festooned with fairy lights flashing on and off with migraine-inducing intensity. Among the Greek goddesses, Santa Claus sat in a sled behind four cavorting reindeer, all in life-size inflatable plastic. A Christmas tree had been sawn vertically in two, and each half fixed to the wall on either side of the front door, both dripping with tinsel and draped with flickering-light ropes. A vast wreath of holly garlanded the door itself. I pressed the doorbell and the chimes of 'Deck the Hall with Boughs of Holly' engulfed me. Sometimes I felt Scrooge had had a point.

There was a long silence. I was steeling myself to ring again when I saw a figure looming through the frosted glass. Then Donovan opened the door. But it was Donovan as I'd never seen him before, swathed in a plum silk kimono that reached just below his knees. A fine sheen of sweat covered his face and he looked extremely embarrassed. 'Bah, humbug,' I muttered. He seemed baffled, but what else could I expect from an engineering student?

'Hiya, Kate,' he said.

I pointed to his outfit. 'I hope this isn't what it looks like,' I said drily.

He rolled his eyes heavenwards. 'You're as bad as my mother. Give me some credit. Come on in, let me get this door shut. We're through the back,' he added, leading the way down the hall. 'You think the outside is over the top, wait till you see this.'

I waded after him through shag pile deep enough to conceal a few troops of Boy Scouts. I tried not to look too closely at the impressionistic flower paintings on the walls. At the end of the hall was a solid wooden door. Donovan opened it, then stood back to let me pass.

I walked from winter to tropical summer. Hot, green and steamy as a Hollywood rainforest, the triple-glazed extension must have occupied the same square footage as the house. Ferns and palms pushed against the glass and spilled over in cascades that overhung brick paths. Growing lamps blazed light and warmth everywhere. The air smelt of a curious mixture of humus and chlorine. Sweat popping out on my face like a rash, I followed the path through the dense undergrowth, rounded a curve and found myself facing a vast swimming pool, its shape the free form of a real pond.

'Hiya, chuck,' Gloria screeched, raucous as an Amazonian parrot.

She was stretched out on a cushion of wooden sunbed, wearing nothing but a swimsuit. Beside her, a younger version reclined on one elbow like a Roman diner, a champagne glass beaded with condensation hanging loosely from her fingers. Gloria beckoned me over, patting the lounger next to her. 'Take the weight off,' she instructed me. I sat, slipping off my leather jacket and the cotton sweater underneath. Even stripped to jeans and cotton T-shirt, I was still overheating. 'Don, sweetheart, fetch us another sunbed, there's a love,' Gloria called. 'This is our Sandra,' she continued. 'Sandra, meet Kate Brannigan, Manchester's finest private eye.'

We nodded to each other and I told a few lies about the house and swimming pool. Sandra looked pleased and Gloria proud, which was the point of the exercise. Donovan reappeared carrying a fourth lounger which he placed a little away from our grouping. Self-consciously, he peeled off the robe, revealing baggy blue trunks, and perched on the edge of the seat, his body gleaming like a Rodin bronze. 'No problems today?'

Gloria stretched voluptuously. For a woman who was fast approaching the downhill side of sixty, she was in terrific shape. It was amazing, given what I'd seen of her lifestyle. 'Not a one, chuck. Nowt but pleasure all the way. We went to Oldham police station and I spoke to a lovely young inspector who couldn't see what all the fuss last night had been about. Any road, young Don's in the clear now, so we don't have to worry about that. And then we went shopping for Christmas presents for Joanna. We had to get a robe and some trunks for Don and all, because our Keith's a tiddler next to him. We've not seen a journalist all day, and there's nobody more pleased than me about that. What about you? Any news?'

'I wanted to ask you about something,' I said, side-stepping the question. 'You remember when I came to fetch you from Dorothea's van the night she was killed? Well, I was busy wrestling with the umbrella and keeping an eye out in case anybody jumped us, so I wasn't really paying attention to individuals. Besides, I don't really know anybody at NPTV, so even if I had noticed who was around, it wouldn't mean anything to me. But you . . .'

'You want me to think about who I saw in the car park?'

'It might be important.'

Gloria leaned back, closing her eyes and massaging her temples. 'Let's see . . .' she said slowly. 'There were two women getting into a car a couple of bays down from Dorothea's. I don't know their names, but I've seen them in the accounts office . . . Valerie Brown came out of the admin block and ran across to production . . . I saw that red-haired film editor with Maurice Warner and Maurice's secretary. They were legging it for Maurice's car . . . John Turpin was standing in the doorway of the admin block, like he couldn't decide whether to make a run for it . . . Freddie and Diane and Sharon from make-up, they were getting in Sharon's car, that lot always go to the pub in town on a Friday . . . Tamsin from the press office, she came out the admin block and went across towards the security booth, but she wasn't running because of them daft shoes she wears.' She opened her eyes and sat up. 'There were one or two other folk about, but either they were too muffled up for me to see who they were or else I didn't know them. Does any of that help?'

I reached for my sweater. 'More than you can imagine, Gloria. Much more than you can imagine.'

'So what's going on?' she demanded. 'Do you know who killed Dorothea?'

'I've got an idea,' I said. 'I don't want to say too much yet. I've got stuff to check out. But if you get Donovan to bring you to the office first thing tomorrow morning, I think I might be able to give you your money's worth.'

Donovan gave me a look of resignation. 'You want me to stick with Gloria?'

'Oh, I think so,' I said. 'You make such a lovely pair.'

21

SATURN IN PISCES IN THE 11TH HOUSE
She is comfortable with her own company and works best alone. Her friends are valued as much for their experience as for their personal qualities. She has a single-minded concentration on objectives, but has a flexible and sympathetic mind. She is intuitive and imaginative. She can be moody.
From *Written in the Stars*, by Dorothea Dawson

When Freddie Littlewood got home from work, I was waiting for him. Stacey of the big eyes and trusting soul had made it back fifteen minutes ahead of him and she'd let me in without a moment's hesitation. She'd shown me into the dining room again, presumably because that was where Freddie and I had spoken before. She'd been back inside five minutes with a tray containing teapot, milk, sugar and a china mug with kittens on it.

'It can't have been easy for Freddie, the last few days,' I said sympathetically.

She gave me an odd look. 'No more than usual,' she said. 'Why would it be difficult?'

Until that moment, the idea that Freddie might not have mentioned his mother's murder to Stacey hadn't occurred to me. People have called me cold in my time, but I don't think I could plan to spend the rest of my life with someone I trusted so little. 'I meant, with the police everywhere,' I improvised hastily, remembering I was supposed to work for NPTV too. 'It's been really disruptive. They walk around as if they own the place, asking all sorts of questions. And it's not even as if Dorothea Dawson worked for NPTV.'

Seemingly satisfied, Stacey drifted off, saying she was going to get changed and get the dinner on, if I didn't mind. I also couldn't imagine marrying someone with so little curiosity about a strange woman who turned up looking for her fiancé twice in such a short space of time. I sipped my tea and wished there was a large lemon vodka in it. The sound of the front door opening and closing was immediately followed by Stacey's footsteps in the hall and the low mutter of conversation.

Freddie stepped into the doorway, looking grey-faced and exhausted. 'What's so urgent it couldn't wait for work tomorrow?' he asked brusquely. More for Stacey's benefit than mine, I suspected.

'I needed the answer to a question,' I said. 'I won't be at NPTV first thing in the morning, so I thought you wouldn't mind if I caught up with you at home.'

He closed the door behind him and leaned against it. 'Have you never heard of the telephone?' he said, exasperation in his voice.

'It's much harder to tell when people are lying,' I said mildly. 'Sorting out the truth is difficult enough as it is.'

Freddie folded his arms over his chest and glared. 'Since you're here, I'll answer your question. But in future, if you want to talk to me, see me at work or call me on the phone. I don't want Stacey upset by this, OK?'

'That's very chivalrous of you,' I said. 'There's not many men who are so concerned for their future wives' wellbeing that they don't even tell them their prospective mother-in-law's just been murdered.'

'What goes on between Stacey and me is none of your business. You said you had a question?'

'You told me that it wasn't you who leaked the advance storylines to the press, and I believe you,' I said. 'But somebody did. I was wondering if Dorothea had ever indicated to you that she knew who the mole was?'

He gave me a long, considering stare, running his thumb along his jaw in the unconscious gesture I'd already become familiar with. 'She once told me that it wasn't hard to work out who the mole was if you looked at the horoscopes. She said there weren't that many people connected with *Northerners* who had the right combination of features in their charts. If you excluded people who didn't really have access to advance stories, she said, it narrowed right down.'

'Did she mention anybody's name to you?'

He shook his head. 'Not then. She said she didn't seem to have much choice about passing me other people's secrets but that she wasn't going to ruin somebody when she had no evidence except her own instinct. But then later . . .' His voice tailed off.

'What happened, Freddie?' I asked urgently.

'Turpin was in make-up one day and somebody said something about one of the stories in the paper and was it true he was going to get rid of the caterers because they were the moles. Turpin said he wasn't convinced that would solve the problem. I turned round and he was staring at me. I thought maybe he suspected me. So I went round to Dorothea's house and told her. I said she'd probably be glad if Turpin did find out, because then she'd be off the hook and wouldn't have to break her precious client confidences any more.'

'She wasn't though, was she?' I said gently.

He shook his head and cleared his throat. 'No. She said she wouldn't let Turpin destroy my career. She said she was as certain as she could be that he was the storyline mole and she was going to confront him.'

'She was going to expose him?' I couldn't believe Freddie was only revealing this now.

'No, she wasn't like that. I told you, she was

obsessed with trying to do her best for me, supposedly to make up for all the bad years. No, she said she'd do a deal with Turpin. If he stopped hunting the mole, she'd keep quiet about her suspicions of him.'

'But she didn't have any evidence apart from an astrological chart,' I protested.

'She said that if she was right, there had to be evidence. All it needed was for someone to look in the right place and Turpin would realize that once she'd pointed the finger, he'd be in trouble. So he'd have to back off and leave me alone. Except of course she wasn't going to come out and say it was me, not in so many words. She was just going to tell him that she was acting on behalf of the mole.'

'When was this?' I asked, trying to keep my voice nonchalant.

Freddie shrugged. 'A couple, three weeks ago? She told me afterwards he'd agreed to the deal. That he'd seen the sense of what she was saying. You don't think that had anything to do with why she was killed, do you?'

'You don't?' I asked incredulously.

'I told you, it was weeks ago.'

I couldn't get my head round his naiveté. Then I realized he wasn't so much naive as self-obsessed. 'There's a lot at stake,' I pointed out. 'You know yourself you'd never work in TV again if I told NPTV what you've been doing. And there are a lot of people involved with *Northerners* who have a lot more to lose than you do. If somebody thought Dorothea was a threat . . .'

Freddie stared at the floor. 'It wasn't like she was blackmailing him. She was too straight for that.'

'She let you blackmail her,' I pointed out.

'That was different. That was guilt.'

'Looks like it killed her, Freddie.'

I got up and put a hand on his arm. He pulled away. 'Don't touch me! It's meaningless to you. You never knew my mother.'

There was nothing more to say. I'd got what I came for and Freddie Littlewood was determined to need nobody's sympathy for the death of a mother he'd barely come to know. I walked back to the car, glad I wasn't living inside his skin.

I'd barely closed the door when my moby rang. 'Hello?'

'Hey, Kate, I'm out!' Dennis's voice was elated.

'Free and clear?' I could hardly believe it.

'Police bail pending results from the lab. Ruth says you played a blinder! Where are you? Can I buy you some bubbly?'

If anyone deserved champagne, it was the long-suffering Debbie. But female solidarity only stretches so far, and I needed Dennis more than she did. I was glad I hadn't done as Ruth suggested and submitted a bill, because tonight I needed payment in kind. 'Never mind the bubbly,' I said. 'I need a favour. Where are you?'

'I'm in the lobby bar at the Ramada,' he

announced. 'And I've already got the bottle in front of me.'

'Take it easy. I'll be there in half an hour.' I needed to make a quick detour via a phone book. I started the engine and fishtailed away from the kerb. The roads had iced up while I'd been indoors. It was going to be another treacherous night. And I was quite sanguine about contributing to the total.

If you walk out of Strangeways Prison up towards town, the Ramada Hotel is probably the first civilized place to buy a drink. It's certainly the first where you can buy a decent bottle of champagne. Following the IRA bomb, its façade reminded me of those mechanical bingo cards you get on seaside sideshow stalls where you pull a shutter across the illuminated number after the caller shouts it out. So many of the Ramada windows were boarded up, it looked like they'd won the china tea service. I found Dennis on a bar stool, a bottle of Dom Perignon in front of him. I wondered how many 'Under a Pound' customers it had taken to pay for that.

He jumped off the stool when he saw me, pulling me into a hug with one arm and handing me a glass of champagne with the other. 'My favourite woman!' he crowed, toasting me with the drink he retrieved from the bar.

'Shame we're both spoken for,' I said, clinking my crystal against his.

'Thanks for sorting it,' he said, more serious now.

'I knew it wasn't down to you.'

'Thanks. This favour . . . we need a bit of privacy?'

I gestured towards a vacant table over in the corner. 'That'll do.' I led the way while Dennis followed, a muscular arm embracing the ice bucket where the remains of the champagne lurked. Once we were both settled, I outlined my plan.

'We know where he lives?' Dennis asked.

'There's only one in the phone book. Out the far side of Bolton. Lostock.'

He nodded. 'Sounds like the right area.'

'Why? What's it like?'

'It's where Bolton folk go when they've done what passes for making it. More money than imagination.'

'That makes sense. I looked it up on the *A-Z*. There's only houses on one side of the road. The other side's got a golf course.'

'You reckon he'll be home?'

I finished my champagne. 'Only one way to find out.' I pointed to his mobile.

'Too early for that,' Dennis said dismissively. Then he outlined his plan.

An hour later, I was lying on my stomach in a snowdrift. I never knew feet could be that cold and still work. The only way I could tell my nose was running was when the drips splashed on the snow in front of me. In spite of wearing every warm and waterproof garment I possessed, I was cold enough to sink the *Titanic*. This was our second stakeout position. The front of the house had proved useless for Dennis's purposes and now we were lying inside the fence surrounding an old people's home, staring down at the back garden of our target. 'Is it time yet?' I whimpered pathetically.

Dennis was angled along the top of the drift, a pair of lightweight black rubber binoculars pressed to his eyes. 'Looks like we got lucky,' he said.

'Do tell me how.'

'He's not bothered to pull the curtains in the kitchen. I've got a direct line of sight to the keypad that controls the burglar alarm. If he sets that when he goes out, I'll be able to see what number he taps in.'

'Does that mean we're going to do it now?' I said plaintively.

'You go back round the front. I'll give you five minutes before I make the call. Soon as he leaves, you shoot up the drive and start working on the front-door lock. I'll get to you fast as I can.' He turned and waved a dismissive hand at me. 'On your bike, then. And remember, we're dressed for the dark, not the snow. Keep in the shadows.'

That's the trouble with living in a climate where we only get snow for about ten days a year. Not even serious villains bother to invest in white camouflage. Neither Dennis's lock-up nor my wardrobe had offered much that wouldn't blend in with your average dark alley. I slunk off round the edge of the shrubbery and down the drive of the old people's home. I nipped across the road and on to the golf course, where I waded through knee-high snow until I was opposite the double-fronted detached house we were interested in. A light shone in the porch, and the ghost light from the hall cast pale oblongs on the ceilings of upstairs rooms. The rooms on either side of the front door had heavy curtains drawn.

I checked my watch. A couple of minutes before, Dennis would have rung the house and explained that there had been a break-in at the administrative core of NPTV and that the police wanted Mr Turpin to come down right away to assess the damage. A quick call to Gloria had already established that he was divorced and as far as she knew, unattached. We were taking a gamble that Turpin was alone. As I watched, the front door swung open and he appeared, shrugging into a heavy leather coat over suit trousers and a heavy knit sweater. On the still night air, I could hear the high-pitched whine of an alarm system setting itself. He pulled the door to behind himself, not bothering to double lock it, and walked briskly to his car. A security light snapped on, casting the drive into extremes of light and shade.

Ignition, headlights bouncing off the garage door, reversing lights, then the big Lexus crunched down the icy drive and swung into the road. I watched the tail lights as far as the junction, then scrambled over the banking, across the road and up Turpin's drive, dodging in and out of shadow and blinding light. The porch was brighter than my kitchen. I'd never broken the law in quite so exposed a way before. I fumbled under my jacket and fleece, fingers chill in latex probing the money belt I was wearing until they closed around my lock-picks. At least I'd be able to see what I was doing.

Oddly enough, it didn't really speed up the process. Picking a lock successfully was all about feel, not sight, and my fingers were still clumsy from the cold. Dennis was hovering impatiently by my shoulder by the time I got the right combination of metal probes, muttering, 'Come on, Kate,' in a puff of white breath.

The door opened and he was past me, running down the hall to the alarm panel, tapping in the code to stop the warning siren joining forces with the klaxon that would deafen us and, in an area like this, have the police on the doorstep within ten minutes. I let him get on with it and checked out the downstairs rooms. A living room on one side of the hall, a dining table on the other. Kitchen at the rear. I ran up the stairs. Four doors, three ajar. The first was Turpin's bedroom, an en suite bathroom opening off it. The second, closed, was the guest bathroom. Third was a characterless guest room. Last, inevitably, was the one I was looking for. As I walked in, the alarm went quiet, the silence a palpable presence.

Luckily, Turpin's study overlooked the back garden, so I felt safe enough to switch on the desk lamp. I took a quick look around. There was one wall of books, mostly military history and management texts. On the opposite wall, shelves held file boxes, stacks of bound reports and fat binders for various trade magazines. A PC squatted on the desk and I switched it on. While it booted up, I started on the drawers. None of them were locked. Either Turpin thought himself invincible here or we were doing the wrong burglary.

Suddenly, Dennis was standing next to me. 'Do you want me to do the drawers while you raid the computer?' he asked.

'I'd rather you kept an eye out the front,' I said. 'I know it should take Turpin an hour to get to NPTV and back, but I'd rather be safe than sorry.'

'You're probably right,' Dennis said. He went out as silently as he'd come in. At least now I didn't have to worry about being caught red-handed. I checked out the computer. It looked as if Turpin used Word for all his documents, which suited me perfectly. I took a CD-ROM out of my money belt and swapped it for the encyclopaedia currently residing in the drive. It had taken all my powers of persuasion to get Gizmo to lend me this disk and I hoped it had been worth it. It was a clever little piece of software that searched all Word files for particular combinations of words. I typed 'Doreen Satterthwaite', and set the program running.

Meanwhile, I started on the desk. Not surprisingly, Turpin was an orderly man. I flicked through folders of electricity bills, gas bills, council-tax bills until I found the phone bills I was looking for. Domestic and mobile were in the same file. A quick glance around revealed that I wasn't going to have to steal them. Turpin had one of those all-singing, all-dancing printers that also act as a computer scanner and a photocopier. I extracted the itemized bills for the last six months and fed them through the photocopier.

When the phone rang, I jumped. After three rings, the answering machine kicked in. A woman's voice floated eerily up from the hall. 'Hi, Johnny. It's Deirdre. I find myself unexpectedly at a loose end after all. If you get this message at a reasonable time, come over for a nightcap. And if I'm not enough to tempt you, I've got sausages from Clitheroe for breakfast. Call me.' Bleep.

I glanced at the screen and discovered that there were two files containing 'Doreen Satterthwaite'. I was about to access them when Dennis's yell made my heart jolt in my chest. 'Fuck!' he shouted. 'We're burned, Brannigan!'

22

MARS IN LEO IN THE 4TH HOUSE

She has combative strength and brings her ambitious plans to fruition. She is honourable and takes responsibility for her actions. She has a temper, acts with audacity and is often prone to involvement in incidents that embrace violence. She has a powerful sense of drama that can verge on the melodramatic. Generous, she hates small-mindedness.

From *Written in the Stars*, by Dorothea Dawson

The adrenaline surge was like being plugged into the mains. Dennis was almost screaming. 'Switch off. Spare room. Now!' No time to exit properly from Windows. I stabbed my finger at the computer power button. I grabbed the photocopies and stuffed the originals back into their folder, thrusting them into the drawer without checking I was returning them to the right place. I leapt to my feet, switching off the desk lamp.

Three paces across the room, I heard the wail of

the alarm siren as Dennis reset it. I dived across the hall and into a spare room bathed with light from the security lamps outside. I skidded round the door to stand against the wall. Seconds later I heard Dennis pounding up the stairs. Then he was beside me, his chest heaving with the effort of silent breathing. 'There's a sensor in the corner,' he said. 'Under the bed. Quick!'

I dropped to the floor and rolled, aware of him following me. As I hit the bedside table on the far side of the bed the alarm finished setting itself and silence fell once more. I heard the slam of a car door. Then the front door opened and the warning siren went off again. By now, every nerve in my body was jangling, and I suspected Dennis was no better. I was going to wake up sweating to the nightmare sound of that burglar alarm for months to come, I could tell. 'How the fuck do we get out of this?' I hissed.

'Worst comes to worst, we wait till he goes to sleep. Just relax. But not too much. Don't want you snoring,' Dennis muttered, clutching my hand in a tightly comforting grip. We endured a few more seconds of aural hell, then blessed silence apart from the thudding of two hearts under John Turpin's spare bed. If he'd had parquet floors instead of carpet, we wouldn't have stood a chance. Then a click, a bleep and a replay of Deirdre's attempt at sultry seductiveness, thankfully muffled. I heard the clatter of a handset being picked up and the electronic stutter of a number being keyed in. Amazing how certain sounds travel and others don't. At first all I could hear of Turpin's voice was a low rumble. Then, as he mounted the stairs and walked into his bedroom, I could hear every word.

'. . . halfway down the motorway when it dawned on me. When I'd asked this supposed security man if he'd called Peter Beckman, he'd said Peter was already on his way in. But Peter's taken a couple of days off this week to go to some stupid Christmas market in Germany with his wife. So I rang him on his mobile, and he's only having dinner in some floating restaurant on the bloody Rhine.' I heard the sound of shoes being kicked off.

'Well, I know,' he continued after a short pause. 'So I rang studio security and they denied any report of a break-in or any call to me . . . No, I don't think so. It'll be some bloody technicians' Christmas party, some idiot's idea of a joke, let's bugger up Turpin's evening . . .' Another pause. 'Oh, all right, I'll check, but the alarm was on . . . Yes, I'm just going to get changed, and I'll be right over. You know how I feel about Clitheroe sausages for breakfast,' he added suggestively. I was going to have serious trouble with sausages for a while, I could tell.

I strained my ears and picked up the sound of sliding doors open and close, then faint sounds like someone doing exactly what Turpin had said. I heard the bathroom door open, the sound of a light cord being pulled once, twice, and the door closing. A door moved over carpet pile, a light switch snapped twice. The study. He was checking, just like he'd told Deirdre he would. My throat constricted, my muscles went rigid. Gizmo's CD-ROM was still in Turpin's drive. Where had I left the CD I'd taken out of it? Dennis's hand clamped even tighter over mine. All round the bed was suddenly flooded with light, but only momentarily. Then twilight returned.

I felt the tension slowly leaking out of my body. We'd got away with it. Turpin was going out again. The terrible irony was that if we'd waited quarter of an hour longer before Dennis had made his hoax call, Deirdre would have saved us the trouble and I'd not have lost five years off my life expectancy. Dennis let go of my hand. I patted his arm in thanks.

Finally, the alarm was reset and the low thrum of Turpin's car engine dimmed in the distance. 'Now what?' I asked.

'He's gone for the night. You've got hours to play with,' Dennis said cheerfully.

'The alarm's on. As soon as we move out from under the bed, Lostock calls the cavalry. And for all we know, Clitheroe sausages is only a couple of hundred yards away.'

Dennis chuckled. 'The trouble with you, Kate, is you worry too much. Now me, I've got the advantage of a commando training. Cool under pressure.'

I poked him sharply in the ribs, enjoying the

squeal that accompanied the rush of air. 'You can't get the staff these days,' I said sweetly. 'I'll just lie here and meditate while you get it sorted.' It's called whistling in the dark.

In the dim gleam from the landing, I watched as Dennis rolled on to his stomach and propelled himself across the floor using toes, knees, elbows and fingers for purchase. Keeping belly to the carpet made it a slow crawl, but it was effective. The little red light on the passive infrared detector perched in the corner of the room stayed unlit. He disappeared round the corner of the door and my stomach started eating itself. I badly needed to go to the loo.

Time stretched to impossible lengths. I wondered if Dennis was going downstairs head first or feet first. I wondered whether the keypad itself was covered by an infrared detector. I wondered whether it was possible to install detectors that didn't show they'd been activated. I even wondered if Turpin was paranoid enough to have installed one of those silent alarms that rang in a remote control centre staffed by battle-hungry security guards. I wondered so much about burglar alarms that night that I was beginning to consider a new profit centre for Brannigan & Co.

Suddenly the main alarm klaxon gave a single whoop. Shocked, I cracked my head on the underside of the bed in my manic scramble to get out from under there. 'It's all right,' Dennis shouted. 'It's off.'

He found me sitting on the landing carpet gingerly fingering the egg on my forehead. 'Don't ever do that to me again,' I groaned. 'Jesus, Dennis, if I was a cat I'd be on borrowed lives after tonight.'

'Never mind whingeing, let's get done and get out of here,' he said. 'I fancy a night in with the wife.'

'I didn't realize you'd been banged up that long,' I said tartly, getting to my feet and heading back into Turpin's study, this time via the loo. I was amazed we'd got away with it; directly in the line of sight from the doorway was a CD gleaming like a beacon on Turpin's desk.

Ransacking his secrets took less time than I expected. Less time, certainly, than I deserved, given how overdrawn my luck must have been that night. We let ourselves out of the front door just after midnight. I dropped Dennis outside his front door half an hour later and drove home on freshly gritted roads. For once, Richard was home alone, awake and ardent. Unfortunately I felt older than God and about as sexy as a Barbie doll so he made me cocoa and didn't say a word against me crashing alone in my own bed. It must be love.

I think.

I was constructing the fire wall between me and the evidence when Gizmo stuck his head round my office door next morning. 'What's happening?' he asked.

'I'm trying to make this stuff look like it came

through the letterbox,' I said, waving a hand at the pile of material I'd amassed from John Turpin's office. 'It's all sorted now, except for the computer files. All I can do is enclose a floppy copy with a printed note of where to find the original files on Turpin's hard disk. But it's not conclusive.'

Gizmo sidled into the room, looking particularly smart in one of the suits I'd chosen. He'd even had a haircut. I wondered if today was the day. I'd find out soon enough, I reckoned. He placed a thin bundle of papers on the desk in front of me and said, 'I think this might be.'

The top sheet revealed John Turpin's present shareholding in NPTV as well as details of his future potential share options. I whistled softly. Even a movement in share price of a few pence could make a significant difference to Turpin's personal wealth. Next came what were clearly commercially sensitive details of NPTV's current negotiations with a cable TV company. I didn't even want to know where this stuff had come from. What was clear from the terms of the deal was that if certain levels of viewing figures were reached in the twelve months either side of the deal, senior executives of NPTV – among them John Turpin – were going to be a lot richer than they were now.

The last sheet was the killer. Somehow, Gizmo had got his sticky fingers on the details of a trans-action carried out by John Turpin's stockbroker on his behalf. The order for a tranche of NPTV shares had been placed on the day of Dorothea Dawson's murder. According to the computerized time code on the order, Turpin had instructed his broker in the short space of time between Gloria and me leaving the camper van and the police arriving in response to my call.

I looked up at Gizmo. 'I suppose he thought he'd be too busy later on to get his order in. And then he'd have lost the edge that killing Dorothea had given him.'

'You mean he killed her just to push up the pro-gramme ratings and make himself richer?' Gizmo said, clearly shocked.

'I think that was just a bonus. He actually killed her because she'd sussed that he was the mole leaking the storylines to the papers. Ironically, she had powerful reasons for keeping quiet about his involvement, but he didn't believe her. He thought she was going to blackmail him or expose him, and he wasn't prepared to take that risk. He just bided his time till he found the right opportunity.'

Gizmo shook his head. 'It never ceases to amaze me, what people will do for money. People always say shit like it buys you privacy, or it lets you live the life you want. But I don't know. I've got all the privacy I need, and I'm mostly skint. But I live the life I want. I reckon most people that chase money only do it because they don't really know what it is they do want.'

Philosophy for breakfast now. It had to be better than Clitheroe sausages, I thought with a bitter smile. I hoped Turpin was making the most of it. He'd be a fair few years older before he tasted anything other than prison food. With a sigh, I picked up the phone and managed to persuade the police switchboard to connect me to Linda Shaw. 'Hi, Sergeant,' I said. 'It's Kate Brannigan.'

'Oh yes,' she said, her voice guarded.

'I've something at the office I think you might like to see,' I told her.

'Oh yes? And what would that be?' She sounded neutral. I guessed Jackson was within hearing range.

'You need to see it to get the full effect. I can promise you it'll help your clear-up rate.'

'I'd heard you've already contributed to that this week,' she said tartly. 'I can't say I'd like to share the experience.'

'This is different,' I said firmly. 'Please, Linda. I'm trying to do us both a favour here. You know and I know that if I approach Jackson his first instinct will be to rubbish what I've got. And that could mean a murderer walking. You don't want that any more than I do. So will you come round?'

'Give me an hour,' she said, a noticeable lack of enthusiasm in her voice.

It couldn't have suited me better. An hour was perfect for what I had to do.

Given the grief I'd already had over the Perfect Son, I'd expected Shelley to rip Gloria's face off and send her home with it in a paper bag. Instead, Gloria got the star treatment. Apparently, according to Shelley, if her boy was with Gloria, he couldn't be getting into the kind of trouble I organized especially for him on a daily basis. But Gloria, being a mother herself, would understand Shelley's concerns. Gloria patted Shelley's hand, sympathized and told her what a credit to his mother the Perfect Son was. Donovan shifted from foot to foot, faintly embarrassed but relieved not to be on the receiving end of another maternal diatribe. Excuse me, I wanted to shout. Who's the one with frostbite and coronary heart disease and a major sleep deficit and a bump on the head the size of Rochdale as a result of this case?

Eventually, I managed to shoo Gloria into my office. She did a double take when she saw Freddie perched uncomfortably on the edge of the sofa. I'd promised him there was no reason why anyone had to know he was Dorothea's son or that he'd been the major mole, but his body language didn't actually indicate conviction. When Gloria walked in, his face spasmed in panic. 'Gloria,' he stammered, jerking to his feet and taking an involuntary sideways step away from her.

'Hiya, chuck,' she said warmly, collapsing on to the sofa. 'You another one of Kate's mystery witnesses, then?'

'Er . . . yes. She never mentioned you were coming . . .' He shot me a look that said he'd never trust a private eye again. I wouldn't have minded so much if I'd lied to him, but I hadn't. Well, not so's you'd notice.

We didn't have long to wait for Linda. She came in with more attitude than a rap band. 'This better be good,' she said even before she got across the threshold. I waved her to a chair and leaned against my desk.

'Since you're all so thrilled to be here, I'll keep it short as I can. There's been a mole at NPTV making a small fortune out of selling scandal stories and advance storylines to the press. Dorothea Dawson thought she had worked out the identity of that mole by studying her astrological charts and matching what they told her against the names of people who had access to advance stories and who were in a position to find out about the murky pasts of the cast.' I nodded towards Freddie.

'You might remember Freddie here. He works in the make-up department at *Northerners*. Freddie witnessed an encounter between Dorothea and a senior management figure at NPTV. Freddie, can you tell DS Shaw what you told me last night?'

He was so overwhelmed with relief that I hadn't after all revealed either of his secrets that he told the story we'd agreed eagerly and openly, with none of his awkward mannerisms to make Linda wonder if there was more going on than met the eye. 'Dorothea had come over to the make-up studio looking for one of the actors so she could rearrange an appointment, but she'd just missed him. Anyway, Turpin came in just as she was leaving. She asked if he was still wasting his time on the mole hunt. Then she said she had a pretty good idea who the mole was, and she'd tell him if the price was right.'

'What did Turpin say?' I asked.

'He went bright red. He told her if he wanted to waste the company's money, there were plenty of perfectly good charities. Then he just stomped out without doing whatever it was he'd come in for.'

'Turpin might well have interpreted Dorothea's comments as an indirect blackmail threat,' I pointed out.

Linda had listened with her head cocked to one side, critically appraising his words. Then she gave a slight nod. I was about to say more, but she raised one finger and made a series of notes in her pad. 'Interesting,' she said.

'There's more.'

'I'm sure,' she said.

'You've already taken a statement from Gloria about the events of the evening when Dorothea was killed. I don't know if you remember, but she had a far better opportunity than I did to take notice of who else was in and around the car park at the same time. Among the people she saw was that same NPTV executive, John Turpin. Maybe you'd like to confirm that for us, Gloria?'

My client nodded avidly. 'That's right, chuck,' she said eagerly. She was loving every minute of it, just as I'd expected. I hadn't really needed her there, but she was paying the bill, and I figured a bit of grandstanding might just be worth a Christmas bonus. 'I saw John Turpin standing in the doorway of the admin block. He looked as if he was wondering whether it was worth chancing getting his good suit wet in the sleet.'

'Thanks for confirming that, Ms Kendal. But we did know that already, Kate,' Linda pointed out, not even bothering to make a note this time.

'I'm just sketching in the background, Linda,' I said apologetically. 'I became involved in this case because Gloria here was getting death-threat letters. She hired me to take care of her.'

'Which you and yours have done admirably,' the irrepressible Gloria chipped in.

'Thank you, Gloria. I may need that testimonial before long,' I said. 'This morning, when I unlocked the office, there was a padded envelope in the mailbox.' I produced an envelope from the desk behind me.

'Inside was an assortment of papers and a floppy disk. The disk contains what I believe are the originals of the letters sent to my client. A note attached to the floppy claims that the originals are to be found on the hard disk of John Turpin's home computer. I'd have thought that might be grounds for a search warrant?'

Linda grunted noncommittally, frowning at the disk and the note I handed her. 'Why would he target you specifically, Gloria?' she asked.

'I haven't a clue, chuck,' she said. 'The only thing I can think of is that I'm the only one of the show's really big names who lives alone, so maybe he thought I'd be easiest to scare. Mind you, he's never entirely forgiven me for our Sandra giving him the elbow all those years ago.'

'What?' Linda and I chorused.

'He took our Sandra out for a few weeks, years ago now. Before she met Keith. Any road, she decided he wasn't for her and she chucked him. He wasn't best pleased. He's never had a civil word for me since.'

All I could do was stare at her and shake my head. I love clients who go out of their way to make the job easier. I just don't seem to get many. I took a deep breath while Linda took more notes.

'Also in the envelope.' I placed more papers in front of her. 'A photocopy of Turpin's phone bills, home and mobile. A photocopy of what looks like a Rolodex card, giving the number of Tina Marshall. She's the freelance journalist who broke a substantial number of the *Northerners* stories in the press. Check out the number of calls to her number. I think you'll find most of them were made a few days before a big *Northerners* story broke.'

Linda was now sitting upright, totally focused on the papers in front of her. Her finger flicked to and fro. Then she looked me straight in the eye. 'This fell through your letterbox,' she said flatly.

'That's right. It seemed to be my civic duty to pass it on to you, Sergeant.' I rummaged inside the envelope. 'There is more.' I handed her the material Gizmo had culled from his electronic sources. More for Gloria and Freddie's benefit than Linda's, I ran through the contents.

'And at the time when he placed that order for NPTV stock,' I wound up, 'only the killer could have known that the viewing figures were about to climb sky-high on the back of Dorothea Dawson's murder.'

'Hellfire, Kate, you've done wonders,' my grateful client said. 'I can sleep easy in my bed at night now.'

'I'm glad,' I said. Not least because I could get Donovan back on the work he was supposed to be doing. I turned back to Linda. 'Taken together, it's a hard conclusion to resist.'

'It'd be easier for my boss to swallow if the information came from somewhere else,' she said resignedly.

'Howsabout if it does?' I asked. 'It won't take five minutes for Gizmo to walk down to Bootle Street and leave it in an envelope at the front counter with your name on it. You can tell Jackson you've been out taking a statement from Freddie about Dorothea's conversation with Turpin and then when you got back to the office, hey presto! There it was. You can leave me out of it altogether.'

'Are you sure?' she said. I could tell she was weighing up how much my generosity might cost her in the future.

I shrugged. 'I don't need my face all over the *Chronicle* again. Besides, there is one thing you could do for me.'

Her face closed like a slammed door. 'I thought it was too good to be true.'

I held my hands up. 'It's no big deal. Just a word with your colleagues in uniform. Donovan is going to be serving process for me for at least the next eighteen months. I'd really appreciate it if you could spread the word that the big black guy on the bicycle is wearing a white hat.'

Linda grinned. 'I think I can manage that.' She got to her feet and took some folded sheets of A4 out of her shoulder bag. 'As it happens, I've got something for you too. I'll see myself out.'

Curious, I unfolded the bundle of paper. There was a Post-it stuck on one corner in Linda's handwriting. 'Printed out from Dorothea Dawson's hard disk. It gave us all a laugh.' I pulled off the note and started to read: *Written in the Stars for Kate Brannigan, private investigator.*

Born Oxford, UK, 4th September 1966.

* *Sun in Virgo in the Fifth House*
* *Moon in Taurus in the Twelfth House*
* *Mercury in Virgo in the Fifth House*
* *Venus in Leo in the Fourth House*
* *Mars in Leo in the Fourth House*
* *Jupiter in Cancer in the Third House*
* *Saturn retrograde in Pisces in the Eleventh House*
* *Uranus in Virgo in the Fifth House*
* *Neptune in Scorpio in the Sixth House*
* *Pluto in Virgo in the Fifth House*

* *Chiron in Pisces in the Eleventh House*
* *Ascendant Sign: Gemini*

Sun in Virgo in the 5th House: On the positive side, can be ingenious, verbally skilled, diplomatic, tidy, methodical, discerning and dutiful. The negatives are fussiness, a critical manner, an obsessive attention to detail and a lack of self-confidence that can disguise itself as arrogance. In the Fifth House, it indicates a player of games . . .

'What is it, chuck? You look like you've seen a ghost,' Gloria said, concern in her voice.

I shook my head, folding the papers away. 'It's nothing, Gloria. Just some sad twisted copper's idea of a joke.'

Epilogue

SATURN TRINES NEPTUNE

She loses her own apprehensions through her profound and penetrating investigative interest in others. She has a strong sense of how her life should be arranged, often bringing order to chaos. She follows her feelings and is sensitive to the subtext that lies beneath the conversation and behaviour of others. She can harness irrationality and factor it into her decision-making.

From *Written in the Stars*, by Dorothea Dawson

If I hadn't known how thoroughly Dorothea Dawson researched her clients, I'd probably have been impressed with her astrological analysis of my character. I wouldn't have minded betting that the minute Gloria told Dorothea she'd hired me, the astrologer had started digging. I wasn't exactly a shrinking violet. For a start, I'd appeared in Alexis's stories in the *Chronicle* more times than I was entirely comfortable with. So it wouldn't have been too hard for Dorothea to pick up a few snippets about me and weave them into an otherwise standard profile.

What she missed completely was my sense of humour. I mean, if I didn't have a world-class sense of humour, why else would I be sitting in the Costa Coffee forecourt at Piccadilly Station drinking moccachino and reading my horoscope when I could be at home, snug as a bug in a phone, working out how to solve my latest computer game with a Stoly and pink grapefruit juice on the side?

The reason why I was lurking among the sad souls condemned to travelling on Virgin Trains was shuffling from foot to foot a few yards away, like a small child who needs to go to the toilet but doesn't want to miss some crucial development in his favourite TV show. Gizmo had clearly had a hard time deciding between style and comfort and he'd ended up wearing one of the suits I'd chosen for him. The trouble was, the only outer garment that went with it was his mac, which wasn't a lot of use in the lowest December temperatures on record. Neither were the thin-soled Italian shoes. Sometimes I wonder what real Italians wear in winter.

As well as hopping from one foot to the other, Gizmo was clutching a copy of Iain M. Banks's cult sci-fi novel, *Feersum Endjin*, the agreed recognition signal. He'd arranged to meet Jan off the London train at half past eight and he'd been dancing his quaint jig since a quarter past. Imagine expecting a train to be early. I'd sat comfortably sipping my brew and dipping into Dorothea's digest of my personality.

There was an indecipherable announcement over the Tannoy and Gizmo stopped jigging. He leaned slightly forward, nose towards the platforms like a setter scenting the breeze. I followed his gaze and watched the dark-red livery of the London train easing into platform six with a rumble and a sigh. I couldn't help crossing my fingers. If this went pear-shaped, I'd get no proper work out of him for weeks.

The carriage doors were opening the length of the train and people spilled on to the platform. First past us were the smokers, carrying with them a miasma of overflowing ashtray after two and a half hours sitting in stale tobacco smoke. Then the usual Friday-night mixture of day-trip shoppers, students coming to Manchester for a groovy weekend, senior citizens exhausted from a week with the grandchildren, sales reps and educational consultants in cheap suits crumpled by the journey and, finally, the first-class passengers in sleek tailoring with their identikit suit carriers and briefcases, men and women alike.

Gizmo bobbed like a ball on the tide of humanity streaming past him, his eyes darting from side to side. The crowd swelled, then steadied, then thinned to the last stragglers. His head seemed to shrink into his shoulders like a tortoise and I saw him sigh.

Last off the train was a blond giant. His broad shoulders strained a black leather jacket that tapered to narrow hips encased in tight blue denim. They didn't leave much to the imagination, especially with his swivel-hipped walk. As he reached the end of the platform, he turned his head right, then left, a thick mane of blond hair bouncing on his collar. He looked like a Viking in the prow of a longship, deciding which direction held America.

He settled for left and moved in our direction. As he grew nearer, I could see the book clutched in the massive hand that wasn't carrying the black leather holdall. I closed my eyes momentarily. Even Dennis might have a bit of bother menacing his way out of this one. Gizmo would have no chance.

When I opened them, Jan was looming over Gizmo. 'You're Gizmo,' he boomed. I couldn't quite place the accent.

Gizmo half turned towards the café, panic in his eyes. 'I never . . . she never said anything about anybody else,' he stammered desperately.

Typical, I thought. Great with silicon, crap with carbon-based life forms. Does not compute.

Jan frowned. 'What do you mean?' I figured he wasn't sure if Gizmo had missed the point completely or if there was a language problem.

Gizmo took a hasty step backwards. 'Look, I never meant to cause any trouble, I didn't know anything about you. Whatever she's said, there's been nothing between us, this would have been the first time we'd even met,' he gabbled.

Jan looked even more puzzled. He waved the book at Gizmo. 'I brought the book. So we'd know each other,' he said in that pedantic way that Germans and Scandies have when they're not sure you've understood their impeccable English.

Gizmo swung towards me. 'Tell him, Kate. Tell him it's all a misunderstanding. She never said anything about having a bloke. I thought she was unattached.'

With a sigh, I got to my feet. 'You're Jan, right?' I said, giving the J its soft Y sound. Gizmo's mouth fell open and the Iain M. Banks tumbled to the concourse floor. Then, suddenly, he whirled round and ran for the escalator down to the tram terminus below. Jan made a half-hearted move to step around me and give chase but I blocked him. 'Leave it,' I said. 'He's not the one, Jan.'

He frowned. 'Who are you? What's going on?' He craned past me, peering anxiously towards the escalators, as if he expected Gizmo to reappear. Fat chance.

'I'm Kate. Gizmo and I work together.'

'Why has he run off? We arranged to meet,' Jan said, sounding puzzled. 'We have been e-mailing each other for months. Getting to know each other. We both figured it was time to meet.' He made the inverted commas sign in the air that pillocks use to indicate they're quoting. '"Time to take things further," Gizmo said.'

'Don't you think it might have been sensible to mention that you were a bloke?' I said, unable to keep the sarcasm out of my voice. 'He thought you were a woman. Jan with a J, not Jan with a Y.'

Jan's fair skin flushed scarlet. 'What does that matter? I'm still the same person. Because I am a man suddenly it's different?'

'Of course it's different,' I protested. His disingenuousness was really winding me up. 'He's not gay, for one thing. I can't believe you never made it clear you're a man. It can't be the first time someone's made that mistake.'

He glared at me. 'Why should I? I'm not responsible for someone else's assumptions. You British are so terrified of anything that is different, that challenges your sad little conventions.'

By now, the entire coffee shop was enthralled, waiting for my response. 'Bollocks,' I said contemptuously. 'Tell that to Julian Clary. Don't try and pretend that deceiving Gizmo was some kind of heroic act of sexual liberation. It was cowardice, that's what it was. You were scared to admit you were a man because you thought Gizmo would end your cyber-relationship.'

'And I was right,' he shouted.

'No, you were wrong,' I said quietly. 'He might have rejected you as a lover, but he would still have been your friend. And I've got good cause to know just how much that signifies.' Three women sitting round a table in the coffee shop gave me a ragged round of applause.

Jan's laugh was harsh. 'In cyberspace, he didn't need a woman to fight his battles.' Then he turned on his heel and stalked off towards the taxi rank.

I gave the women a sardonic bow and walked out into a heavy drizzle. Underneath the entrance canopy, the Salvation Army band was playing 'In the Bleak Midwinter'. A beggar with a dog on a string was trying to sell the *Big Issue* to people with a train to catch. A traffic warden was writing a ticket to stick on some poor sucker's windscreen.

I couldn't see Gizmo turning up for work on Monday morning as if nothing had happened. It looked like Brannigan & Co had just lost their computer expert. And when I got back to my car, the back tyre was flatter than my spirits.

If this was what was written in the stars, there was a scriptwriter somewhere who'd better watch his back.

Dead Beat

Val McDermid

Dead Beat introduces Kate Brannigan, a female private detective who does for Manchester what V.I. Warshawski has done for Chicago.

As a favour, Kate agrees to track down a missing song-writer, Moira Pollock, a search that takes her into some of the seediest parts of Leeds and Bradford. But little does she realize that finding Moira is a prelude to murder . . .

'Solid pleasure . . . this moves along with the speed of a Porsche, so smooth you can almost kid yourself you haven't been sitting on the edge of your seat throughout'
Mail on Sunday

'Zippy action, a well-crafted plot and some refreshingly gritty northern truths'
The Times

ISBN 13: 978 0 00 7142910

Crack Down
Val McDermid

There was only one reason Manchester-based private eye Kate Brannigan was prepared to let her boyfriend help out with an investigation into a car sales fraud – nothing bad could happen. But by now Kate should know that with Richard you have to expect the unexpected.

With the unexpected being Richard behind bars, Kate seems to be the obvious choice to look after his eight-year-old son – who proves even more troublesome than his father. Kate finds herself dragged into a world of drug traffickers, child pornographers, fraudsters and violent gangland enforcers . . . bringing her face to face with death in the tensest, toughest and most terrifying investigation of her career.

'Touch, funny and intensely topical. McDermid stands out as one of the few contemporary writers actually nourished by the here and now'　　　*Literary Review*

ISBN: 978 0 00 649008 1

The Mermaids Singing

Val McDermid

You always remember the first time. Isn't that what they say about sex? How much more true it is of murder . . .

Up till now, the only serial killers Tony Hill had encountered were safely behind bars. This one's different – this one's on the loose.

In the northern town of Bradfield four men have been found mutilated and tortured. Fear grips the city; no man feels safe. Clinical psychologist Tony Hill is brought in to profile the killer. A man with more than enough sexual problems of his own, Tony himself becomes the unsuspecting target of a battle of wits and wills where he has to use every ounce of his professional skill and personal nerve to survive.

A tense, brilliantly written psychological thriller, *The Mermaids Singing* explores the tormented mind of serial killer unlike any the world of fiction has ever seen.

Winner of the 1995 CWA Award for Best Crime Novel of the Year

'Truly, horribly good'   *Mail on Sunday*

ISBN 13: 978 000 721711 3

The Grave Tattoo

Val McDermid

Summer in the Lake District and torrential rain uncovers a bizarrely tattooed body on a hillside. But that is not the only thing to come to the surface: centuries-old tales involving the legendary Pitcairn Massacre are being told again. Did Fletcher Christian, mutinous First Mate on the ill-fated Bounty, stage the death of his men in order to return home in secret?

Wordsworth scholar Jane Gresham wants to know the truth. There are persistent rumours that the Lakeland poet, a childhood friend of Christian's, harboured the fugitive and turned his tale into an epic poem – a narrative that has since remained hidden. But as she follows each new lead, death follows hard on her heels. Suddenly, a 200-year-old mystery is putting lives on the line. And against the dramatic backdrop of England's Lake District, a drama of life and death plays out, its ultimate prize a bounty worth millions.

The superb new thriller from Val McDermid. Available now in hardback.

'Our leading pathologist of everyday evil'   *Guardian*

'McDermid's capacity to enter the warped mind of a deviant criminal is shiveringly convincing'   *The Times*

'Val McDermid is a roaring Ferrari amid the crowded traffic on the crime-writing road'   *Independent*

ISBN-13: 978-0-00-714285-9